School of Sight

Alisha A. Knaff

Published by Razorgirl Press.

First U.S. Edition: November 2015

Cover design by EK Cover Design

This book is a work of fiction. Names, characters, places, and incidents either are products of the author's imagination or are used fictitiously. Any resemblance to actual events or persons, living or dead, is entirely coincidental.

All rights reserved. Except as permitted under the U.S. Copyright Act of 1976, no part of this publication may be reproduced, distributed or transmitted in any form or by any means, or stored in a database or retrieval system, without the prior written permission of the publisher.

Copyright ©Razorgirl Press, 2015

Originally published as part of the *Four Windows: Seattle* periodical, September 2014

*To my mother, who taught me to read
and introduced me to stories worth reading.*

PART ONE

I could not have defined the change—
Conversion of the Mind
Like Sanctifying in the Soul—
Is witnessed—not explained—

'Twas a Divine Insanity—
The Danger to be Sane
Should I again experience—
'Tis Antidote to turn—

To Tomes of solid Witchcraft—
Magicians be asleep—
But Magic—hath an Element
Like Deity—to keep—

-Emily Dickinson

Chapter One

THE THING ABOUT being maybe-kind-of-almost-sort-of-perhaps crazy is that...well, you start to get paranoid. At some point in the maybe-kind-of-ness, you start to wonder if everyone around you notices the maybe-kind-of and if maybe-kind-of they don't think there's any maybe-kind-of about it. Thinking you're crazy? *Makes you fucking crazy.*

I see things. And I don't mean that in an 'I'm so hyper-observant I see the things that most people overlook because I'm super deep and can stare into your soul until you can't help seeing what an incredibly sensitive, deeply caring, perfectly empathetic individual I am and falling madly in love with me because I'm the only one who understands your painful, tragic past, now take me in your scintillating arms and let me show you just how much I *feel*, Edward' kind of way.

I just...see things.

For the past two or three years—no, I know exactly how long it's been. Of course I do. You notice when you start going maybe-kind-of crazy. For the past three years, since I came out here for school, I've seen things. The kind of things other people just ignore, sure, but I also see things that other people just don't. Or if they do, they never talk about them.

Like, there's this homeless lady that I walk past on my way to the bus stop every morning. And I know other people see her; they give her money or smile or do that thing where you casually look away because you don't want to be hit up for spare change. So other people definitely see this lady. But I *see* her.

She's an artist. Whenever she thinks nobody's watching, she pulls out this battered notebook—you know, the kind with holographic unicorns and things on it—and starts to sketch. She isn't drawing what's around her, not really. She's drawing what's in her head. I know that doesn't sound all that crazy, right? But the thing is, sometimes I see what she's drawing. Not in her notebook, not on paper, but when I see that she's drawing, I look around, and I *see* things I know aren't there, people who aren't there and who aren't...well...people, really. They're blue or winged or have too many limbs or eyes or heads. Sometimes other things too, trees or buildings that don't exist or don't exist anymore. And when I look back, she's drawing all that.

Or like, there's this kid at school. Total, hardcore, 90s throwback, Marilyn Manson, goth kid. Pale face, black lipstick, huge black duster. He puts off this *massive* 'DO NOT TALK TO ME' vibe. But I saw him last week feeding bits of his lunch to this stray cat that's always hanging around campus, and he gave a black-lipsticked smile when the cat brought him a dead mouse. Only, it wasn't really dead. I mean, it was, right? I knew it was, but then it stopped being a mouse and became this tiny talisman, very much alive in its own way.

And then there's my Econ professor. She is the dorkiest, dippiest, dweebiest person I have ever met. I mean, if she were a man, she'd have a comb-over and ninety-five different bow ties. As it is, her hair is always frizzy, and I think she has the world's largest collection of mustard-colored cardigans. Everybody knows this. Everybody sees this. But every day, when she walks into the lecture hall, I have to look away because she is fucking *glowing*. I'm not even being metaphorical here. She's not secretly pregnant; she's *literally glowing*.

And I figure, if this were a commonly recognized phenomenon, I would have heard about it, right? Someone would have said to me at some point, "Oh, you have Econ with Sternquist? Man, you better bring shades to class. You know she glows, right?" But nobody has ever said this to me in my tenure at this fine establishment of higher learning, so I am pretty damn sure I'm the only one who sees it.

Or I *was* pretty damn sure.

I'm not sure what gave me away. Maybe I was squinting up at the lectern, or maybe I shaded my eyes or something, but one afternoon in Econ, the guy sitting next to me snorted and whispered, "I know, right? Should have brought my sunglasses."

That paranoia I was talking about earlier? Yeah, it comes out in times like this. Was it a trap? Was he trying to get me to admit that I was crazy? The things that go through my head in moments like this are bordering on ridiculous.

Beyond bordering, really

But he looked completely genuine, and I must have looked completely gobsmacked because he just grinned and turned away, and I was left feeling maybe-kind-of crazy all over again. (It doesn't go away, this feeling, but sometimes I can ignore it for a while.)

I made it through Econ just fine. I was overly conscious of squinting and shading, but I felt like I'd been pretty normal for the hour and a half it took to ignore the glowing and the cardigan and take copious notes on a subject I had absolutely no interest in. I headed out after class, and it was something of a relief to be back in the cloud-filtered sunlight that Seattle was so good at. I had a little time before my next class, and I thought I'd go grab some coffee and finish my essay for my Personal Writing class. (Let's not get into what it's like to write about yourself when you're worried about your sanity.)

But when I turned toward the coffee shop I liked to write in, I almost ran into sunglasses guy; he was grinning again and very definitely looking to converse, which I'm not normally opposed to but really didn't want to get into with someone who might blow my 'no really, I'm totally sane' cover.

Sunglasses, of course, were not the dominant feature of sunglasses guy. (He hadn't brought them, after all.) Actually, he didn't seem to have any particularly dominant features. He was your basic College Guy. Indeterminately sandy-ish hair color, browny-hazely eyes, Seattle U sweatshirt, jeans, sneakers, messenger bag slung oh-so-casually over one shoulder. And that grin.

It wasn't like the grin made him glow like Dr. Sternquist. It just sort of...brightened him. It made him almost pleasant looking where he otherwise would have been almost painfully average.

"I'm not crazy," was his opening salvo, and my return shot was, "That's my line."

He laughed and pushed the indeterminate hair in its indistinguishable, shaggy cut out of his face. "Okay, then *you're* not crazy."

"That's what I just said."

"You wanna get some coffee?"

Five minutes ago I really had, but I had really not wanted company for that. Now, though....

Well, he had just told me I was not crazy when I was pretty sure I maybe-kind-of was, and that was a lead I had to follow up.

"You're buying," was my answer when it finally came, but even the really-probably-too-long time it took me to decide on an answer didn't seem to make him change his mind on his previous statement. He just smiled again and pushed the hair back again and tilted his head toward my coffee shop.

"Fair enough."

There wasn't much talking on the way. Awkwardness in social situations is a by-product of paranoia, I think. Just before we got there, though, he said, "I'm not a psych major."

"...okay."

"I mean...I'm not trying to use Intro Psych to diagnose you, and I'm not probably actually qualified to say conclusively that you're not crazy, but I'm pretty sure you're not crazy for the reasons you think you are, unless you think you are for more reasons than seeing Sternquist's aura."

That was a whole lot to process, so I took really-probably-too-long again before my brilliant mind came up with, "Her what?"

"Her aura," he repeated like this was a thing that people just knew and accepted and talked about casually as they held open coffee shop doors for Econ classmates. "Do you know what you want? They do a kickass Mexican mocha."

I had heard often about the Mexican mocha and never really been interested in trying it, but honestly? I was still stuck on the aura thing, so I just nodded and said, "Yeah, sure, sounds good."

"Awesome. Get us a table?" And then he was off ordering coffee, and I was left to look around the room helplessly and try to act normal even while thinking this guy was also maybe-kind-of crazy, and that's probably why he didn't think I was. Really, I was just enabling his delusion, and he was enabling mine. Not that it mattered. Being crazy with another crazy person had to be better than doing it on your own, right?

I had to think it would be, at least, so I found a table back in the corner, away from most of the other occupied tables, and in a few minutes he came over with two steaming mugs and set one in front of me. I didn't quite know how to transition from 'thank you for the coffee' to 'what do you mean I'm not crazy?' so I just ended up blurting out, "What's an aura?" and then, because I knew that sounded kind of stupid, "I mean...I know what an aura is, but what did you mean by it?"

"That's what you see when you look at Sternquist. That glowy thing." He was casually sipping his coffee and getting foam bubbles on his stupid smile and making no sense at all, but it was better nonsense than I'd been making for the past few years, so I decided to run with it.

"How do you even know about that?"

"Isn't it obvious?"

I wanted to flick mocha in his face because if it were obvious, I wouldn't be asking. Obviously. But I was trying not to look insane, and I'd had a lot of practice at it lately, so instead I very calmly said, "If it were obvious, I wouldn't be asking."

"Right," he said. "Sorry." And he did look sorry, so I stopped having mocha-flicking ideas for the moment. "I see it too. It's not because you're crazy. It's really there."

I decided to go for the obvious question, then, the one that had been nagging me since I sat down in Econ the first day. "So how come nobody else sees it?" I didn't mean it to come out as a challenge, but I could hear the skepticism in my voice. I tried to mask it by taking a sip of my own drink. (Which was, indeed, kickass. Damn him.)

He shrugged. "They're not seers."

Well, that was just...beyond maybe-kind-of. "What?"

"Seers," he said again, like I just hadn't heard him the first time. "At least, that's what my grandma called us. I've heard other names. Augur, channeler, prophet, not a big fan of that one.... I kind of like sibyl myself. The group I'm with here says witches, but I think that's a little broader."

"So you think I can see the future." My hopes of being sane after all were rapidly dwindling if this guy was the best the 'you're not crazy' front had to offer.

"No, not really. I mean, sometimes? There are some seers who really can. That's why I don't like prophet, though. Misleading. You're just...well, a few centuries ago they would have said you had the Sight."

"The Sight. Right." My skepticism was showing again, and I'd started to rhyme, but I didn't try to stop it this time. "And you think I'm some kind of chosen something or other who can see special things and whatever?"

"Yes!" he said, vindicated, it seemed, and totally missing the Skeptical Eyebrow of Doom I was giving him. "Well, maybe not chosen something or other, but...well, you *can* see special things, can't you?"

I thought back to the goth kid and the homeless lady and the glowing dweeb in the Economy department. I really didn't want this to be true, though. "Maybe," I offered after a moment. "But it's not like I get psychic readings on people or anything."

He laughed again, finally wiping the bit of foam from his upper lip with a distracted thumb. "No, of course not. It's not *Long Island Medium* here. 'I'm getting someone whose name starts with J,' or any of that bullshit."

It was a bit rich that he was spouting crazy talk while telling me a reality show was bullshit, but I loved that a little.

"Look, I know it's weird, but that's what it is. I promise. I'm not crazy and neither are you."

I sat back and for a moment I just sipped my mocha. He really didn't seem crazy, despite all the weirdness coming out of his mouth. He definitely didn't look crazy. Just your average Joe College with a great smile and good taste in coffee. I was not by any means ready to just accept this as truth, but something about it just...felt right.

That's a lame excuse, I know, but it did. It just felt right. It felt like all the questions I'd been having lately could be easily answered with this one wacko explanation. I'm not one to believe in things like this. I wasn't even sure I believed in some kind of higher power, really, so when I say that this explanation spoke to my soul, I know exactly what that sounds like, and I know it doesn't sound like I'm not crazy.

"Okay, smart guy," I said finally. "If I'm not crazy, how come I don't see this aura thing with other people?"

I didn't really think I'd caught him with this question, but I thought maybe, just maybe, it might give him some kind of pause. Either that or it might give him a chance to say the thing that would convince me he was actually telling the truth.

"Well, there aren't that many vampires around."

That was not the thing I was looking for.

And anyway, that was just too much for me, and I laughed—snorted, really—into my mocha, spraying a little foam as I did. "Okay, right. Yeah. My roommates put you up to this, didn't they?" I hadn't exactly confessed my fears about my sanity to my roommates, but they did think I probably had a crush on Sternquist after I drunkenly mentioned her glowing issue one Friday night in a moment of utter weakness.

"I don't even know your roommates," he said, looking perfectly genuine and not at all offended that I didn't believe him.

"Okay, but...that's just stupid."

He shrugged again. He was way too good at shrugging like he wasn't saying insane things. "Why is it more stupid than you seeing her aura?"

"Because...because...." I was stalling, casting around for any viable reason one of these crazy things was more crazy than the other. "Because Econ is in the middle of the day?"

He waved a hand dismissively. "Okay, but you're going off one particular mythos for vampires that is entirely fictional."

"As opposed to all the non-fictional vampire mythoses?"

"Well, yes."

This is the other problem with being maybe-kind-of crazy. You can never tell if other people are actually rational or if it's just your crazy showing. Either way, he definitely seemed to believe what he was saying, and he had just enough of an air of knowing it sounded crazy to make him seem not crazy without him actually sounding like he really thought what he was saying was crazy. It was a whole lot of crazy. This was probably the maybe-kind-of craziest table on Capitol Hill at that given moment.

"Look," he said, "vampires have become hugely popular in fiction and film and all sorts of other pop culture media lately. But those ideas came from somewhere. Even Bram Stoker didn't actually make it all up. He was drawing on folklore. And...some of that folklore was drawing on actual fact. Stoker sort of doctored it to make vampires vulnerable to God, but there's still some truth in a lot of it."

"So what you're telling me," I started, speaking slowly so I could get my thoughts in some kind of order before they came out of my mouth, "is that Dr. Sternquist — dorky, cardigan-collecting Sternquist — goes out hunting at night and drains innocent victims of their blood in order to sustain herself for the taxing life of being a professor of the single most boring subject offered at any university ever."

"Don't be silly," he said with another hand wave. "I'm pretty sure her partner is a willing donor. And everybody knows that accounting is the most boring subject."

Well. He had me there.

"She has a partner?"

I didn't know when this had become more implausible than the blood-sucking, but it seemed like pertinent information at the time.

"That or a really, really close roommate."

I laughed. I couldn't help it. Still wasn't sure I believed in a god or gods, but I was maybe-kind-of starting to believe in vampires.

God or gods help me.

"Okay," I said, leaning forward, mug in hands, kickass coffee basically forgotten about. "I don't believe you, but tell me about vampires."

So. Here is the rundown on vampires as it was given to me in that coffee shop.

For one thing, all that church, holy water, crucifix crap is a load of bull. Which would go a long way toward explaining how or why one of them was teaching at a Jesuit university in the first place. Kind of makes sense, too, since they've been around, or so I'm told, since way before the Christian church was just some weirdo sect of Jews getting thrown to the lions on occasion.

Second, sunlight. Not that big a deal, as it turns out. They're just pretty sensitive to sunburn, which apparently comes from the fact that most of them hail from northern Europe. Hence Sternquist, my very Scandinavian professor. There are enclaves in other parts of the world, of course, but I guess it started up north, and of course, European literature and folklore deals mostly with European-style vampires. And I guess the pale skin thing is a pretty dominant gene for them.

Which leads me to the third thing. VAMPIRES CAN TOTALLY HAVE LITTLE VAMPIRE BABIES.

Take that, Bella.

The undead thing is, I guess, sort of true? But all their bits are still working. So. Yeah. Vampire babies. And I thought human ones were terrifying enough. They don't have them often, and they have to have them with other vampires. But Finn said, oh, right. His name was Finn, the guy with the smile. Apparently a lot of seers come from Irish families, and his was big on Irish heritage. Anyway, Finn said that vampires don't manifest until they're teenagers. Most supernatural sorts work that way, which also explains why I didn't start thinking I was maybe-kind-of crazy until after I went to college. I was a bit of a late bloomer.

(And yeah. There are *other* supernatural sorts. I'd get to those, eventually. One thing at a time.)

So, we've got church and sunlight and babies.... Oh, yeah. The blood thing. So vampires do totally need blood to survive, but I guess most of them come by it honestly. That is, they have what Finn called 'willing donors' or humans who let the vamps feed on them, and they don't hurt these people, other than the biting, and it makes the humans live longer? Because the vampires sometimes give them some of their own blood. It's this whole weird, freaky, blood-swapping thing. Mostly they're like Dr. Sternquist and her partner, where it's a long-term relationship, at least as long term as it can be. Vampires still live longer than humans. They're not immortal, but I guess it's not weird to see a 300-year old vampire. You know, other than the fact that it's a *300-year old vampire*. (Finn's definition of weird was not exactly the same as my definition of weird, as it turned out.)

Anyway. Blood donors. There's also a roaring trade in black market blood bags for those vamps who just aren't ready to settle down with a human yet.

And there are your rogue vampires. Because this couldn't be that easy. These are your power-hungry Vlad-the-Impaler types who get off on taking unwilling victims. Now, it's to everybody's advantage that there aren't just all kinds of exsanguinated bodies showing up all over the place and blowing the big, vamp cover for all the little bloodsuckers, so they tend not to kill their victims. Can't have them running to the police with a crazy vampire story either, though, so that glamour thing? The one where vampires can make humans do what they want by looking at them hard or whatever? Yeah, that's real.

Finn said they don't usually turn people, though. Don't want the responsibility. And mostly when they do turn people it's one of two things. Either it's the nice way (because there's a nice way to turn people into vampires?) where a vampire just can't stand the thought of living without their donor, so they turn them and do this sort of weird vampy marriage thing. Or it's the not-so-nice way, where some rogue vamp is looking to build an army and he (or she, let's not be sexist here) starts turning people basically to cause a ruckus.

But like I said, it's to everybody's advantage that nobody starts looking into the possibility of the vampire subculture being an actually legit thing, so Finn assures me that this is not a common thing to happen. Comforting, no?

Things that kill vampires? Not much. Mostly just decapitation and fire. Wooden stakes, not so much. They're not *exactly* undead? I mean, you have to die to become a vampire, and they do run a little on the chilly side, but they're very much alive. And they can regenerate from a lot of things.

All this came out over several hours and two more mochas in the coffee shop, and I still did not feel even close to having all my questions answered. Not to mention, I hadn't even touched on the whole seer thing. Somehow it was easier to ask about the weirdness I wasn't really a part of than to get down to the meat of what was actually going on with me. By the time Finn had to leave to get to his evening class, I was no closer to believing I wasn't actually crazy, but I had a whole lot to think about. Finn gave me his number before running off and promised to take me for coffee again after our next class if I still had questions.

"My treat. Least I can do for dumping this all on you at once."

I guess I must have seemed pretty overwhelmed. I *was* pretty overwhelmed, to tell the truth, but I was trying not to be obvious about it.

I still had that personal essay to write, but I didn't think I was going to get to it that night.

I walked home instead of taking the bus. It wasn't too far. A couple miles, maybe, but I wanted time to think about things before facing the roommates. I stopped to grab teriyaki for everybody before I got there so I'd have something else to focus on.

The door to our half of the duplex squeaked like crazy when I opened it, and Noah greeted me from the couch with a, "Hey!" and then an, "Ooh, teriyaki! I knew you loved me."

"Always and forever," I said with a smile. This was normal. This I could handle without worrying about my sanity or whether vampires were real.

I took dinner into the cramped kitchen where my other roommate, Yael, was sitting at the table doing her homework like the studious little nerd that she was.

"Hey, dinner!" she said when she looked up from her homework to see me at the table. "But it's Wednesday."

We each have one night a week when we're supposed to provide dinner, either making or buying, and on the other nights, we're all on our own. My night is Tuesday.

"Yeah." I shrugged. "Teriyaki just sounded good, and I know Noah would get all pouty if I didn't bring any for him."

"I don't pout," Noah protested from the doorway, somehow having managed to drag himself away from his video game to answer the call of food. "I protest in a perfectly manly fashion."

"You are such a pouter," Yael argued with a sweet smile. "But we love you anyway."

"You're too kind," he said, and for a while I could just ignore everything else that had happened that day. This was normal enough to push it all from my mind. My roommates and I might have originally joined forces because of a weird confluence of birthdays, but they'd become like family to me over the last year and a half.

So I got through dinner and I finished my essay after all—with no mention of vampires or auras or sibyls, just a boring account of falling out of a tree when I was twelve—and I went to bed like nothing had changed. It was really just another part of the maybe-kind-of I'd been living with for a couple years now. Just a different shade of crazy.

"Nobody in your family has it?"

I was sitting across from Finn at the corner table again, another Mexican mocha in front of me, somehow talking rationally about all the reasons neither of us was crazy.

"I don't know," I said. "I don't think so? But really? If something like this ran in my family, nobody would talk about it." Repression was a family value as far as my parents were concerned.

"That is so weird," Finn said, like everything else we were talking about was normal.

"Yeah, that is definitely the weirdest thing I've said since sitting down."

"Well, I wasn't going to bring up the whole 'I don't like baseball' thing. That's not weird, that's just un-American."

I had to laugh. Not because it was particularly funny, but because we were having this conversation at all, and because we'd actually gone from baseball to witches in about ten minutes flat.

"Okay, okay, but why is that so weird?"

"Well, it tends to run in families. Sometimes it crops up after a few generations' gap, but I've never heard of it showing up in families with no history of it."

"So...is everybody in your family like this?"

"No." He laughed this time, shaking his head and pushing his hair back. "Usually it's just once a generation. Sometimes it skips a generation or slides across. Like, my grandma has it? But it was her uncle who had it before her."

"So, it's like...genetic?"

"Sure!" He grinned into his coffee. "I mean, magic genetics, but same sort of idea. I'm pretty sure nobody's done any scientific studies on it."

I smiled a little and sipped my coffee. I wasn't really sure where to go from here. I thought I was starting to believe some of the stuff he was telling me, but I wasn't sure what was supposed to happen next.

"So...what do I do with it?"

"Well...there's kinda two schools of thought on that. The easy answer is obviously: nothing. You don't have to do anything you haven't already been doing. Just...now you know why you see stuff."

I'd definitely thought of that. Why did anything have to change? Why couldn't I just go about my business now being fairly sure I wasn't even maybe-kind-of crazy? I'd actually been wrestling with that one a lot over the past couple days. It should really be that easy, but something in me said it wasn't.

"What's the other school?" I asked, though I wasn't sure I wanted to know. Once it was there, once the option had presented itself, I couldn't ignore it anymore. Schrodinger's box was open, and I was stuck with that damn cat. (I've mentioned science is not my thing, right?)

Finn shrugged, and for the first time he looked like he was aware that he was going to tell me something that was important, that could potentially change my life. "Well, the other school is that we have an obligation to use our gifts, that we've been entrusted with them for a reason."

Yeah, that seemed about right. The thing in me that had been telling me I couldn't just ignore this was satisfied with his answer.

"Gifts? Plural?"

"Maybe? Some people have more than one."

Great. Like seeing visions wasn't enough. "How do you know if you have more than one?"

"You don't until you start developing them. The Sight is the most common. I've never met a sibyl who didn't have it. Never even heard of one. But when you start working to strengthen the Sight, sometimes other gifts manifest."

"Like what?" I didn't want to end up seeing more or start glowing myself.

"Commonly some kind of magic. A proclivity for one of the elements, maybe? Usually that only happens if there's werewolf in your blood, though. Most of the time, there's just some kind of domain you're particularly good at."

"Werewolf in my...no, never mind. I don't want to go there. How do I...how *would* I go about strengthening this?"

I couldn't believe I was actually contemplating this. But what Finn said made some kind of sense. I may not have believed in a higher power, but it did feel like if I had this thing in me, there must be a reason for it. I do believe that we're supposed to use what we're good at to make the world better.

"What are you doing Monday night?"

"Nothing important, why?" It was Noah's night for dinner, but he always picked something that could be reheated.

"Come to my coven."

"Your coven."

"Yeah, it's like a group of—"

I cut him off. I wasn't totally ignorant, after all. "A group of witches. I know. Why are you in a coven?"

He shrugged again, and I wanted to strap his shoulders down. "Like I said, they prefer the term 'witches' out here. It's just a group of people with gifts. We get together and study and practice."

"Like a mini-Hogwarts."

"Sure, if you wanna look at it like that. It's not weird, I promise."

"I'm not sure we agree on what that word means."

There was this smile on his face that I was starting to notice he got from time to time. It wasn't condescending exactly, but it was definitely knowing. "I know this is a lot to take in, but I really think coming on Monday would help. If it's too weird for you, you can leave any time." He glanced at his watch. "I've got to get to class, but...call me? If you decide you want to come."

I nodded and said goodbye, but I had no intention of calling. I wasn't a witch. I didn't need to get involved with some hippies or Wiccans or whatever they were. It was too much. The nothing option seemed like a way better deal, really. I could do that. I could do nothing.

And I was absolutely going to do nothing. Except that now that I knew what the things I was seeing were, or at least where they came from, I was starting to see more of them. The homeless lady by the bus stop? Her drawings started talking to me. The cute waitress at the pho place down the street? She suddenly had cat eyes.

That Saturday, Noah, Yael, and I went out to this bar by our place that does cheap margaritas and doesn't mind that Yael can't turn down a drunken bet and sometimes has to be talked out of taking her top off because she lost at darts.

(Yael is...well, she's Yael. I don't know anybody who doesn't like Yael. She's sweet in a way that should be annoying but somehow isn't, and she makes up for all of Noah's academic failings—and they are many—by being the best student I have ever seen. Obsessively so. She also loves tequila and has been known to stand on tables in bars and serenade everyone. She's a violinist, and she's really incredibly good at it. Probably the only reason she doesn't play the violin in bars is that people will hear her better if she belts it at the top of her lungs instead.)

Most of the people there are regulars, and most of them go to our college—proximity and price make it pretty popular.

We'd been there maybe an hour, and I was going to get us some refills. A guy a little taller than me squeezed his way up to the bar on my right, and I did a little double take. Sternquist glowed, but this guy was like a freaking sunlamp. He grinned and gave me a little wink that let me know he knew I could see it. Probably I was squinting at him, but I made a mental note to ask Finn if vampires could sense sibyls somehow.

"Hello, gorgeous. You going to drink all that yourself?" he asked, nodding to the three glasses the bartender had just slid over and leaning in a little too close for my comfort.

"Just picking up for friends," I said, still a little thrown off by how *bright* this guy was and how it didn't actually seem to hurt my eyes so long as I looked at him straight on.

"Why don't you drop those off and let me get you another," he suggested, looking me dead in the eyes, a faint smile playing at the corners of his lips.

I didn't want to, and I knew that. This guy was Creepy McCreepface in the flesh, and every rational part of my mind told me that I should be getting on my way now, thanks. But all the irrational parts of me—and it seemed there were a lot of them—really wanted to take him up on the offer. It sounded like a great way to spend my Saturday night. Both parts were pretty intent on getting me to go along with their plan, and I was frozen between the two. The longer I looked at this guy—this *vampire*—the more the irrational parts seemed to be winning.

They probably would have if I hadn't felt a familiar hand on the small of my back and heard Noah's voice saying, "There you are, babe. Thought maybe you got lost."

So about Noah. I met him freshmen year in my Functions and Algebraic Methods class. He was the TA, and I was hopeless. I would not have survived that class without him. Noah's a civil engineering major, and he's super smart with all that math and physics and whatever else you need to be an engineer and build safe bridges and all that. He also works as a bartender and never does his homework. Ever. He'll help me with math or science any time, but if it's his own work, it just doesn't get done. Basically, though, he's been helping me out of jams since we met, and my sixth sense (or would it be a seventh?) told me Noah thought I was in a jam right now. His interruption was enough for me to pull my gaze away from the light fixture in front of me, and that seemed to clear my brain a little. It still took me a moment to smile at Noah and say, "Nope, sorry. Just a little delayed. You wanna help me with these?" I handed him his glass, and he took it with a grin that he turned on the vampire before steering me back to our table.

I could feel the guy's eyes on the back of my neck all the way there.

I watched him for the rest of the night as surreptitiously as I could manage. When he finally left, he had a guy with him, and I couldn't help wondering if he knew what Creepface was or if he was in for a surprise.

I didn't even wait to get home before pulling out my phone and texting Finn to tell him we were on for Monday. It was starting to look like if I didn't embrace the crazy, it was going to embrace me, and that couldn't be a good thing.

Chapter Two

THE COVEN MET in a condo in West Seattle, just off the waterfront with a view of the city. We stopped at Trader Joe's on the way for some Two-Buck Chuck. Apparently booze was a thing you brought to coven meetings.

"There should be a name for these things," I said as we wound our way down towards Alki in Finn's 1990 Dodge Spirit.

"We just call them meetings."

"Yeah, but that's boring. There should be a better name." I don't know why I was so intent on this other than that it gave me something to think of other than what was waiting at the end of the drive.

"Suggestions?"

I shrugged. "Covenages? Coventries? There's got to be something better than just...meetings. Y'all are doing magic here."

"Coventries. I like it." He glanced over with that smile, and I smiled back.

"Okay. So what's going to happen at this coventry?"

"Well, there's wine."

I held up the bottle to show I got that part already, thanks.

"And you know...snacks and things."

"So it's a party?"

"It's a gathering."

"Of witches."

"Yeah. And we usually talk about what we've been doing and practice some things we're having trouble with. You know, see if we can help each other with anything."

Even I had to admit that didn't sound so terrifying. Practically normal. Like a supernatural study group. None of that really helped as we pulled up to the condo. It was pretty nice. I had to wonder if witching was a lucrative business. I could think of a few ways you could turn a profit with it, but Finn seemed to be a little down on that sort of thing, so I couldn't imagine his friends were into that.

I had been thinking study group, but the woman who answered the door was in her late forties. I guess I had been been living in the college bubble so long I forgot there were people of another age who weren't professors. She was tall and lanky, dark hair just starting to grey, pulled back into a ponytail.

"Hi!" she said, way too cheery for my taste, giving Finn a brief hug and offering me her hand. "You must be Finn's friend. He said he found a new one for us."

"Hey, Sharon, come on. Don't scare the newbie." This from the guy behind her, probably in his thirties, total hipster, complete with waxed handlebar mustache. If I hadn't been so focused on not coming off as an idiot, I would have thought he was a douchebag.

"So," Finn said, ushering me inside, I guess so that we didn't spend the whole night out on the front step. "This is Sharon and Fred. Sharon hosts our coventries."

And this is the reason I should never open my mouth when I'm nervous. Whatever I say is sure to come back and bite me.

"Our whats?" Fred asked, taking the wine bottles from Finn.

"That's what we've decided to call the meetings from now on. If we're gonna be a coven, we should make some use of it." I was glad Finn hadn't foisted the blame for that all onto me, even if that was exactly where it belonged. Nobody else needed to know that.

"I like it," Sharon said, giving me an approving nod. We headed to the living room, then, and it looked like everybody else was there already. Finn introduced me to Katie, a petite blonde with purple streaks in her hair; Davis, an older guy with a goatee and a serious widow's peak; Eleanor, a slightly chubby girl who somehow managed to look like she was walking on air when she moved; and Jerod, who looked like he hadn't gotten the memo that the grunge age had ended.

Hellos were exchanged all around, and Sharon invited everyone to the kitchen to grab snacks and drinks.

It wasn't exactly a festive atmosphere, but it was clear that they all knew each other and were comfortable. Everybody got a glass of wine—even Katie, who was probably underaged—and some cheese and crackers and fruit and cookies, and then we all made our way back to the living room. There was a lot of chatting and laughing and they all seemed to be having a good time. Except for Eleanor. She seemed like she was trying to have a good time, at least, but her brow was pinched together at the bridge of her nose like she was thinking about something else, something not altogether pleasant. I kind of wanted to ask her what was wrong, but considering I'd known her for about three minutes, I didn't think it was my place.

I took a seat on the couch with Davis and Sharon, and Finn just dropped to the floor next to me, legs tucked under him. Everybody else scattered themselves on several chairs around the room.

"So," Sharon said. "Everybody's probably wondering why Eleanor is with us today."

I hadn't been, but there were nods all around me.

"Eleanor has her own coven over on Queen Anne," Finn explained quietly. "We get together with them sometimes, but we usually meet separately."

"Got it."

Eleanor smiled, but that pinched brow was still there. "It's probably nothing," she started, and everyone sort of leaned toward her a little as she spoke. She had a faint accent to her voice, possibly Irish. "But we've been hearing some troubling stories coming from the shifters."

"Shapeshifters," Finn clarified for me.

"Wow, you really are a newbie, huh?" Jerod said, half into his glass of wine.

I tried to smile in response, but I'm pretty sure it was more like a grimace. "Yep, sorry. Prepare yourselves for all the stupid questions."

"Don't worry about it," Eleanor jumped back in. "We've all been there. Even those of us who grew up in the community." Her expression cleared a little, probably from having something else to focus on than whatever the shifters were saying.

Speaking of which, "So the shifters?" Fred prompted.

Eleanor nodded, and I noticed that her eyes were a deep, deep blue with tiny flecks of...well...sparkle in them. I wondered if that was a sibyl thing or if there was more going on with her. Nobody else's eyes seemed to be sparkling. "There have been some going missing. And others report blacking out and not being able to remember where they were the night before."

"Full moon?" Katie asked, pushing her hair behind her ear with a frown.

"Not always," Eleanor said. "And it's not just werewolves. It could be nothing. Most shifters are transient anyway; they may have just moved on to their next city."

"But you don't think so," Finn put in.

"No. We think there's something going on. Eli Jefferson blacked out for an entire weekend."

There was a collective intake of breath from everyone but Jerod, who was the next most recent addition to the coven, and I felt completely stupid, but I sort of raised my hand like I was in class and said, "Um...who?"

Finn nudged my ankle. "Eli. You know...Hagrid."

Hagrid was the mostly-affectionate nickname the campus had collectively given our most visible groundskeeper. He was an aging old hippie, and as far as I could tell, his only actual similarity to a Harry Potter character was his enormous beard. I liked him. Most people did. Rumor was he'd sit and talk to anybody who wanted to sit and talk about anything at all.

"Eli's sort of the deputy leader of the shifters in Seattle," Fred offered, tugging on his mustache a little. "Like Eleanor said, most shifters aren't like the werewolves. They move along pretty quickly. Eli's been here for three decades, and he hasn't touched a drop of alcohol or so much as puffed a joint for as long as I've known him."

"So no chance he just got a bad batch of something?" Jerod asked.

"It's highly unlikely," Eleanor said, nodding. Her eyes sparkled a little brighter, and then she took a deep breath and they dulled back down again. "So far only two have actually gone missing, so I'm just going around to the other covens to let everyone know to keep an eye out for unusual behavior or suspicious characters. Especially anyone you haven't seen around before."

"We'll keep our eyes open," Sharon responded for the group. I was wondering how I was going to know what constituted unusual behavior when everything I'd seen in the last week seemed like it was pretty damn unusual.

Eleanor smiled and said, "Thanks," and the conversation moved on to other topics.

The rest of the evening was basically what Finn had described. Katie was having some trouble with her power—she could levitate small objects—and Sharon and Fred walked her through some concentration exercises to help her focus. Eleanor taught Jerod a spell for temporarily altering his facial features, briefly making him look like Paul Rudd. Finn admitted that he'd almost singed his eyebrows the week before trying to light a candle across the room, and Davis gave him a long list of tips ranging from meditation to fire safety.

Once everybody's problems seemed to be sorted, Katie turned to me. "So what's yours?"

"My what?"

"Your power, silly," she said, nudging my foot with her toes from her chair next to the couch.

"Oh, um...I don't really know yet? I only just found out I was...whatever I am on Wednesday."

Finn nudged my other foot from his seat on the floor. "It's not like there's a rush. These things come in time. Sometimes they don't come at all."

"I didn't get mine until I'd had the Sight for a year," Davis admitted. "I thought it wasn't going to happen for me."

"Everybody's different," Eleanor affirmed. "Sometimes it takes necessity to draw it out."

"What do you mean?" I asked, pulling my feet away from both of the nudgers, tucking them under me on the couch.

"Sometimes it manifests only when you need it," Finn explained. "If you're in danger or something."

"Or you really need to look like Paul Rudd," Jerod added. Everybody laughed, and I sat back a little, sipping my wine.

There were vampires in the city, shapeshifters not only existed but were disappearing, the girl next to me had just levitated her wine glass, and I was sitting in a coven on a Monday night wondering what my mutant power was going to turn out to be. I still felt more sane than I had in a long time.

I'd gotten so involved in the coventry (yes, it's a stupid name, but it stuck) on Monday, that I'd completely forgotten to ask Finn about the vampire I'd seen at the bar. I didn't remember it again until we were having coffee after class on Wednesday.

"When you say 'brighter,' how much brighter are we talking?" Finn asked after I explained to him about the creeper I'd run into.

"Like...if Dr. Sternquist is a nightlight, this guy is a flood lamp."

"Okay, wow. So...brighter."

"That's what I said."

It was getting to be entirely too comfortable sitting in my coffee shop with Finn talking about vampires. I felt like I should still be pretty weirded out by the whole deal, but it just seemed natural at this point. I guess it made sense that I had a pretty high tolerance for maybe-kind-of crazy.

"And he tried to glamour you?"

"Um...I guess?" With my vast, pop-cultural knowledge of vampires, I'd decided that had to be what he did that made me want to act so monumentally stupid.

"He must have been pretty cocky or pretty old or both then."

"Why's that?"

"Sibyls are hard to glamour. We have a natural resistance. Some stronger than others, but everybody's got it a little. It's kind of a defense mechanism."

"But if he was old, it would be easier?"

"Yeah, and it might explain the brightness. I've never seen a vampire older than about 150 before, but I guess if he was really, really old, he might get brighter."

I thought about that for a moment. I didn't know how old Dr. Sternquist was, so I couldn't really make a comparison, but it did seem to make pretty good sense. "Do you think he could tell I'm a...sibyl?" That, at least, still felt weird to say.

"Oh, definitely. Vampires can smell us."

"Smell us?" I tended to come off a lot like an echo chamber in these little chats, but now I was wondering if I was going to have to start buying stronger deodorant.

"Yeah. Their sense of smell is pretty heightened anyway, but I guess there's something distinctive about a sibyl's scent that they can pick up on."

"Do you think that's why he tried to pick me up?" I really didn't need to have vampire-attracting pheromones. If I did, I was going to have to find a new bar.

"Maybe? As far as I know, our blood doesn't taste any different than a regular human's, but maybe he's got a thing for sibyls. Was the guy he left with one?"

"How do you tell?"

"You can't see it?"

Someday, I was going to get Finn to just sit down and write me a list of all the things I was supposed to be able to do with these gifts of mine.

"I'm gonna go with no."

"Oh!" He sat back a little, looking like this was the most surprising revelation he'd had about me to date. "Well, sibyls have an aura too. Maybe you just aren't looking for it."

"What's it look like?"

"Usually green. Sometimes blue. It's not as bright as a vampires, but it should be noticeable."

I leaned forward to get a better look at him then, arms braced on the table, squinting to see if that would help the aura come into focus. It wasn't until I thought I saw maybe a flicker of green by his ear and grinned, my eyes sliding to his, that I realized just how close I was.

I sat back quickly and took an unconvincingly casual sip of my coffee. "I, um, think I saw it."

He blinked and pushed his hair back and gave me a smile I couldn't categorize. "Cool. Um...well, it should get stronger from here on out. It's like your other gifts. Recognizing them gives them power."

"Is that why that guy's ears are pointed?" He looked over his shoulder to see where I was pointing, making it completely obvious that I was...well...pointing.

"Oh hey, Steve!" he said, waving at the guy, who smiled and waved back. He turned back to me, and I was mortified to see I was still pointing. I put my hand down quickly. "Yeah," Finn said. "Steve's part fairy."

"Oh, god. Now there's fairies."

"To be fair, there have always been fairies. You just haven't always seen them."

"Does he read people's minds or something?"

"This isn't *True Blood*."

"Hey, I don't know! I'm new to all of this."

"Well, he doesn't. He is kind of an empath, though...."

I threw my hands up. "I am never going to learn all this!"

"And you thought Econ was bad," Finn joked, pushing his hair out of his face.

He definitely looked green now. Just a tinge around the edges. Kind of like light filtering through leaves.

"What?" he asked, sitting up a little straighter and rubbing his cheek. "Do I have something on my face?"

I hadn't realized until then that I'd been looking at him intently. "No, nothing. Just...your aura."

"You can see it!"

I glanced around to see if anyone else had noticed his outburst, but everyone was just sipping away at their coffee like normal. "Yeah," I said quietly. "I can see it. No big deal."

"Hey, every step forward is good. The more you take, the easier it is."

This guy was full of platitudes. They were true, but still. Platitudes.

"I really don't think this is ever going to get easier."

That made him frown, and I almost regretted it. He really did have a great smile.

"What do you mean?"

"Well...I mean, if I just keep seeing more and more and doing more and more, it's never going to normalize."

"Sure it will," Finn said, leaning back and looking at me carefully. "I think you're just...looking at it wrong."

"How should I be looking at it?"

"Like you do anything else new. Think about it like learning a new sport or starting a new class. At first there's just *so much* to learn, and it's overwhelming, and for every new thing you learn, there seems to be another five things that show up that you don't know. But eventually you know enough that learning more is fun instead of daunting."

"This is going to be fun?"

"Sure! Didn't you have fun on Monday?"

I was starting to hate it when he was right.

"Yeah, okay. But that's different."

"How?"

"Because how can a coventry not be fun?"

He laughed, and the green around him got a little brighter. I didn't want to like him, but I was definitely starting to.

He was right about that too. Recognition made it stronger.

Finn and I settled into a sort of routine. We had a standing coffee date after class to talk about things that were freaking me out or questions that I had. We talked about other things too. Mostly because I didn't always have questions or freaking out things, but the coffee was natural by now. I was going to have to pick up another couple shifts at the shop where I worked to pay for them if they kept up, but it was nice to have some normalcy around all this crazy. Noah started teasing me about the 'mystery guy' and asking when he was coming home to meet the family.

Mondays were coventry nights, and that was going pretty well too. I still didn't know what my other gifts were, but it was nice to talk to someone other than Finn about the things I was finally starting to think weren't a sign of insanity. We didn't hear about any more shifters disappearing, and I think we all just sort of pushed it to the back of our minds.

I saw Hagrid—Eli, that is—around campus a few times, and I smiled at him more, looking at him more closely to see if I could pick up any signs that he was a shifter. I thought that I saw a bit of a yellow-ish aura once, and his eyes seemed a little more gold than hazel, but otherwise he was just the same.

I was starting to think this new side of my life wasn't going to be so bad after all. Totally manageable.

Of course, that's when I ran into him again: the vampire from the bar.

I was walking home from the bus stop after my evening class, and when I turned the corner he was leaning casually against a streetlight, illuminating the street far better than the actual lamp. I froze, and for a moment all I could do was stare and blink and try to convince myself it was really him.

He looked straight at me and smiled. "Hello, gorgeous," he said and beckoned me closer with one hand. It was the same as it had been in the bar. I didn't want to, but I found myself walking closer, one slow step at a time. I'd closed about half the distance between us when I remembered what Finn had said about sibyls being resistant to glamouring. I thought, too, about recognition making things stronger. *Well*, I thought, *I recognize that this asshole can't control me.*

It wasn't like anything big happened. I didn't feel anything. I still sort of felt that tug to move closer, but I just stopped instead.

He frowned. I couldn't quite bring myself to look away from his eyes, and when he said, "Come here," in a low, commanding tone, I felt that tug even stronger. I *wanted* to go to him, but I recognized that the desire to move wasn't coming from me.

"No," I said firmly, annoyed that my voice shook a little but still standing my ground.

The noise he made in response to my refusal sent a shiver of fear down my spine. It was a deep, inhuman sound, a sort of growling hiss, and when he opened his mouth, I was certain that even a mundane human could see those fangs gleaming in the glow of the streetlight. My hand moved to my pocket for my phone, but before I could reach it he came at me in a blinding blur of movement and light. His hand curled around my bicep like a vice, and his other arm moved around my waist. And then he took off.

He *took off*. Into the air. Carrying me. Nobody told me vampires could *fly*. We were a couple hundred feet off the ground, and all I could think was that this really should have come up in the several hours Finn spent explaining the undead to me or the weeks I'd spent at the coventry since then. How had nobody ever thought to mention that vampires could fly? Clearly this was pertinent information, though I don't know what I could have done with it in the moment.

I was so shocked by this lapse in my supernatural education that I didn't think to yell or struggle or really anything. Probably good in retrospect. I didn't want him dropping me, after all.

Before I could gather myself enough to do something about the situation, we were landing. I looked around and saw that we weren't actually that far from my place. He'd taken me to Lake View Cemetery. I was still reeling from the flight and more than a little out of it, and I started to laugh. He took me to a *cemetery*. Somewhere in my clearly damaged psyche that level of cliché was *hilarious*.

I didn't laugh for long, though. In a few seconds he had me pushed back against a tree with his hand at my throat. I could feel the prick of his nails, and I wondered if this was something else Finn had forgotten to tell me or if this guy had actually filed his nails into points. He seemed the type.

"If you make a noise, I will not hesitate to rip your throat out, understood?"

I figured 'yes' would count as a noise, so I cautiously nodded.

"Good." His hand stayed at my throat, and he laid his other arm across my shoulders, presumably to keep me against the tree in case I had any notion of trying to escape. (I didn't.)

"I'm going to ask you a few questions," he said, locking eyes with me again. "And you're going to answer them quickly and quietly. You will not speak otherwise."

I felt that tug again, like a prickling in the back of my mind, making me want to obey. I nodded.

"Very good. So much better like this, isn't it?"

"No," I said honestly. He'd asked for answers, after all.

"Very funny, but I'm not laughing. You're a seer, yes?"

"A sibyl," I corrected him.

"Whatever you want to call yourself. You're new to the area?"

"Not really," I said. I'd been in Seattle for three years now.

"But I haven't seen you or heard of you before."

It wasn't a question, so I kept my mouth shut.

"New to your powers?"

"Yeah, you could say that."

"How new?"

"I only found out what they were a month or so ago."

His expression turned almost sympathetic. "That must have been hard for you to deal with."

"It was. I thought I was going crazy."

He nodded, satisfied, and his gaze intensified. I don't have another word for it. He looked at me *more*, and his arm against my shoulders pressed back harder. There would be bruises tomorrow, I could tell. "You're going to help me with a little project."

The light he was emitting was practically enveloping me, his eyes bored into mine, and that itching in my mind was almost physically painful, but I thought of the recognition. There wasn't much I was sure of in that moment, but I was sure I didn't have to do what he said.

"No," I ground out, teeth gritted with the effort of speaking that one word.

His grip loosened slightly; he was clearly surprised by my answer. "No?"

"No," I said again, and it was easier the second time, like knowing I could do it meant it didn't take as much work.

He looked at me hard again, like he was trying to work out if I'd actually said that. And then he laughed, high and cold, as cliché as the setting. "Oh, you're going to be so sorry you said that, gorgeous."

"Am I?" I was standing in a cemetery, pinned to a tree by a vampire who had his claws to my throat. It wasn't like I had much to lose at this point by being snarky.

"Well," he said thoughtfully. "Not for too long."

What happened next, I still can't quite explain. He took his hand from my throat and leaned in, clearly ready to bite me, drink my blood, leave me in the cemetery, whatever it was he was planning. Only, he never got there.

I closed my eyes, and for half a second I thought I was done for, but then it was like this little voice in the back of my mind, the same place that itched when he tried to glamour me, just said, "Don't give up so easy."

My eyes were still closed—even his light was shut out—but I could see something in the blackness. It looked like rope, and I just sort of...called for it. In my mind. I didn't even have a clear picture of what I wanted to do with it, but I knew I needed it, so I called. It came flying toward me, and then next thing I knew, the pressure of the vampire was off my chest, and I felt him being pulled away from me. I wasn't done, though; the voice wouldn't let me stop there. I was working off instinct, and I could see something behind me, something big and heavy with spikes protruding from it. Without hesitation, I sent one of the spikes flying toward where I could see the ropes struggling to hold the vampire. I heard it impaling him, and I knew that it had pinned him to the ground.

I opened my eyes.

In front of me, tangled in a mess of ivy, a branch protruding from his chest, was the vampire. He wasn't moving. I approached him slowly, not sure if he was faking or if he really was held by the plants.

His eyes were wide, and his face was livid.

"You'd better run, gorgeous. This won't hold me long."

I knew I should, but I was still held by his gaze. It was somehow even stronger than before. Maybe his anger made it more powerful. I don't know, but I couldn't look away. I think it took him a moment to realize this, and then he smiled.

"None of this is real, you know," he said. His voice was calm, soothing, like a friend very gently telling you something you knew was true but didn't want to admit. "There aren't any vampires. There aren't any sibyls. None of the things you see are really there, and there are so many of them, aren't there? You see so many, many things. So many, many creatures. They can't all be there. Someone would notice."

I frowned, brow furrowing. I knew that wasn't true. It couldn't be true. It couldn't be true because... "Finn. Finn sees them too."

"Even Finn isn't really there," he said, shaking his head sadly, disappointed to break this news to me. "Poor thing. You're just going crazy, and you've made up this explanation to make it seem like you're still sane."

He was losing a lot of blood.

I only say this because it's the only explanation I can come up with for why his gaze stopped being quite so powerful, why it lessened enough for that itching to come back in my mind, for me to remind myself that he couldn't do this to me.

"Liar," I said, and as I did, the ivy tightened around him. He gave a gargling, choking gasp, and I did what I should have done in the first place.

I ran.

Chapter Three

It was about a mile from the cemetery to my house, and I ran the whole way. I miraculously still had my messenger bag slung across my shoulders, and it whacked my hip with every step. It was raining, pouring really, but I just kept running right to my street, through the gate, across the yard, up the steps, and into the door where I almost bowled Yael over.

"Jesus," she said as she caught me just before I face planted into the living room. "What happened?"

I was way too out of breath to answer her right away, which was good, because it gave me a chance to come up with an explanation. No way was I telling her I'd just sent a tree branch through a vampire's chest in the cemetery using only the powers of my otherwise unimpressive brain. I held up one finger to indicate she should wait for a response and racked my brain for a good—or at least plausible—reason for having run home.

By the time I could breathe again, I said, "Sorry. Just...saw this dog thing? It was dark and late and..." I knew it sounded stupid, so I just finished with, "And I'm a moron. Sorry. It was really nothing. But we got out of class early, and I hung out with some guys from class to watch *The Mothman Prophecies* in their dorm. I just...got a little freaked out."

There. That was...slightly better? Not perfect, but I was hoping she'd buy it. I'm really not good with scary movies.

"Oh my god, you asshole," she said, smacking my shoulder. "You scared me half to death. I thought you were being chased by an ax murderer or something."

"Sorry," I said again, rubbing my shoulder. "And ow."

"Sorry," she echoed and gave my shoulder a quick rub, not really helping the soreness. "But seriously. Freddy Kruger better be hot on your heels the next time you pull something like that."

"Yes, ma'am," I said, giving her a quick salute as I headed to my room, and pondering just how likely that was to actually happen someday.

That Friday, I was sitting across from Finn in the coffee shop, hands curled around my mug, contemplating how to ask the question that had been itching in the back of my mind for the last couple days.

"Hey, vampires can't...fly, can they?"

He snorted into his drink. "Not *True Blood*, remember?"

"Just checking," I said, and I could feel the frown tugging at the corners of my lips. "I just thought maybe they were like sibyls. You know, like they each had a particular power in addition to their vampiness."

"I'm pretty sure it doesn't work that way," he said, and I nodded.

"I gotta go," I said a moment later. "Paper to write."

"For the essay class?" he asked. I nodded again.

"Yep. About an issue of personal and cultural importance."

"Sounds like a blast. See you Monday?"

"Yep," I repeated, slinging my bag over my shoulder. I gave him a quick wave and headed out into the misty rain.

I didn't go home.

I just walked along Broadway. I needed time and space to clear my head because this? This was bad.

I'd just been starting to think I was maybe-kind-of sane.

But vampires didn't fly.

If vampires didn't fly, then I had no idea how I'd gotten to Lake View the other night. I took a left down Pike, heading toward downtown. I didn't really have any specific destination in mind, but I needed to be away from...everything.

A woman bumped into my shoulder as she passed me. Her eyes were orange.

A few blocks further down, a busker smiled at me. His teeth were sharpened to points.

A mounted policeman reined in across the street from me. His horse wasn't the only one with a tail.

Everywhere I looked I could see something that wasn't right. Something that shouldn't be there. It had been bad enough when it was once or twice a day. Now I was being bombarded with it.

What if I really was going crazy? What if none of the things I saw were really there? What if I'd just made the whole thing up as a coping mechanism? My subconscious had picked a hell of a time to perk up and bring me back to reality if that was the case.

But it almost had to be. Yesterday, I had seen maybe three new supernatural things a day. On a busy day. I had just seen three in the last twenty minutes. There were so many, many of them. They couldn't all be there. Someone would notice.

I had intended to keep walking until I could calm my brain down and get some idea of how I wanted to handle things, but there were just too many people around, and too many of them were not what they seemed. I got as far as Fourth Avenue, and I couldn't deal with it any longer, so I ducked into the nearest Starbucks, figuring it was the least likely place to encounter anything but perfectly normal human beings. All I really needed was a place to sit and think and not have to be confronted with evidence of my possible psychosis.

I stepped into the line and kept my eyes down just in case, letting the muted music piping into the shop calm me down a little. By the time I got to the counter, I was almost relaxed.

"Yeah, can I get a grande americano with room?" I said automatically, my eyes scanning the bakery case to see if anything looked good.

"Of course," said the guy behind the counter, and then, "Hey! You're Finn's friend, right?"

Finn. Oh god, Finn. Was he even real? Had I just spent fifteen minutes in a coffee shop talking to myself? Or was he real but not really a sibyl? Had I just made that up, too?

I finally looked at the guy, and it took me a moment to place where I'd seen him before. Not at the coven meetings, surely. And then I noticed his ears, and it hit me. "Steve, right?" Steve the half-fairy. "You...work at Starbucks?" I quickly glanced at the other employees, but they seemed to all be human.

"Yeah," he said with a sheepish laugh. "Don't tell my boss I go to other shops on my days off, huh?"

That was not the cause of my incredulous tone, but I didn't exactly want to point that out just now, so I mumbled, "Secret's safe with me," and tried for a normal, friendly smile.

I must have fallen short of the mark, because Steve said, "Hey, are you okay? You don't look so good."

I really didn't think I needed to be getting help from a half-fairy while I was almost sure that fairies maybe-kind-of weren't a thing, so I just shrugged and gave that smile another attempt and said, "Yeah, fine. How much do I owe you?"

He gave me the total, and I handed him my debit card. As he ran it, he gave me a shrewd look, and when he handed it back, he said, "You're really bad at this, you know."

"Bad at what?"

"Pretending everything's okay."

I tried once more for a super convincing 'everything's okay' smile and gave him my name for the order. "Really, it's fine."

I didn't think it had actually worked, but he nodded, and said, "It'll be up in a minute," handing my cup to the barista and turning his attention to the next person in line.

I was more than happy to shuffle out of the way and wait for my drink at the other end of the counter. I fully intended to take that coffee to Westlake or the nearest bench I could find, hunker down with my headphones over my ears and shut off all my senses until they started actually *making* sense, but by the time I got my coffee doctored up and was ready to leave, Steve was sitting at a table near the corner waving me over.

I contemplated, briefly, pretending I hadn't seen him, but the things is, Steve is tall and burly and basically built like the platonic ideal of a lumberjack, complete with the ultimate in manly—and still somehow perfectly groomed—beard. When he waved his whole arm at you from across a downtown Starbucks? You saw it. Half the customers in the shop were looking over at him.

"I was actually just going to—" I started, but he cut me off with a wave of his hand and a gesture to the seat across from him.

"My shift just ended, and you look like you need to talk."

I probably did need to talk. I wasn't sure I needed to talk to someone who may or may not actually have elf ears. Still, even though I'd just met Steve, I could already see he was basically a giant puppy dog and I didn't want him to pout at me. I was sure he was way better at it than Noah.

So I sat. I didn't put my coffee down, though. I was definitely ready to bolt if he sprouted wings or something.

"You don't have to," he continued. "We can just sit and sip overpriced coffee if you'd rather."

I would rather have. I was pretty sure about that. But I had this lumberjack puppy sitting across from me looking all kinds of sincere, and if I could just block out the ears, he seemed pretty normal too. And maybe there was some kind of fairy dust floating around or something because I found myself saying, "How much do you know about Finn?"

"Like do I know he's a sibyl?"

And just like that, I felt a little better. Because Steve was definitely real. He'd helped customers before and after me in line, and everyone in the room had looked when he waved. He was not a figment of my imagination, and he was definitely acknowledging the thing I was most afraid of not being real.

"Yeah, that. Basically."

"Of course," he said with a wide grin. "The supernatural community is generally pretty tight. We all kind of know each other. I mean, vampires keep to themselves for the most part, the werewolves are kind of pack-intensive, and the shifters have their own thing going, but otherwise, we're close. You're new to it, right?"

Something I was having trouble really wrapping my head around was the way these people—I guess I was one of them—treated this like it was no big deal. At first, I'd thought it was just Finn, the way he talked about vampires with the same casual acceptance as he talked about last night's Sounders match, but the others at the coven did as well, and here was Steve now, telling me about the supernatural community like it was a book club.

"Yeah," I answered, and even I could hear the weary resignation in my voice.

"It'll get easier," he said, reaching across the table to lay his massive palm across my forearm. There was a certain level of comfort in the touch, and I didn't want to read too deeply into why that was.

"How do you know? You probably grew up with this just like Finn."

"I did," he admitted easily, pulling his hand back like my refusal to be comforted hurt him somehow. "But I've also seen a lot of people go through what you're going through. Not everybody in the community grew up with it, and everybody has to learn to accept what they are and what the world is. It takes time, but I haven't seen anybody fail at it yet."

"How long have you been watching?" He looked twenty-five at most.

"About eighty years?"

I choked on my drink, and he laughed. It was a deep, rich, lumberjacky laugh, but when he spoke there was almost a twinkle in his voice. "Fairy," he said, with a shrug and an almost delicate wave of his beefy hand.

"There's got to be a book with all this stuff in it somewhere."

"There is. Several, actually, but I don't recommend trying to slog through them. Better to learn as you go."

"It's kind of a steep learning curve."

"It can be," he agreed, pure sympathy in his tone. I remembered what Finn had said about him being an empath, and I wondered how much of what I was feeling he also felt. "So what part of the curve's got you down today?"

He was so sincere, and so clearly actually interested, that for a moment, I wanted to tell him all about the vampire and the cemetery and my worries that I was making all this up. I hoped he was studying counseling because something about him made me want to tell him everything that was wrong. I didn't know if it was the fairy thing or if he just had that kind of face.

I opened my mouth to start the story, but something held me back. Something in that itching place in the back of my mind. Instead, I said, "I think I'm still in the adjusting period. There's just *so much*. I saw a cop with a tail on the way down here."

"Derek? Yeah, he's a shifter. Nice guy. Bit of a temper, but he just turns into a chinchilla, so it's not like he's gonna do any real harm."

I honestly couldn't tell if he was joking or not, but I laughed anyway, and he joined me in it. "It's pretty overwhelming, huh?" he asked, and I nodded. Understatement of the...I don't even know. Some really big measurement of time. Epoch, maybe. "Have you told anyone outside the community?"

It hadn't even occurred to me to do this. I'd already resigned myself to keeping it to myself for maybe-kind-of forever. "Do you think I should?"

He shrugged. "It's up to you. I definitely don't recommend running around telling everybody you know. You'd end up in an asylum for one thing, if the supes didn't stop you first. Some people find it easier to confide in someone, though. Your parents, maybe? Finn mentioned you don't have a history of this, or don't think you do. They might surprise you by knowing already, though."

I tried to imagine my mom at something like our coventries, or my dad turning into a hamster. The very idea was ludicrous. "Yeah, somehow I doubt it."

Steve nodded, and for a minute or two we were both just quiet, sipping our coffees. It wasn't until then that I realized I had calmed down a bit. Insanity seemed slightly less likely than it had half an hour ago, and there was something about Steve that was just comfortable.

"I think the thing that most people struggle with is the way it cuts you off from other people," he mused after a moment. "We're a close community, sure, and if you need support, pretty much everyone is here for you, but it can be difficult suddenly having a part of your life you can't share with the people you've always been closest to."

That made sense. More than made sense. My parents, my friends, my roommates, they were all outside this new world of mine. When I came back from coventries, I couldn't tell Yael that Katie had managed to lift a whole couch. I couldn't tell Noah about Davis accidentally spraying wine all over Sharon while attempting to turn it into beer. I couldn't call my dad and tell him Finn had learned how to tune a radio to pick up telepathic communications. It was a huge, new thing in my life, and I couldn't share it with anyone I'd known before.

"I don't wanna tell you what to do," Steve continued. "But I think maybe you ought to see if there's someone in your life you feel like you can trust with this. Maybe not with all of it, but with a little bit."

I nodded, not sure yet who I might tell, but considering the people I knew and trying to figure out who might take it the best. There was no way my mom and dad could handle this. Noah was too sciencey to accept it. Maybe Yael?

He sat back in his chair as he finished his coffee, then smiled. It warmed me all over. I was definitely going to have to ask Finn about fairies. "I've gotta get going, but if you ever need to talk…." He held out his hand, and I passed my phone over for him to put his number in. When I took it back, I saw that he'd labeled himself 'fairy-boy.' "See you around," he said as he pulled himself upright, and then, with a quick smile, he was gone.

Everyone else in the shop was just a regular, boring old human, but I didn't need to sequester myself from the supernatural anymore, so I finished my drink and headed out, pulling out my phone to text Yael: *Drinks tonight?*

I almost followed it up with a text to Finn about flying vampires, but that little voice came back and whispered that there were maybe-kind-of some things I still wasn't sure were real.

Noah was on a date that night with his fling of the week, so it was just Yael and I at the bar. We weren't exactly deep into our cups, but we'd definitely had a few, and I was starting to work up the courage to tell her about, well, not everything, but maybe some of the things. It was my round, and I made my way up to the bar, determined to tell her when I got back, or at least to start to tell her.

I had just put in the order when I was surrounded by light. I didn't want to turn around, didn't want to acknowledge what I knew was behind me, but I took a deep breath and made myself look.

"Hello, gorgeous," he said, just as smarmy as ever other time. He leaned against the bar a little too close for comfort, and I took a tiny step back. He really needed to cut back on the Old Spice.

"Not interested," I answered, pretty sure he wouldn't try anything in the middle of the bar but not entirely convinced.

He looked at me hard, and I tried to look away, to break the contact I knew he needed to try and glamour me. But I couldn't. "No, of course not," he said, his voice pitched low and slightly hypnotic. "Because you think I'm something I'm not. You think I'm something that doesn't even exist. Vampires? Fairies? Sibyls? What kind of a person creates an entire fantasy world just to convince themselves they're sane?"

As he spoke, the itching came back, getting worse and worse with every word, almost maddening now. I tried to think of Finn and Steve. I tried to recognize that he couldn't glamour me. He wasn't allowed to.

He's not glamouring you, the little voice said. *How can he? That's not even real.*

I was still trying to come up with a good argument against this perfectly reasonable-seeming objection when two things happened. Looking back on it, I think if they hadn't both happened at the same time, I would have still been standing there staring back at Creepface. On one side of me, the bartender slid my drinks across the bar and asked for $8.50. On the other, Yael slid up and gave me a hug from behind, grinning first at me and then at the vampire, so much like Noah I almost laughed.

"You forgot your wallet, doofus," she said, sliding a ten over to the bartender.

"Ah," Creepface said, turning his smile toward Yael. "You should ask your little friend to join us."

"Sorry," she said, only half looking at him as she picked up the drinks and handed me mine. "This little friend has a date with Jose. Gonna have to get a raincheck on that."

"I'll hold you to it," he called after us as Yael pulled me through the crowd back to our table. I was really hoping he'd forget that promise.

As I slid into the booth across from Yael, she said, "Hey, you were gonna tell me something, weren't you?"

All of the nerve I'd worked up before getting drinks was gone, and that voice was telling me that I was imagining things anyway. "It's nothing," I said after a moment. "Just wanted to say I got an A- on my essay."

"Good for you!" she said, lifting her glass to me. "Jell-o shots to celebrate?"

"Sure," I answered, giving her the same smile I'd given Steve earlier and hoping she accepted it easier.

While she went to the bar, I kept an eye out for Creepface's streetlight, but I couldn't spot him anywhere. I couldn't decide if I hoped that was because I'd only imagined the glowing or if I wanted him to have picked his victim for the night.

I didn't like what it said about me that the latter might be true.

Yael came back with a tray of brightly colored shots, and once we started losing ourselves in theories about what, exactly, made Creepface's face so creepy, I let myself forget all about it.

That worked just about until the time we stumbled out of the bar at closing, arms flung over each other's shoulders. Yael was telling me about this guy in her O-Chem class she had an enormous crush on, lamenting his obliviousness to all her best flirting.

"It's like he doesn't even notice that I'm female. Or maybe he does! Maybe that's the problem. Do you think he's gay?"

"Haven't met the guy," I pointed out, steering her out of the street, even though I was unsteady myself. "Probably, though. You're definitely female."

"Ugh. I could totally be a boy if he wanted me to," she mused. "I mean…hey!" She straightened up suddenly, leaning across me to peer into an alley as we passed. "Isn't that Creepface from the bar?"

Sure enough, when I looked over, he was there with his face buried in some girl's neck. I couldn't see any blood, but I wasn't in any condition to be looking closely.

"Looks like he did okay finding another little friend," Yael said, giggling and leaning against me.

Her giggles resounded in the nearly empty street, and Creepface looked up from his victim/partner. He turned right to me, shining brightly in the dark alley, and he grinned.

There were no fangs, no blood, no sign at all that he was doing anything worse than making out in an alley. I shook my head to clear it and rubbed my eyes a little, sure that I was missing something, too drunk to see what was right in front of me. The girl made a little noise of disapproval and pulled his face to hers to kiss him.

"Get a room!" Yael shouted, still giggling.

It was enough to draw my attention back to her. "Let's get you home, kid," I said, tugging her along the street. I couldn't help glancing back over my shoulder as we went, but I never saw anything more than a beacon of light making out with a very drunk college student.

Chapter Four

By the time I woke up the next morning (okay, afternoon), I had only a vague recollection of what had happened the night before. I remembered tequila and Jell-o shots and running into Creepface, but everything else was hazy. I was pretty sure I hadn't told Yael about being a sibyl, and I was glad for that. It seemed like a monumentally bad idea now. The more I thought about it, the less convincing my evidence seemed. Even the undeniable realness of Steve didn't seem to make a strong case for me not simply hallucinating. And even if it was true, it *sounded* crazy. There was no way to get around that. Keeping it to myself was almost definitely a solid plan.

I was tempted to text Steve just to see if he wanted to hang out. I felt better when I was around him, and I could use a little better.

I didn't, but only because I got a text from Finn saying coventry was moved to Sunday that week because it was supposed to be a beautiful day, and Fred had a thing for communing with nature as a group. I figured I could wait for Sunday to get some support in the craziness, so I texted Finn back that it was okay with me and to make sure he could pick me up again. Then I slithered out of bed, pulled on a sweatshirt, and stumbled out to the kitchen where Noah was at the stove making an enormous pan of scrambled eggs with all manner of good things in them.

"Morning, sunshine," he said, pressing a mug of coffee into my hands and directing me to the table.

"You are my favorite person in the universe," I said.

"You only love me for my coffee," he returned.

"Hey, what about me?" Yael asked in a subdued voice that let me know she felt just as bad as I did that morning.

"You are the reason I'm in this condition in the first place. It's okay to celebrate with other things than shots, you know. Cupcakes are always nice."

"Nobody forced them down your throat."

She had a point, and before I could come up with a good retort, Noah dropped a plate in front of each of us, the clattering pounding in my head. "Now, children. No fighting over breakfast. Eat up."

I looked around the kitchen, taking in Yael hunched grumpily over her eggs and Noah scrubbing the pan in the sink, and I felt good about my decision not to say anything. It was just about the only thing I felt good about just then, so I figured it better be enough.

Sunday's coventry was at Volunteer Park. "Beautiful" in Seattle terms in November meant that it wasn't raining, but it was still colder than a penguin's ass. For our purposes that was just fine. It meant that we could have our nature time but we weren't likely to be interrupted by curious civilians, though Sharon was working on a spell to mask our activities if someone came too close.

We had hot chocolate and coffee in thermoses, and Fred had brought chili in a crockpot. On top of that, Finn showed off a new trick he'd learned where he could light a piece of wood on fire without actually burning it up, so we found a log and Finn set it blazing while we all gathered around. It was a fairly normal coventry except for the being outside part. Everybody had something they were working on, and people helped where they could, offering suggestions for exercises or walking them through a process that had worked in the past. Despite the weather, I was actually comfortably warm. Probably this was because on my right Finn was playing with making the fire burn in different shapes and colors and on my left Sharon was magnifying the effect where she could, and they always got warmer when they were working with flames. I closed my eyes for a moment to settle into the heat around me.

Almost as soon as my eyes closed I could see shapes in the darkness, just like that night in the cemetery. Now that I knew what they were, though, it was easier to recognize them as plants. I could see the outlines of the trees around us, the spiky coldness of the grass at our feet. If I concentrated a bit more, I thought I could see the sleeping perennials in the flower beds by the gazebo. I focused still more, and I could see the outlines of the plants in the greenhouse on the other side of the park. It wasn't until I started pushing out toward the homes on the borders of the park that I realized everyone had gone quiet.

I slowly blinked my eyes open, and they were all staring at me.

"Well, damn," Jerod said, eyebrows raised.

"What?" I said and Finn nodded toward my feet.

I looked down to see grass and clover covering my boots and tendrils of some plants I didn't recognize winding their way up my jeans, twining around my legs. Even the log Finn was keeping ablaze was starting to send out new growth.

"Oh," I said.

"Looks like somebody's found their gift," Sharon said, watching me with interest like she was waiting to see what I'd do next.

"That is so cool," Katie squealed, grinning over at me.

"It's really unusual for a gift to manifest in a moment of peace like that," Fred commented, looking impressed.

I probably would have kept quiet about things if it hadn't been for that. I didn't want them thinking I was some kind of prodigy or something. "Actually," I began, a little sheepish. "This isn't the first time it's, um, manifested." I knew I should have said something sooner, but there was nothing I could do about that now.

The whole story sort of spilled out then. Well, not the whole story. I left out the part where Creepface tried to convince me I was imagining things. In the middle of my coven, it seemed like such a ridiculous thing to think that I couldn't bring myself to admit I'd even been questioning it. That and the little voice was telling me I'd look stupid if I brought it up. Suspicious even, maybe. Like I didn't trust them.

It took a while to tell the whole story. They kept interrupting with questions, but eventually I got the whole thing out. I didn't realize how difficult it had been until I'd finished, and I noticed that Finn had his hand on my back, just a little gesture of support, but it felt nice. Not much but just what I needed, confirmation I wasn't in this alone.

When I was done, everybody was thoughtful. Eventually, Finn said, "This is why you asked me if vampires could fly, isn't it?"

"Yeah," I admitted. "You said they couldn't, though, so I figured I must be confused." I didn't want to say crazy. I'd been over that ground with Finn already.

"They can't," Davis said. Everyone's gazes turned from me to him. "I mean, we're all thinking it, but it's true. Vampires can't fly. Can't even turn themselves into bats."

"That's the part that really concerns me," Fred put in.

"I know it sounds maybe-kind-of...." I still couldn't bring myself to say the c-word.

"We all believe you," Finn said after I trailed off. "Don't we, guys?" This last was addressed to the group like a challenge, and everybody chimed in their agreement, though Sharon and Davis seemed a little skeptical.

"It's not a question of not believing you," Fred added. "But if this is true, we've got some things to figure out. I might have to talk to Soren and see if any of his pack have heard or seen anything like this before. Sharon, you should call Eleanor and let her know what's going on."

"I'll talk to her this evening," Sharon agreed, but Fred shook his head.

"I don't think we should put this off if we can help it. The sooner we get the word around, the sooner we can hear some news on it."

"You're right," she said, pulling out her phone and moving a little ways away to make the call.

Fred turned to me next. "If something like this happens again, I want you to call me immediately, okay? I don't care what time it is or how trivial you think it is. Have you seen this vampire around anywhere else?"

I told him about the couple times at the bar, leaving out seeing him in the alley on Friday.

"I wish you'd said something the first time," he said with a frown.

"That's my fault," Finn said. "I didn't think anything of it, other than the brighter glowing. I should have brought it to the coven when I found out."

"No, Fred's right," I offered. "I should have said something. I.... You guys are the only people I really know in this community." I thought of Steve and how he'd said they'd support me. "I should have known to come to you."

"Don't beat yourself up about it," Katie said, coming over to hug me around my waist. "You're new still, and we're obviously terrifying." She put on her best stern and scary face, and it was enough to get a quiet laugh out of everybody.

The sound faded quickly when Sharon came back, her expression grim.

"What is it?" Jerod asked, worry etched all over his face. "Did Eleanor have any news?"

"Yes," Sharon said. "But not about the vampire." She paused and looked around the group slowly. "Eli Jefferson has gone missing."

PART TWO

I stand amid the roar
Of a surf-tormented shore,
And I hold within my hand
Grains of the golden sand—
How few! yet how they creep
Through my fingers to the deep,
While I weep—while I weep!
O God! can I not grasp
Them with a tighter clasp?
O God! can I not save
One from the pitiless wave?
Is all that we see or seem
But a dream within a dream?
-Edgar Allen Poe
from "A Dream Within a Dream"

Chapter Five

I never used to dream.

Yeah, okay, I know that's not actually true. I know that you need to dream or your brain doesn't rest properly or something, but I never used to remember my dreams. Maybe they just weren't interesting enough. Maybe my subconscious thought better of letting me know what it was up to while I wasn't looking.

After the coventry in the park, though, I started having dreams I couldn't forget.

I was riding a wave of vines through a cemetery. The vines undulated like an ocean, rippling under my feet, carrying me on past headstones and mausoleums. Finn was chasing me, but his feet kept getting tangled in the vines, and he was calling after me to wait for him. I tried to tell the vines to stop so he could catch up but they kept carrying me on and on, toward this bright, glaring light. I never quite reached the light, but there was a voice in it saying, "None of it's real, gorgeous. Wake up."

So I did.

I didn't realize how much of an impact Eli Jefferson had on my life until he disappeared. He'd always just been this person who was in the background, milling around campus in his Facilities fleece, smiling his grey-bearded smile at anyone who needed it. I hadn't really ever given him much thought.

Suddenly, though, it was like there was this Eli-shaped void on campus. He was, as they say, conspicuous in his absence.

Of course, there was an article about his disappearance in the school paper and a candlelight vigil to pray for his safe return. He was well-loved, more than I had realized. I went to the vigil, not because I had known him at all but because I wanted to see who had. Eleanor was there—I hadn't seen her since that first coventry—and so were Finn and Katie, who looked tiny next to Finn, the pink in her hair somehow seeming duller than usual, but I felt sort of weird joining them when clearly Eli meant so much more to them than he had to me, so I just gave them a little wave when they beckoned me over and moved further into the crowd. I saw Steve as well, burly and solid in the midst of all this nebulous grief, and he nodded as I passed. Even Dr. Sternquist was there, her usual glowing dimmed, even in the darkness.

The director of campus ministry said a few words, and then she led us in a couple prayers. I didn't know what to feel or what to say. I'm not exactly religious, but the communal aspect of this gathering was something I could appreciate.

No one had any answers, and no one was trying to pretend they did. It almost made me want to tell them what little I did know, just to ease some of the confusion. Mostly, though, it was a comfort. I was in the middle of this strange thing I didn't yet understand, but I could still be part of this community.

I felt a hand on my shoulder and turned to see Noah there, his wide smile and perpetually unkempt hair like a beacon of familiarity in this sea of mostly strangers. "Hey," I said quietly. "What are you doing here?"

"I used to work with Hagrid at the P-Patch," he said with a shrug. "What are you doing here?"

I shrugged as well. "He's a friend of a friend."

"The mystery guy?"

"And a couple others," I said, nodding.

He slung an arm over my shoulder and I slung my arm over his, and I was struck by this intersection of the two parts of my life. Despite Steve's advice, I couldn't help but think of them as completely separate. Noah was all numbers and angles and science, and Finn was all maybe-kind-of and magic and vampires. Bringing them together like this made me wonder again if I should tell someone about it all, someone outside of it.

We didn't say anything else. The quiet around us sort of seeped in, and I let out a slow breath and closed my eyes.

Since the coventry in the park, I hadn't really done much with my gift. I knew —and Finn kept telling me—that I should be trying to develop it, playing with it to see what I could do and where my limits were. Mostly, though, I'd just been ignoring it. There was too much else going on. I hadn't felt either the urgency of the cemetery or the calm of the park, and forcing it never really occurred to me.

Standing there with Noah I felt that calm again. When my eyes closed, I could see the outline of the grass and the reaching branches of the trees, the scattered flowers and the roots digging in deep. It was comfortable, comforting. I tried to focus more carefully this time, being aware of the plants instead of reaching out to them. In particular, I kept my focus on the grass around my feet, and when it seemed like it wanted to get a little friendly with my ankles, I made myself open my eyes and let go of all the tendrils I could feel creeping at the edges of my consciousness.

"Hey," Noah said quietly. "You okay?"

I thought for a moment before answering. "Not yet. But I'm working on it."

"Aren't we all?"

For an engineer, Noah was pretty good at cutting to the heart of things.

The trouble with being caught up in the middle of a maybe-kind-of secret club that had a full-scale supernatural mystery on its hands was that, since it was maybe-kind-of secret, the world didn't shut down for us to figure out what was going on. I still had work. I still had school. I still had to go about my daily business. The only real difference I noticed was that Dr. Sternquist seemed to be a little dimmer when I went to class. She was clearly upset about something, and I had to wonder how involved the vampires were with other supernatural creatures. Finn had said that they liked to keep mostly to themselves.

This might sound weird, but it made me a little sad to know that. Everybody else seemed to be relatively close. Steve had described it like a family. For all her frizz and cardigans, Dr. Sternquist was a pretty good person—or whatever you considered vampires—and even though I knew she had a partner, it bothered me to think of her dealing with this alone. It didn't seem right, somehow. Creepface might have been one of the bad ones, but as far as I could tell, Sternquist wasn't anything that deserved to be isolated like that. Maybe all the community spirit since the vigil had been getting to me. Probably I should have talked to her to see if she was okay, but that felt like crossing a line. If vampires wanted to be left alone, who was I to ruin that for her?

I at least made an effort to smile at her when I left class that week.

My Personal Writing class was still going too, and that week Dr. Pearce decided it would be a good idea to assign us dream journals.

"Sometimes," he said, pacing the front of the classroom and nudging his glasses up the bridge of his nose with his forefinger, "when the world seems to be in such...such turmoil, the subconscious is much better at making sense of things than our conscious mind can afford to be." He rubbed chalk-stained fingers over his elbow, leaving a spread of white dust on his shirt. How someone with this particular tic ended up in one of the few classrooms on campus to still have chalkboards was beyond me. By the end of any given class he had streaks of white covering both elbows, dusted along the hem of his shirt, and peppered throughout his prematurely thinning hair.

"I know a lot of you are still trying to come to grips with the disappearance of Mr. Jefferson. I think keeping track of your dreams might help with that. Now," he continued, passing out a stack of forms with questions like, 'What symbols recur in the dream?' and 'What was the prevailing emotion?' complete with helpful suggestions, "whenever I give this assignment, I have students who tell me that they don't remember their dreams. A lot of people don't, and that's okay, but I want you to try. Keep your dream journal forms by your bed, and when you wake up after a dream, immediately write down anything from the dream that you remember—even if it's gibberish, even if it's only snippets. You may find that, after a few times jotting blurred details down, your dreams become more vivid and you remember them better. It's an exercise in strengthening your subconscious."

Awesome. Just what I needed was for my dreams to get more vivid and more memorable.

As I left class that day, he stopped me. "Hey, how are you doing?"

I was so taken aback by the question that it took me a moment to come up with any sort of answer, and even when I did, it was only, "Um...fine? I mean...yeah, okay."

He reached across to touch my elbow briefly, leaving us with matching smudges of white on our shirts. "I know it's been a rough few days for everyone. Were you close to Eli?"

"I...no, not really," I stammered. I guess it must have been more obvious than I thought that I was not okay with this dream journal thing. Maybe finding people who didn't think I was crazy was robbing me of my ability to hide what was going on in my head.

"Well, if you need to talk, I'm here," he said after an awkward pause. "Or if you're not comfortable talking to me, the counseling center is open late all week for anyone who needs them."

There was no way in hell I was going to the counseling center to tell them why a simple journaling assignment had me so rattled. I was likely to end up committed if I did. "Yeah, thanks," I muttered, hitching my bag up higher on my shoulder.

He nodded and raked his hand through his hair, leaving a streak of white across his forehead, and I hustled out of there.

Chapter Six

My first journal was complete bullshit:

I'm sitting in my elementary school playground on the merry-go-round. All around me my classmates are holding hands, forming a circle that wheels around and around. They're whistling something. I can't tell what it is, but it's creepy. My first grade teacher, Miss Jessup, comes out and blows her whistle and everybody scatters on the breeze.

My next one wasn't much better:

I'm standing on a hill, and there's this winding, Seussical conveyor belt all around me, covered with miles and miles of turkey sandwiches on plates. They're all making their way into a tiny opening in a beehive-shaped building, and I know that it's my job to get all the sandwiches into the hive, but I know that there's no way they will all fit.

By the third night, I was running out of bullshit ideas, so when I woke up at two in the morning, I just wrote down what I had actually dreamt, though I didn't intend to turn it in.

Everything is quiet and dark, but I can hear something breathing, and I can see the tendrils of vines climbing up a wall.
I open my eyes.
He's standing there, beckoning me forward with one hand, smiling benevolently. His voice is calm, much more soothing, much more appealing than it ever really has been. "Don't be afraid, gorgeous. You and I, we're going to do amazing things. Incredible things. Things you have never dreamed of. Just stop fighting, stop resisting what you know is

inevitable, what you know is right."

Everything he says seems so true. I know it down to my bones.

Behind me, I hear a deep, resonant voice, saying, "We're here for you, if you need us, if you want us. You're not alone in this."

I turn to see who's talking, but I can't see anyone, and when I turn back again, he's gone.

After that, the dreams came more and more frequently, and I had the cynical thought that recognizing them had given them power. They weren't always the same. Little things changed here and there—sometimes big things—but a few things were always the same. Creepface was always there. Sometimes he was friendly, sometimes he was violent, sometimes he made an awful attempt at seduction. But he was always there and he was always trying to get me to join him. There were always plants as well. I didn't always manipulate them, but I could always feel them. And there was always someone else, someone who was clearly on my side. Sometimes it was Finn, sometimes it was Steve, sometimes it was Katie. Once, it was Yael.

It wasn't always easy to tell if they were nightmares or not. Sure, Creepface was there, but occasionally he was maybe-kind-of pleasant, which was fine when I was asleep but incredibly disturbing once I woke up.

It was starting to get colder, fall drizzling its way into winter, so there was no more coventry in the park. Coventry, for the most part, remained the same. We still got together for booze and snacks. We still practiced our various powers. Sharon had bought a few houseplants specifically for me to mess with. I was getting good at impromptu topiary.

All the surface activities remained the same, but underneath it all was this tension that never seemed to go away. Fred's lips under his impressive mustache seemed permanently turned down. The bridge of Davis's nose was pinched at least half the time I looked over at him. Even Katie stopped playing with the toe of my boot when she sat by my feet.

Only Finn seemed unchanged. He was clearly concerned about the disappearances—though they seemed to have stopped with Eli, which was disconcerting in itself—but he still had that nonchalant ease that made everything appear status quo. He'd started sitting next to me, and he was trying to convince Sharon to invest in some bioluminescent plants so I could make them grow and he could light them up. Sharon said she'd look into it, but she was pretty sure they wouldn't grow in Seattle.

I suppose there was a little more wine flowing than usual, but that was to be expected. Sharon seemed to be compensating for the tension by becoming extra welcoming. She baked cookies and bread and pastries and basically everything heavy and full of spice. I think she invited me to come over for dinner about three times on average every week.

"Any time, really. Or if you need a place to do laundry? Or if you just need someone to talk to. Seriously, my door is open whenever you want."

Much as I was getting to really like the people in the coventry, it was still nice to have Finn there as a sort of barrier. I wasn't planning on accepting any of those invitations, but I tried to turn her down as gently as possible. She wasn't deterred.

"At least you should come for Thanksgiving. Nobody should be alone at Thanksgiving."

"I'll think about it," I eventually capitulated, if only because she really seemed to want to help me in some way.

I wasn't sure I needed help, though. Sure, things were tense, and I was having weird dreams, and the campus still felt incomplete without Eli around, but I figured I was probably doing better than most of them. I hadn't even seen Creepface around in weeks. In the midst of the mystery of the disappearances, my little bloodsucking problem hardly seemed worth agonizing over.

So far our little group had not been hit with anybody going missing. We hadn't even had any blackouts. There were mixed theories on this. Jerod thought we were just lucky. Katie postulated that we were so badass nobody wanted to mess with us.

"That must be it," Davis said dryly. "They're terrified of having pillows thrown at them." Katie sent the cushion she was levitating toward his head. He only just managed to duck.

"Don't be a dick," Jerod said, and Sharon passed me another glass of wine.

"I'm not being a dick," Davis argued. "I just think it's ridiculous to pretend we aren't at risk. We've got nothing protecting us. We don't even know what we need protecting from."

"Davis," Sharon chided, but he didn't let her finish.

"Don't 'Davis' me. We're in a fucking mess, and none of us have the slightest idea how to get out of it."

"That doesn't give you the right to be an asshole to Katie," Jerod practically growled. I looked over to where Katie was sitting, curled up smaller than normal on the couch, arms around her knees looking like she was trying not to cry.

"Yeah, come on, Davis," I said. "Let's not make this...."

"Make this what?" he interrupted. "Bigger than it is? Well, guess what, kid? It's big. It's bigger than us, and it's bigger than anything we know how to deal with. What are we gonna do if something comes for one of us? Throw a book at it? Change its color? Tickle it with ivy?"

"All right, asshole," Jerod said, lurching to his feet and lunging for Davis.

Fred stepped in between them, grabbing the back of Jerod's shirt. "All right, I think it's time you went home," he said carefully.

For a moment, I thought Jerod would struggle, but he just shot Davis a death glare and said, "Yeah, I think you're right."

"Sorry about this," Fred muttered as he grabbed his coat and steered Jerod out the door. "I'll take him home."

Everybody was quiet for a long moment after they left until Sharon looked around the room and said, "More wine, anybody?"

By the time I left that night, I was definitely tipsy. My face felt warm and my limbs felt heavy, and I leaned my head against the window as Finn drove me home.

"Want me to walk you in?" he asked when he pulled up in front of the duplex.

"I'm good," I said, feeling pretty relaxed about everything in general.

"I'm walking you in," he insisted, cutting the engine as I got out of the car.

"It's really okay." I was already moving up the walk, but he caught up with me, one arm around my waist, though I wasn't that unsteady.

"I got you."

"Nobody's got me." I didn't mean for it to sound like I was complaining. All I meant was that I could walk perfectly well on my own.

"Lots of people have you," he said, pausing at the foot of my front steps and holding onto me firmly enough that I had to pause too. "You're not alone in this, you know."

Probably because I was a little bit drunk, I actually stopped to think about that before answering. My processing systems were moving a little slow, so I had to take a moment. "Yeah," I said eventually. "Yeah, I know."

I don't really know what was in my voice that he took as invitation, and maybe if I'd been sober, I could have sidestepped it, but before I had a chance to realize what he was doing, Finn was kissing me. I made a noise in my throat that wasn't quite a protest but also wasn't an encouragement. Once I got with the program, I put my hand on his chest and pushed a little. To his credit, he backed off.

"Whoa," I said. "I'm...um...I'm not sure if this is.... I mean, you're nice and all, and there's the hair and the smile and everything, but just.... Yeah. No." I liked him, sure. Probably a few weeks ago and without any alcohol, I might have been willing to give that a shot, but there was so much else going on right now that my head wasn't in it at all. Or my heart. Or whatever other body parts were supposed to be in it when someone you thought you might have been starting to like against your better judgment kissed you out of the blue.

His nose wrinkled, and he pushed his hair back again before rubbing the back of his neck. "Oh. I just.... I thought.... Never mind. Oops?"

"Yeah, let's go with that. Oops." I tried to smile, but it was a little wobbly. He just shrugged.

"It's okay," he said, like I'd apologized. "I'll see you in class?"

"Yep."

Neither of us was sticking around after that. He went straight back to his car, and I continued up the steps and fumbled with my key for a bit before Yael opened the door for me.

"I wasn't spying," she said. "But I was sort of spying."

"It's not what it looked like," I assured her, stepping inside and tossing my bag on the floor next to the door.

"Really? Because it looked like mystery guy finally made a move and you shut him down."

"Oh. Then it's totally what it looked like."

"Cupcake?" she said, holding up a telltale, pink box.

"No shots?"

"I think you've had enough. Besides, there's booze in these."

"Random act of intoxication?" I asked, moving toward the kitchen to get two plates and two glasses for milk.

"You should suggest that to Cupcake Royale for a new slogan, but if you can get drunk off one of these, you are a bigger lightweight than I thought." She dropped onto one of the mismatched chairs at our kitchen table and flipped the box lid open. The scent of buttercream and caramel filtered through the kitchen.

"Only two?" I asked, pulling one of the cakes from the box to slice it carefully in half.

"Noah's on a date again."

"What's that make, four with this one?"

"Five. I think he might actually be settling down. The other day, he almost actually let me dress him up before he went out"

"Never."

She laughed and split the other cupcake, putting half on each plate before moving to the fridge to get the milk.

"You know," I said, "you can still get three, even when he's not here."

"You get them next time, then."

The cupcake sharing was a ritual of sorts. When the new cupcake flavors came out, someone picked up three, and we all had a third of one. As roommates, we tended to bond over either booze or treats.

Once I had the cakes divvied up and Yael had poured the milk, we settled in to eat. For a moment, we didn't do anything other than enjoy our sugary delights and compare the flavors. We weren't exactly food critics, but we'd both eaten enough cupcakes to talk about them in a way we told ourselves sounded intelligent. There was a lot of musing over the spices in the pumpkin ale cupcake and wondering about the particular type of apple in the Tipsy Apple.

It wasn't until we were finishing the last of the milk that Yael said, "So tell me about mystery guy. Why'd you leave him out in the cold?"

I shrugged. It was way too complicated to explain how everything had started, all the things that were on my mind, and why, with all of that, kissing Finn seemed like the absolutely wrong thing to do.

"He's just...Finn," I said, eventually.

"I really hope that's his name and not a weird fish metaphor."

"It is."

She got up and grabbed us each a beer from the fridge. When she sat back down and slid the bottle opener over to me, she said, "Okay, obviously you know what you mean by that and you decided him being Finn was a reason to give him the brush off. So good for you. I support your choice."

"But?" I asked, because I could practically see it hanging in the air.

"But if you're not interested, what's with the standing date? You're with him every Monday, and I know you two have coffee a lot."

The great thing about having a bottle of beer is that it gives you an excuse to not answer a question while you think of what you want to say.

I took a really long drink.

"Can I tell you something maybe-kind-of crazy?"

"You tell me maybe-kind-of crazy things all the time," she pointed out, and while I knew this was a whole new level of maybe-kind-of than what she was talking about, I had to admit to myself that she was right. It was why I'd almost told her that night in the bar.

I nodded. "Okay. I'm...going to show you something, and I want you to try not to freak out."

She sat up a little straighter. "You got it."

There was a row of terra cotta pots on the table where Yael had started a mini indoor herb garden. I looked hard at the little sprouts of rosemary, my face scrunching up as I concentrated. This would have been way easier without the wine and beer.

"Um...what are you going to show me?" she asked, glancing between me and the pot I was staring at.

"Just...watch the plant."

"The plant?"

As she turned to look, I closed my eyes, settling myself as I'd been practicing at the coventries. As I did, I could feel the tiny, curling outlines of the sprouts, and with a bit more concentration, I called one of them toward me. Its outline grew, reaching up and over the edge of the pot, leaning toward me.

"Oh my *fucking* god," Yael said. "How are you doing that?"

I opened my eyes again, and when I looked back to Yael, the tendril of herb drew itself back into its pot. Her eyes were wide, and I could tell she was struggling not to freak out, likely because she'd promised to try. "That's...what I do on Monday nights," I said, watching her face for any subtle changes.

"You learn to talk to plants?" Each word was measured carefully, a sure sign she was still schooling her reaction.

"Sort of?"

This was the part I'd been worried about. I knew exactly what it would sound like when I tried to explain the last few months. I had been starting to feel sane, but bringing this to someone outside all the weirdness stripped me of any of that confidence in my sanity. I wondered briefly if there were any sibyls who had the power to reverse time so I could go back and never had said anything in the first place.

I was about to try and backtrack a little, see if I could get to a place where my footing was firmer, but Yael just sat back, took a sip of her beer, and said, "Okay.

Tell me about the plants."

I didn't mean to stay up quite as late as I did, but Yael had lots of—perfectly understandable—questions. A lot of her questions were ones I hadn't even thought of. She wanted to know about Finn's family and how everybody else had gotten into magic. (Finn never called it magic. Just powers or gifts. I guess that went along with him not liking the term witch.)

"So wait," she said, several hours and a couple beers later. "Creepface is a *vampire*?"

"Yeah...."

"You definitely should have mentioned that sooner."

"Would you have done something different?"

She thought about that for a moment. "No, I guess not. Still, if I'm standing up to a vampire, I wanna know it."

"So you can be scared?"

"No. So I can know what a badass I'm being."

I laughed, getting up to recycle our bottles. "I really need to sleep. Is there anything else you can't wait until morning to ask me?"

"If I think of anything, I'll come banging on your door."

"You're a terrible person."

"You know you love me."

"Goodnight."

Despite the weirdness with Finn, I felt better than I had in a long while. I should have told her sooner. After all that, I was pretty sure I would sleep well that night.

There is rosemary all around me. The smell is overwhelming. I hear Yael's voice, but I can't see her anywhere. I look and look and look, but she's nowhere, though her voice echoes around me, calling my name, pleading for help.

I close my eyes.

Under the vast tangle of monstrous herbs I see her, hands outstretched, fingers clenching, pulling at the plants as they grow thicker and thicker around her. I cry out, telling her to wait, that I'm coming. I tell the plants to leave her alone, but they only tangle more tightly.

"It's your fault, gorgeous," comes his voice in my ear, and I can't make myself open my eyes to look at him. "You brought her into something she can't hope to understand. She'll hate you for this. She'll always hate you."

Chapter Seven

Finn was in class on Wednesday with his customary, indeterminate hair and his bright smile, and it seemed like things were going to just go back to normal on that front until he backed out of coffee.

"I just have this paper to write for History of Design," he said shrugging it off per usual. "It's kind of stressing me out. I don't think I probably need the caffeine right now."

"No worries," I said, smiling, probably a less-than-convincingly, and adding, "Good luck with that," as he turned to go. It was stupid to feel like I was being abandoned, especially when I was the one who had turned him down, but there was a disappointment that I couldn't quite link to any rational cause hovering in my subconscious. I wanted to hang out with Yael just to have the support, but when I pulled out my phone to text her about it, something stopped me. I didn't need to involve her in any more weirdness in my life. She had enough to process already without playing therapist to my emotional insecurities.

I didn't mean to start avoiding Yael. In fact, I don't know that I actually was. I just incidentally stopped running into her on a daily basis. We still texted. I let her know I was alive and that I'd picked up extra shifts at the shop. She told me the guy in her O-Chem class was definitely not gay and that they'd started meeting for dinner at the Student Center twice a week. It was easy to justify not seeing her by blaming our new schedules.

I'd picked up a shift after Econ, too, so not having coffee with Finn became less and less of an issue. If he was upset about it, he didn't let on, and things gradually settled into a new routine.

November was winding down, and we were firmly in the grip of winter. I hadn't been able to come up with a good excuse to skip out, so when

Thanksgiving rolled around, I got myself onto a bus to West Seattle and ended up on Sharon's doorstep, holding a bottle of Riesling and a cloth-covered basket full of croissants I'd picked up at a bakery I'd found on Yelp with good reviews. It was really weird showing up there without Finn, but I tried not to think about that too much.

"Hey, come in! Glad you decided to join us," Sharon said, pulling me into an awkward hug that I couldn't easily return with my hands full. "Everyone's here already," she added, taking the wine from me as she moved away.

"Everyone?" I really hoped she just meant the coventry. I wasn't sure I could handle any new people just then.

Sure enough, I felt the basket tugged from my hand and looked up to see Katie levitating it toward the kitchen. "You're not late or anything. We just showed up early to help finish pies."

"I can finish pies," I protested, nodding hello to Davis and settling into something like the comfortable ease of our usual meetings. "Jerod didn't come?" I asked. Davis shifted in his chair, looking a little guilty.

"He and Finn went to Portland to see Jerod's parents," Fred answered, pressing a full glass of wine into my hand.

"Oh," I said, the syllable falling flat in the warmth of the room. "I...didn't know....'

"Jerod's been having a hard time with this disappearance thing," Sharon clarified, ushering me into the living room and onto a couch. "His parents are worried. I think Finn mostly went to reassure them."

"He's good at that," I offered, realizing suddenly that this was the first time I'd been here without him. I was missing that reassurance.

"He is!" Katie piped in. "I'm sure he'll help them out."

"Are Jerod's parents sibyls?" I asked. We hadn't talked much about anybody's families in our meetings. It occurred to me that I hardly knew anything about these people outside of magic. I wondered how they'd known about Jerod's parents. Was I really that distant from everyone?

"Nope. Totally normal. His aunt is, though," Katie said.

"And his grandpa," Davis added.

I felt more and more disconnected, and I had to admit to myself that I really hadn't made an effort to get to know any of them aside from our meetings. Perhaps I shouldn't have been so quick to turn down Sharon's invitations. If things were going to be weird with Finn for a while, I should expand my magic circle, as it were. There was more to missing Finn than just missing him. I felt disconnected in a way I hadn't considered when I'd shot him down.

"Are there disappearances in Portland too?" I asked, taking a good, long sip of my wine to compensate for being Finn-less.

"No, they seem to be localized to the Seattle area." Fred took the seat next to me as Sharon vanished into the kitchen.

"That's something I'd be more than happy to share with our little sister," Davis grumbled.

"Davis!" Katie looked horrified, her pixie-like face contorting in shock.

"What? I don't have any friends in Portland," he argued. "I'd rather spread the love and get it away from people I actually care about."

"Isn't it easier to figure out who's behind it if we're only looking in one city?" I wondered.

Davis drained his glass. "Except we're not looking, are we? We're not doing a goddamn thing."

"Davis!" Katie chastised him again.

"Ow!" he exclaimed as a picture flew over to thwap the back of his head.

"It's Thanksgiving," Fred reminded us, glancing to the kitchen where Sharon could be heard putting finishing touches on whatever she was doing. "Let's not add any more stress to the day than we already have."

"Do you think she needs some help in there?" I asked, half getting up.

Katie shook her head. "I wouldn't if I were you."

"Why not?"

"She's a total dragon lady," she said. "It's better for everyone if we just leave her to it."

As if she knew we were talking about her, Sharon, poked her head around the corner and caught my eye. "Would you mind setting the table? We're almost ready in here."

I didn't know who 'we' was, but I nodded, taking another healthy drink before getting up to move to the dining room as the others exchanged surprised glances at my being recruited into the dragon's den. Sharon handed me a stack of plates and pointed out the china cabinet.

"Any of the cutlery is fine. I think everyone has wine glasses already."

I set to work, more meticulous than I would have been otherwise, not wanting to find out why I'd gotten the dire warning I had from the others.

"How have you been?" Sharon asked as I set out the plates.

"Oh, you know," I said. "Okay. We're getting close to finals now."

"Is everything okay between you and Finn?"

I hesitated, straightening the plate in front of me unnecessarily. "Yeah, of course. Why?"

She shrugged, turning to check something in the oven. "He told me what happened. I wouldn't want things to be awkward."

It bothered me a little that Finn had talked to her about it, especially when he hadn't talked to me at all. "Well...I think things are okay," I said, moving to find cutlery and set it up neatly around the plates. "I mean, I guess they are." Weird as it was to be talking to Sharon about this, I remembered the decision I'd made to stop distancing myself from the coven.

She didn't say anything else, just went about her final preparations, and for a little while, I just let her dance around me, depositing various dishes on the table as I finished the place settings. Somehow the fact that she was willing to let me keep things to myself made it easier to open up, and I found myself saying, "We stopped having coffee."

Nodding, she handed me a heaping bowl of mashed potatoes. "And you miss it?"

"I guess? It was nice to have someone to talk to about these kind of things. I told one of my roommates about it, but...." I trailed off, not sure how to explain the accidental detachment from Yael that had been occurring since that night.

"But it's never the same with people outside the circle," she offered, placing my croissants in the middle of the table.

"Yeah." I wasn't sure that was exactly it, but it was certainly one possible explanation.

"Well, if you need someone to talk to, my invitation still stands. I don't mind going out to Capitol Hill if this is too far for you."

I was about to decline again, but my earlier resolution came back to me once more. "Yeah? Yeah, cool. That would be great," I said after a little hesitation. "Thanks."

"Of course." She smiled at me and touched my back lightly, a gesture that was much more comfortable than I would have expected. I couldn't tell if it was the wine or my new resolve, and I didn't have the chance to wonder for long as she moved to call everyone in for dinner.

It wasn't probably the most comfortable Thanksgiving that I'd ever had—Davis was a little grouchy, Fred was playing peacemaker, and Sharon was overly solicitous to pretty much everyone—but the food was amazing, Sharon refilled my glass every time it got close to empty, and I managed to mostly forget the weirdness of Finn not being there. After dinner Katie and I rigged a game of catch where she levitated a baseball toward a rubber plant, and I made the leaves form a catcher's mitt and then toss it back. There was more wine, and everyone lamented Jerod not being there to try and turn it into pumpkin ale.

Eventually people started trickling out, starting on their way home or wherever they were going next. Fred was the next to last, and then it was just me and Sharon. I was helping her wash the dishes and trying not to admit to myself that I was avoiding going home in case I ran into Yael there.

"You can stay if you want," Sharon offered, and I glanced up, surprised. I was pretty sure I hadn't said anything about not wanting to go, but things were getting a little wine-hazy, so I couldn't be certain.

She laughed a little, taking the last plate from me to dry and put away. "You're really not in any condition to take the bus right now."

"Pfft, I'm fine," I said, waving a hand dismissively.

"I have a spare room," she insisted. "And I make a mean omelet."

"Well, for the sake of omelets...." I smiled, again feeling warm and comfortable in a way that I wasn't sure should be written off to the wine or something else. "Thanks," I added, recognizing that this was something I really needed, even if I wasn't ready to face that recognition.

"Any time," she said with a shrug. "I know we're not quite like the werewolves, but I like to think of the coven as family. We take care of each other."

It was a nice thought, especially with my actual family so far away. Most of the time I didn't really notice it, but with the loss of Finn and Yael—or at least seeing them less—recently, I had definitely been feeling a little afloat.

Once the dishes were put away and the leftovers had been squeezed into the fridge wherever they'd fit, Sharon found me a toothbrush and set me up in the guest room. It had gotten to the point where I didn't want to sleep if I didn't have to anymore, but between the tryptophan and the booze, there wasn't much I could do about that. I was out before I even heard Sharon's door close.

It's different than the other dreams. I'm not really there, even. Voices filter into my mind, but I don't see anything, don't feel anything.

Nothing here is growing.

"You're taking this too far, getting too reckless," one says, but it's not talking to me.

"You let me worry about how far is too far," comes the other. His.

"I didn't sign up for this."

"You signed up for whatever I ask of you, and you're in way too far to back out now. Trust me on this one. It will be worth it in the end."

Silence, staticky and broad.

"Fine. Tomorrow, then. On the taxi."

"I knew you'd come around."

In the morning I found a bottle of water and a couple aspirin on the nightstand, and I finished them off almost without thinking. I shimmied into my jeans and sweater and ran a hand through my hair before padding barefoot out of the room. It must have been the smell of bacon that had woken me. When I got into the hallway it was wafting from the kitchen like those visible scent-hands they always used to have in cartoons. I followed it and almost as soon as I stepped into the room, Sharon had a mug of steaming coffee in my hands. I grunted my thanks and leaned against the counter, holding it up to my nose for a moment to let the smell of it pull me into consciousness.

Sharon smiled at me, but she didn't say anything until after I'd taken my first sip. "How's your head?"

I meant to say that it was fine, but my answer was still mostly nonverbal.

"Yeah, I figured," she said, laughing and plating up an omelet, setting it on the breakfast bar with a fork and another plate piled with buttered toast.

"How are you not hungover?" I asked. I was pretty sure she'd had as much wine as I did yesterday.

"Lots of water," she answered with a shrug and another smile, settling herself on an empty stool with her own plate and gesturing for me to sit. "I promised you an omelet. You should at least eat some."

She chatted lightly through breakfast, but she was pretty good at acknowledging that I wasn't up for fascinating conversation. When we finished, she waved off my help in cleaning up, so I went to brush my teeth instead. She was just putting away the last dishes when I came out.

"Taking the bus home?" she asked.

"Yeah, that's what I was thinking," I said, though the prospect of the bus didn't seem all that appealing just now.

"How about the water taxi?" she suggested. "It's a nice day for it." I glanced out the window. The sun was sparkling off what I could see of the water from her kitchen. "I can give you a ride to the dock," she added. "Then you don't have to take the shuttle."

My head was still pounding a little, and I still had some uneasy thoughts about Finn and Yael chasing each other around my head. A ride across the water was an appealing option. "Yeah, thanks," I said, nodding as I pulled on my coat.

By the time we got to the taxi, I was feeling almost human. Sharon saw me off with a smile and a reminder of our tentative coffee plans, and I made my way onto the boat.

It was cold enough that most people were staying inside, but I really needed the fresh air, so I braved the wind and went out onto the deck. There were a few others out there, mostly couples keeping each other warm. I pulled my coat more firmly around me, and leaned against the railing, letting the wind blow in my face. Lately, it had become pretty common for my mind to reach out for any plants in the area whenever I closed my eyes. It was harder since we were moving, but if I concentrated a little, I could feel the seaweed and algae in the sound and, further away, the trees along the shore.

"Don't think too hard, gorgeous. You'll bring the whole boat down."

His hand came to rest between my shoulder blades, and I stiffened. It took all of my concentration *not* to call up ropes of seaweed to get him away from me, but I figured the same thing that held me back would keep him from getting too carried away himself. Just to be sure, I opened my eyes a little to see the few people still scattered around us, none of them paying any attention to what probably looked like yet another couple staying close to keep warm.

"If you don't get your hand off me, that's going to seem like a good option," I said, teeth gritted but still trying not to draw too much attention to us.

He tsked at me. "Is that any way to greet a friend?"

"Pretty sure we're not friends."

His hand started to move over my back, rubbing slow circles in some weird mockery of friendly comfort. I tried to feel disgust for it, but that itching was back in my mind, and before I really knew what I was doing, I was leaning back into the touch.

"There. Isn't that better?" His voice was low and resonant, right in my ear.

"No," I lied. It was awkwardly disturbing how easy and natural that touch felt, and while I wanted to know why, I didn't want to delve too deeply into that.

"Keep telling yourself that, gorgeous," he said, and his laugh huffed out against my ear.

"What do you want?" I asked, now having to concentrate to keep myself from relaxing against his hand.

"I want you to look at me."

"Not happening," I said, but it was a struggle not to turn and face him, and I couldn't understand that. Always before, so long as I hadn't looked at him, I could keep his influence down, keep him from telling me what to do. Hell, sometimes I could do it even if I was looking at him.

"Look at me," he said again, gentle and persuasive. I couldn't focus on my confusion and resisting him at the same time, and I shifted the few inches it took for me to turn my face and meet his gaze. "There you are, gorgeous," he murmured, the sound washing over me with the same rhythmic hypnotism of the water hitting the boat.

"What do you want?" I asked again, but even I could hear the difference in my tone: warmth and curiosity rather than wariness and contempt.

His hand came up to my cheek, and though I tried again to recognize that he *couldn't* make me do anything, I leaned my head toward it, surprised by the warmth of his skin. "I want you to do something for me."

I opened my mouth, and it was only through incredible effort that I didn't promise to do anything he asked. "What?"

"Nothing difficult. I just want you to keep your eyes open."

"What for?"

"Interesting people." His hand moved from my face, thumb taking a brief detour to stroke across my throat—almost too firmly—before it moved down further. He leaned close to me. Too close, really, but I didn't even think of pulling away. I was pressed back against the railing, and to anyone watching, it probably looked like we were getting a little too friendly for such a public place. His hand slid into my coat pocket, and he pulled out my phone. His eyes never left mine, and I couldn't have looked away even if I had tried. I didn't think of trying. His thumbs moved over the screen quickly, adding himself as a contact. I wanted to laugh because I couldn't help picturing the number listed as 'Creepface.'

"If you see anyone, just give me a ring. And I don't think I need to say it, but don't tell anyone about our little arrangement," he said, slipping the phone back into my pocket. I could hear the engines slowing down, and I knew we were almost at the end of the trip. "Stay out here a couple minutes longer," he said, and I nodded.

He was gone, then, and I leaned heavily against the railing until someone came to tell me I had to disembark.

As I got off the boat, I shoved my hands into my pockets, fingers curling automatically around my phone. When I pulled it out, there was a text from someone named Sebastian: *See you soon, gorgeous.*

Chapter Eight

It would have been nice, after a long, boozy Thanksgiving, to have a day off to recover and try to process the encounter with Creepface that was already sliding out of my memory, but retail waits for no one, and Black Friday was not a day that anyone at my shop had off. Most of my afternoon was spent running back and forth between the back and the floor, checking on sizes and colors and accessories—most of which we didn't have enough of—or working the increasingly frustrating and outdated register which required a hell of a lot of manual calculating when it came to applying discounts.

It's not like I'm a paragon of fashion—jeans and t-shirts and boots are pretty much my standard—so whenever a customer actually asked my opinion, I tended to get pretty flustered. So when a semi-familiar face popped up behind the rack I was restocking and said, "Hey, what do you think of this top?" it took me a moment to get past the initial paralysis and recognize the face as belonging to the cat-eyed pho waitress I'd only recently started wondering about. After that fact settled in, I couldn't help but be relieved to see she was still around. We weren't friends or anything, but enough incidental people in my life had already gone missing to last me through the next several lifetimes.

"Hey!" I said, smiling and exhaling at the same time. "It's you! Christine, right?" I was pretty sure that was the name on her nametag.

"Last I checked," she said, tucking a strand of dark hair behind her ear and clacking her lip ring against her teeth. I was about to remind her where I knew her from when her face shifted into recognition. "Oh, you're the triple small chicken! I didn't realize you worked here."

"I get that a lot." Common Threads was not the trendiest boutique on Broadway, but we had our little niche. Sort of a gothy, punky, outdoorsy combination that should be too eclectic to work but somehow fit right in for Seattle. It was just fashionable enough to be popular but not so hip that someone like me couldn't work there. Still, we did tend to pick up employees with a certain quirky style that I did not possess.

"Anyhow," she said after a brief, awkward silence in which I probably grinned at her a little too hard. "This top?" She waved it in my face again.

It was...a lot like most of our tops, but I did honestly take a moment to try and picture her in it before nodding. "Yeah, it's good. You should definitely try it on. Want me to get you a room?"

"Nah, I'll take a chance on your eye," she said, flashing me a grin and then narrowing her eyes at me a little. "Ah," she added. "You're one of them."

"One of them?"

"A seer." She tilted her head, looking me over, and took a step closer, nose twitching a little like a cat scenting the air. "And...something else."

No one had ever picked up anything other than 'seer' from me, so I frowned a bit, trying to take that in. "Something else?"

"Yeah." She nodded firmly. "Can't pick it out, but there's something else there too."

"Is that a shifter thing?" I asked, taking a stab at what sort of supernatural she was.

"It's a cat thing," she answered, smirking and tugging at her lip ring a little with her upper lip. "Anyway, can you ring me up?"

"Jordan's at the counter," I said, nodding toward the line at the register. "Say I helped you. You might get an extra discount."

"Hey, thanks! Next time you come by the restaurant, I'll slip you some extra cream puffs."

"Awesome," I said as she headed toward the front. I didn't think pastries were probably what Steve had in mind when he told me the community was close, but I wasn't going to pass that up.

I worked through the weekend, and Noah and Yael were both out of town for the holiday, so the house was pretty empty for the next few days, and I was starting to feel it. I wondered if that was a seer thing too. I hadn't ever thought of buildings feeling one way or the other before. Not unless they were extremely creepy or something. When I got home on Sunday night, though, it definitely felt empty. Lonely in some way that surprised me until I realized I was almost never the only one home. Even when Noah was off on a spree of hookups, Yael was usually around.

I thought about calling Finn to see if he wanted to come over for a movie or something, but I didn't think we were at a place yet where that wouldn't be weird. I pulled out my phone anyway, flicking through the contacts until I stopped on Sebastian, thumb hovering over his name. I knew that I should know who Sebastian was. I knew he was important. I just couldn't remember why. I stared at the contact for a long moment before finally tapping the screen to call him.

It rang twice before he answered. "I wondered when I'd hear from you, gorgeous."

The memory of the water taxi was still a little hazy, but I could remember enough to be annoyed at both him and myself for the fact that this conversation was even happening.

"I didn't mean to call."

"Yeah, I bet you didn't. Don't let it worry you. You're still settling into things."

"What things?" Despite my unease with the situation, I was toeing off my shoes and dropping onto my bed.

"Never mind. Tell me what you've been up to."

"Work, mostly."

It was so bland, so innocuous that I started feeling more and more comfortable. It was like my conversations with my parents: meaningless small talk about things that never really changed.

"Any interesting customers?"

"It's the weekend after Thanksgiving. We were swamped with people."

"So there must have been someone interesting," he prompted, and I knew he was looking for something specific, but I didn't know what.

I just said the first thing that popped into my head. "The waitress at the pho place down the street bought a top."

"Good," he said. "And she's interesting?"

"I guess? She's kind of cute."

He laughed, and the sound sent a shiver down my spine that felt a little too like his hand on my back. "Careful, gorgeous. I might start getting jealous."

"Sorry." The apology was out before I had the chance to think about it.

"I forgive you. What's her name?"

"Christine, I think."

He laughed again. "You've done pretty well. Get some sleep."

"Thanks."

I don't remember hanging up.

"Did you get the pho?" Yael is asking, digging through a pile of plastic bags on the kitchen table.

"Of course," I say, reaching for chopsticks.

"Where are the cream puffs?"

I start digging as well, certain they should be there.

"You lost them," Noah says before dissolving into a tangle of vines juggling cream puffs between tendrils.

"Lost them lost them lost them," the plant sing-songs. "Lost her lost her lost her."

Chapter Nine

When I woke up the next morning, the house felt a little less empty, but I didn't know if that was wishful thinking or if Noah had actually come back after I went to bed. At least, I didn't know until I stumbled into the kitchen and came face to chest with a broad expanse of hirsute pectorals that definitely did not belong to Noah.

"Shit," I mumbled, looking up and up until my bleary vision coalesced into a half-familiar, pointy-eared face.

"Oh my god, hey!" boomed Steve, looking far too comfortable for standing in my kitchen wearing nothing but boxers. (I hoped he was wearing boxers. I wasn't quite sure I wanted to look.)

"Hey, um, Steve," I managed, still working my way toward asking him what in the seven hells he was doing in my house.

"I didn't realize you were Noah's roommate."

Right on cue, Noah wandered in, scratching his belly and looking between the two of us. "Oh, hey. So...this is Steve," he said, shuffling over and leaning against Steve, arm looped around his waist (which I was still not looking below). "Steve this is...," he started before finally taking in the way Steve was grinning at me. "You two know each other?"

"Yeah, we...uh...met through Finn," I said, moving to the coffee maker because I could not process this much coincidence this early without some serious caffeine.

"Right. Mystery guy with the wandering lips."

"You talked to Yael."

There was coffee in the pot already, and I was pretty sure that was Steve's doing. I made a mental note to try and be nicer to him, even if he was (hopefully only) mostly naked in my kitchen at the moment.

"A little," Noah said, and I tried not to wonder too hard if that 'little' sounded more like 'she told me he kissed you and you blew him off' or 'she told me you can do freaky things with plants.'

"Yael?" Steve piped in, and I glanced over to see his eyebrows shoot up toward his hairline, then down to see that he was, in fact, wearing boxers.

Much relieved (it was way too early for fairy dick), I nodded. "Other roommate."

"Right. With the violin."

I added sugar to the coffee I'd managed to pour while not freaking out over Yael's potential indiscretion and took a long, blissful sip.

"How much have you told him about us?" I asked Noah, nodding toward Steve.

"A little," he said again.

"Huh."

I wanted to ask how much Steve had told Noah about himself, but this didn't seem like the right time for the fairy conversation. Part of me hoped they'd have it soon. Noah didn't usually see someone more than two or three times, and he almost never brought them home, so if Steve was in the kitchen, things had to be pretty serious. Telling someone you were a fairy seemed like a pre-kitchen conversation to me.

Another part of me, though, hoped they never had it. If Noah found out Steve was a fairy then it would only be a matter of time before my own story had to find its way out. Seeing what had happened with Yael after the rosemary incident didn't give me high hopes for Noah.

"Nothing bad," Steve assured me, though the way he looked at me made me think he knew what I was really worried about.

"Right. Good," I answered with a nod. "Well, I'm gonna take my coffee and leave you two to your boxers," I added. "I mean breakfast. Leave you to your breakfast."

"Good," Noah said, grinning. "Because the boxers might not last…"

"Don't want to know," I called over my shoulder, already escaping to my bedroom to the sound of Steve's lumberjack laugh.

Finn still couldn't make it to coffee that week. I was trying to believe that it had nothing to do with the kiss, but that was getting harder and harder to convince myself of. I went anyway. Those Mexican mochas were difficult to resist.

I had planned to just grab a drink to go, but then I saw a burly figure at a corner table waving me over. Somehow Steve was less obvious here than at Starbucks. Something about the eclectic decor made him just another part of the scenery. Since I had no real reason to be avoiding him, I got my drink and the daily pumpkin pastry and joined him.

"Sorry for surprising you like that yesterday," he said once we'd gotten past greetings.

I shrugged. "I was more surprised to find one of Noah's friends hanging around than that the friend in question was you."

"So you're okay with that?" he asked, for once not looking like he knew what my answer would be already.

I gave it some thought before saying anything. "Yeah? I mean...yeah. Is it weird to say I think you might be good for him?"

He laughed, settling back in his chair with his mug dwarfed in his hands. "A little? But I'm pretty sure I know what you mean."

"Yeah, about that," I started, not sure how to broach the subject. I opted for blurting it right out. "Can you read people's minds?"

He laughed again, more twinkle than lumber. "Not exactly."

"Then what exactly?" I wanted to be annoyed by his answer, but his laughter was too twinkly to inspire that.

"It's a fairy thing. We're sort of...empaths."

I nodded, remembering Finn saying something like that and trying not to think of him too much. Instead, I asked, "Sort of empaths or actually empaths?"

"It varies."

I rolled my eyes. "Of course it does."

"Sorry." He shrugged, smiling. "I've got it pretty strong. Not everybody does. If you're full fairy it's usually stronger."

"Right. I really need to get that book."

"It's still long and boring, but I'm happy to answer any questions. Or Finn. He's pretty good about that."

"I'm not sure he's good about that for me anymore," I muttered into my mug.

"Oops. Landmine issue, huh?"

I sighed. I had really been hoping this wouldn't be a landmine thing, but that seemed less likely by the hour. "Maybe? I don't know. It's weird, and I haven't seen him outside of class in a while now."

"Do you wanna talk about what happened or should we change the subject?"

That was another question I didn't know the answer too, but I figured the second option was better, so I just said, "Have you told Noah about the fairy thing?"

"Yet another landmine issue," he said, but he was smiling, so I assumed he didn't mind too much. "I don't like to spill the beans on that until things are a little more serious."

"Noah brought you home," I pointed out. "That's pretty serious for him."

"Is it?" His face twisted into this weird sort of half-smile that couldn't seem to make up its mind between being pleased and being confused.

"I thought you were an empath."

"Yeah, but it gets a little hazy when our own emotions are involved. Sometimes it's hard to tell who's feeling what."

"You thought you were the only one getting serious," I postulated.

"Yeah." He rubbed his neck, transforming into an enormous, flannel-clad bundle of sheepishness.

"Well, you're not."

"Oh."

It wasn't at all fair for one person to look that much like a pleased puppy. I bet nobody ever skipped out on coffee dates with him.

"Yeah. Oh."

He grinned, unsuccessfully trying to hide it by taking a sip of coffee. "Cool."

"Dork," I said affectionately, shaking my head. "So does this mean the fairy conversation is going to happen?"

"It probably should," he said, face twisting a little. "That's...never a fun one."

I figured in eighty years, he'd probably had every imaginable variation on that particular talk. "Sorry."

"Have you told him yet?" he asked, a hopeful expression flittering across his face.

"Nope." I'm not sure what look I was trying to mask by taking a long sip, but I guess it didn't really matter what with the empathy and all.

"It's harder the longer you wait," he offered. "But you shouldn't do it if you're not ready."

"I told Yael," I said, trying not to sound as defensive as I felt.

"How'd it go?"

"Okay? But I haven't talked to her in a while. It's like she just disappeared after that night. I think she's avoiding me."

"She disappeared, or you did?"

I didn't say anything. That hit a little too close to the mark.

He reached across the table to touch my hand briefly. I let him this time, partially because I remembered the hurt in his eyes when I'd pulled away before but mostly because Steve was just comfortable to be around, and knowing he was with Noah meant I didn't have to wonder what he meant by the gesture or if things were going to get weird because of it. "It's hard to share something like this, I know, but it doesn't actually help to hide away from it. She'll think you don't trust her, and that's exactly what you need to do."

I gave him a wry smile. "You sure about that?"

He squeezed my hand and pulled his back, shrugging and smirking in a decidedly un-puppy-like fashion. "Fairy."

I was going to text Yael when I got on the bus to see if she was home, but when I pulled out my phone, I had a text from Sharon asking if we could meet for drinks on Friday. She offered to come out to Capitol Hill, but I was starting to feel a little claustrophobic in my own neighborhood. Crossing the bridge out to West Seattle seemed like it might be a bit of a respite for me, so I texted back to ask her to pick someplace near her, and by the time we'd settled on happy hour at Talarico's, I was at my stop.

Even as I got off the bus, I could admit that I'd let myself get distracted by Sharon's texts as an excuse not to contact Yael. Not that it mattered. I could see her bike chained to the inside of the fence as I walked up to our front door.

It would be nice to think that I squared my shoulders and walked in thinking, 'No time like the present,' or some other horrible cliché, but the truth is that I sort of slinked into the hallway and called out a tentative, "Yael?" half-hoping she'd gone for a walk or taken the bus somewhere or even that she wouldn't hear me.

This trust thing? Not as easy as it sounds.

"In here!" she called from the living room. I found her curled up in one corner of the couch under a pile of blankets with a composition book open in her lap. Looking at her, it was hard to justify having been so nervous — still being so nervous. She was just Yael, and she smiled a little as she looked up at me expectantly, tucking a swath of hair behind her ear.

"You know, you're allowed to turn on the heat."

"But this is so cozy!" she argued, holding up one end of the blanket in invitation. "Roomie cuddles?"

I figured it couldn't make things any more awkward, so I shrugged and slid under the pile. "Jesus, woman," I said when I got settled. "It's like a furnace in here. What have you been doing?"

"Wouldn't you like to know," she said, waggling her eyebrows before settling against me and putting the notebook aside.

"I really wouldn't, actually." It was comfortable enough to fall back into this with her that I almost ignored the whole issue I'd wanted to talk about.

Until she said, "God, I feel like I haven't seen you in *years*."

"It hasn't been years," I scoffed, squirming a bit as she poked me in the side.

"You know what I mean. When did life get so crazy?"

No time like the present.

"When I showed you how I do unnatural things to plants?"

"Okay, that definitely makes you sound like a tree fucker."

"Eww." I laughed in spite of myself.

She twisted a little to look at me straight on-ish. "Have you been avoiding me?" she asked, as though the thought had only just occurred to her.

"Apparently."

"I'll take Non-Answers for 2000, Alex."

I rolled my eyes but snorted out a laugh. "I didn't mean to? But I guess I kind of have been."

"Because of the rosemary?"

"Because of all of it." I shifted to lean back against the couch, closing my eyes like that would make this all easier to admit. "It's....I was worried you thought I was a freak or crazy or...or I don't know. I guess I was worried you'd look at me different."

"Kid," she said, adopting a vaguely Bogart-esque tone, "the only thing different is that I might start only buying one apple at the store and making you turn it into a tree."

"I really don't think I'm ready for that yet," I said dryly.

"Yeah," she agreed. "Apple trees are a big commitment. Maybe we'll start with a strawberry plant." I laughed and then her eyes lit up a little. "Oh, man, can you imagine? We could have fresh strawberries in December! You're the best roommate ever!"

"Don't count those strawberries before I've grown them," I threw back at her. "I haven't ever tried growing something from a seed."

"Well, there's no time like the present!"

It took me a good five minutes to stop laughing.

Tiny, winged fairies all wearing plaid with big, booming laughs zoom in and out of my frame of sight, sprinkling sparkling dust in their wakes. I walk across a still, cold lake on a bridge made of boxers.

"Told you so," the fairies rumble from chests too small to resonate like that. "Fairy."

Chapter Ten

I STILL FELT a little weird around Yael, and I spent a lot of time watching her closely to see if she was feeling any discomfort she wasn't sharing with me, but she seemed to be her usual, Yael-y self all week. I was still working extra shifts at the shop, but we did manage to run into each other a little more. She asked about doing drinks on Friday, and I was a little disappointed to have to tell her I had plans already.

"Ooh! Who with? Is it that fish guy?"

"Finn?" I asked, frowning a little because I still hadn't seen him outside of class. "No, um...Sharon.

"Sounds promising," she said, perching herself on my bed. "Is she a witchy friend?"

"She's in the coven, yeah."

"Is she a *special* witchy friend?"

"She's, like, forty."

"So? You should go for it! Get your mind off Mr. Fish."

"I really don't think she's interested."

"Her loss," she said with a shrug. "We should dress you up a little anyway."

"Why?"

"There is no why to fashion," she answered sagely. "There is only beauty and the relentless pursuit thereof."

"Fine," I said with a sigh, actually a little pleased to have things back to normal. "Make me beautiful."

I don't know that she made me beautiful, but Yael did insist on going through my entire wardrobe until she came up with a shirt that my mom had sent me for Christmas, a vest I picked up at Value Village when I'd thought that vests were a thing I would wear, and a pair of pants I was sure were too tight but that Yael insisted made my ass look amazing. I drew the line when she tried to get me out of my boots, saying that I needed some measure of practicality or I wouldn't feel like myself.

Yael was right, though, I did feel a bit more confident as I stepped into the dimly lit restaurant and glanced around for Sharon.

I spotted her quickly, and she waved me over.

"Hey! Glad you made it. How was the bus?"

"It was a bus," I said with a shrug, smiling a little so I didn't come off too snarky. I slid into the booth across from her.

"I got you a drink, I hope you don't mind."

"No, that's cool."

"You look great, by the way," she said. "Trying something new?"

"Nah, my roommate insisted." I picked up a menu and glanced over it briefly.

"Good! Dressing up sometimes is a great way to get out of a funk."

I was about to protest that I wasn't in a funk, but I knew she'd call bullshit. Or whatever the Sharon version of bullshit was. Instead, I said, "You're probably right. Let's beat the funk tonight."

"Let's," she agreed, raising her glass in a toast I met with mine.

I didn't realize how long it had been since I'd been out for drinks until I took my first sip. "Wow," I said, nose wrinkling as it fizzled down my throat. "What is in that?"

"It's good, right?" Sharon said. "They do great cocktails here."

"I just wasn't expecting it to be so strong."

"Like I said, they do great cocktails," she repeated with a laugh just as our waiter approached to take our order.

We worked our way through an enormous slice of pizza each and three or four more drinks before we left. It was comfortable in a way I wasn't used to being with anyone who wasn't Finn or the roommates. Steve probably came the closest to it of anyone outside that circle, but Sharon was starting to get there. It was nice.

I blamed Yael for the way I was maybe-kind-of sizing her up as a potential *special* friend, and that, combined with the few-too-many drinks in me, made me offer her my arm when we left the restaurant. She took it with a smile and leaned against me a little as we walked to my bus stop.

"Are you okay to get home?" I asked since we were both a little wobbly.

"I'll get a cab," she said with a wave of her hand.

"I'll wait with you."

"You don't have to."

I shook my head, ignoring the wind biting at my cheeks. "No, it's cool. Don't want you waiting alone."

"Well, aren't you sweet," she said, feeling a sudden warmth in my face and blaming *that* on the alcohol. I was going to blame a lot of things on the alcohol just then.

She pulled out her phone and ordered an Uber car. "You sure you're okay to wait?" she asked again, and I nodded.

"Not like I'm rushing back to anything."

"Still. It's freezing out here."

"Here," I said, and without thought shifted to put my arms around her. It was more like roommate cuddles than anything more, but it still had that degree of comfortability that I was starting to enjoy.

"Thanks," she said with a laugh that made her seem much younger than she was.

We didn't have to wait long for her car, and when it arrived, she gave me a quick hug. "You're okay to catch the bus?"

"It's just around the corner," I pointed out, and she laughed again.

"So it is. Well, this was fun. We should do it again soon."

"Yeah," I agreed. "We should."

She hugged me again and pressed a warm kiss to my cold cheek before sliding into the car. I stayed to wave her off and stumbled toward the bus stop.

When the bus arrived, I found a seat near the back, away from people as much as I could be.

That lasted about two stops and then I looked up to see him calmly striding down the aisle toward me.

"You smell like a distillery, gorgeous," he said as he dropped next to me. "Having a little fun?"

"None of your business," I grumbled, nervously avoiding his glance, though it came back to me now that eye contact didn't seem to be something he'd needed the last time we met. "What do you want?"

"Same as usual. Meet anyone interesting?"

My mind immediately went to Sharon, and I could feel a warmth in my cheek where she'd kissed me. "No," I said, hunching further into my seat.

"Let me rephrase: meet up with anyone interesting?"

I knew what he was getting at, even through the mist of booze-brain. But I didn't want to tell him about Sharon. About any of the coventry. That wasn't for him. I screwed up my face and my resolve and through gritted teeth said, "No."

"Well now," he murmured, leaning a little closer, turning my face to look at him. "That is definitely interesting."

"There's nothing interesting here," I insisted.

"That's what you think, gorgeous. Thank you. You've given me something to think about. I'll be seeing you again soon, I suspect." And then he'd pressed the stop button and was calmly striding back down the aisle and slipping off the bus like a smarmy shadow.

He'd given me something to think about too. Assuming I remembered it.

Finn was back at the coventry the next week, and if things weren't quite back to normal between us, at least we weren't avoiding each other anymore. Sharon seemed just the same, just maybe a little more eager than usual to refill my glass when it got close to empty. Jerod seemed just as eager to change its contents as I brought it to my mouth, so between the two of them, it was hard to feel any tension with Finn. There was a lot of laughing that week, more than there had been since Eli's disappearance. I had a brief pang of conscience at that, wondering if it was bad that we were moving on so easily, wondering too what constituted 'easily' in this situation. Was a month long enough? Two? Six? How long before we had to accept that he was really gone for good?

And what about the others? I hadn't known any of them, but the fact remained that they were gone. Some of them had turned up dead, others with no memory of their time away, still others written off as just shifters moving on the way that shifters do.

I watched as the Riesling in my glass darkened into amber and felt my face slipping from a smile into something more contemplative.

"What's wrong?" Finn asked, nudging my foot with his, frowning in my direction.

I nudged his foot back before answering. "Do we have a list of people who have disappeared? Do we even know when it started?"

Sharon topped off my glass, and I watched again as the contents settled into something stout-like. "What's got you thinking about that?" she asked.

Jerod sat back, frowning at my glass and muttering, "Trying for PBR...."

"I don't know," I answered with a shrug, setting the glass aside for now. "I was just wondering. Do we even know for sure when it started? Have we tried tracking down the people we think just moved on?"

"Oh, honey," Sharon said, her free hand falling to my shoulder and rubbing a little. "Thinking like this isn't going to do you any good."

"There has to be *something* we can do," I protested.

Sharon looked like she was about to argue, but Fred interjected. "No, it's a good point. Up till now we've mostly been leaving it to Soren and Eleanor and their pack to work out, but...there are things we can do."

"Start with a list," Davis suggested, setting his glass aside as well.

"Maybe look for patterns in the timeline," Finn added, tossing me his usual, encouraging smile.

I sat back, and all around me the room slid into a sedate activity. Pencils and notebooks appeared, Sharon passed around a plate of cookies, and we spent the rest of the evening jotting down everything we knew about anyone who had gone missing for any length of time. I couldn't do much more than provide moral support, really. Fred and Sharon were the biggest contributors, but we all chipped in where we could. By the end, Sharon's floor was strewn with scraps of paper and my stout had stayed exactly as it was when we began.

"Tut tut, gorgeous. Keeping secrets isn't nice."

"No secrets here..."

But I know it isn't true. He doesn't chase me but I run anyway, tripping through a tangled forest, boots sliding through moss and underbrush, no clear path to follow.

I skid into an open glade, sunlight streaming down, warming me all over. In the middle, on a bright orange picnic blanket, Sharon is sprawled, sunbathing, nude and perfectly beautiful.

"Come here," she beckons, but my feet are already carrying me over to her. "You did so well. You deserve a reward. I knew you'd keep me secret."

I don't know where my own clothes went, but it hardly matters as her arms slide around me, legs tangled like vines with my own. Overhead, the trees knit together, enclosing us in a green canopy.

"Tut tut," echoes Finn's voice.

Chapter Eleven

I DON'T KNOW how much we accomplished that night, but even the attempt to do something made me feel a little better. Things started getting back to normal that week, or settling into a new normal at least. Finn and I met for coffee after Wednesday's class, and I bused it out to West Seattle to meet Sharon for drinks on Friday. Obviously none of our problems were solved, but it felt like we were getting somewhere, like things were getting better. I couldn't even remember the last time I'd seen Creepface. Maybe he was finally gone for good.

Steve was still occasionally taking up space in our kitchen and Noah had a perpetually goofy grin whenever he was around. It was cute. Nice to see that Noah was happy, satisfied. Even the continual reminder of the way the two parts of my life were starting to collide didn't bother me as much as I'd worried it would.

On Saturday, I'd stumbled my way out to the kitchen just as Steve was leaving, and even before I managed to pour myself a cup of Steve's surreally delicious coffee, I noticed the frown on Noah's face.

"What happened?" I asked, more concerned than I probably should have been. I just wasn't used to having to worry about Noah's heart in these situations. It was always the other person I felt a little bad for.

"Hm?" He looked over like he was just noticing me. "Oh, it's...um...probably nothing."

"Probably nothing or actually nothing?"

"Steve was just...telling me about his family."

"Ah," I said. I didn't need the coffee to wake me up anymore.

"Yeah, I don't think that covers it," Noah said, chewing on his bottom lip a little.

"What does cover it?"

"I don't know. What would cover 'my boyfriend thinks he's a fairy.'"

"Part fairy," I corrected.

"Like that makes a difference," Noah argued, and then his eyes narrowed a little in suspicion. "Wait. How did you…?"

"Um…yeah. We might need to talk."

It was even less ideal than spilling to Yael over beer and cupcakes, but it was pretty clear I wasn't going to be able to put this off any longer.

"We need to talk about my boyfriend thinking he's a fairy and you knowing about it already? Yeah, we might need to talk about that. Why didn't you tell me he was crazy?"

I flinched a little at that word. "He's not…crazy," I said, knowing full well I was maybe-kind-of coming off that way myself. "He really is part fairy."

Noah stared at me for a moment. A long moment. And then another. I wanted to give him a minute to come to grips with what I'd just said, so I didn't add anything else right away. Eventually he shook his head. "I don't even know where to start with that."

"Yeah," I said, grimacing. "I get it. I really, really do."

"Is this about the mystery guy? Does he think he's a fairy too?"

"It's not about…." I paused, rethinking that. "Okay, it's a little bit about Finn, but he's not a fairy." That made me pause again. I didn't think Finn was part fairy. I was pretty sure he would have told me, but it occurred to me that I didn't know much about the backgrounds of anyone else in the coven. This wasn't the time to worry about whether or not I was fully participating in the coventry, though. "It's…well, okay, let me just…"

I looked around, hoping to see the rosemary plant nearby, but my eyes landed on a potato instead. It had been hanging out in the kitchen long enough to have sprouted several eyes of its own, and that's what I went for. I closed my eyes and tried to coax them toward me.

"What the hell are you doing?" Noah asked. And then, a moment later, "Jesus! Seriously, what the *hell* are you doing?"

I opened my eyes. The chunky, white tendrils of potato root were creeping across the counter, but they stopped when I looked at Noah. *I* stopped when I looked at Noah.

His expression was horrified, and his eyes flicked between the potato and my face in something not too far from terror.

"Let me explain," I began, but he shook his head vehemently, cutting me off.

"No. No, this is...this is too much. This is seriously fucked up and seriously too much, and I...need to go. I can't just....I have to go." As he spoke, he backed away from me, reaching blindly for the jacket he'd left on the back of a chair. "You just...stay there, and I'm...I have to go."

And he was gone.

Somewhere in my head, a voice whispered that I'd known it would go this way, that Yael was a fluke, that he was right to be scared of me.

I glared at the potato, and the roots pulled back almost sheepishly until there was no evidence at all of my ill-advised kitchen gardening.

I wanted to call Finn. I wanted to call Yael. For a second I even wanted to call Sharon. None of that was an option right then. What I *needed* to do was go to work, and that would have to come first.

I rushed through dressing and making myself somewhat presentable, and as I jogged down the street to catch my bus, I fired off a text to Yael: *I fucked up. Talk to Noah?*

Noah and Yael were both out when I got home, and the house seemed way more empty than it ever had before. I wished we had a dog or something and briefly succeeded in distracting myself by wondering what it would be like to have a shifter for a roommate: someone to help pay the rent and lick your face when you felt down and lonely.

I tried texting Noah, but there was no response. I sent one to Yael a few minutes later, and got back: *Staying over w/ T. N's crashing on his couch. Home 2morrow?*

T was Yael's O-Chem crush, who was becoming more than a crush, albeit slowly. It was short for Tiberius, which explained why he went by T. Noah crashing on his couch made me like T more, but it made me worry about Noah even more than that. Did he feel like he couldn't come home if I was there? Was he scared of me? If he wasn't staying with Steve did that mean he and Steve were over? It was hard not to think of all the ways that I had potentially ruined everything here.

What good was being sane if my sanity drove everyone I loved away from me?

There's a mountain of potatoes, weeping vines from all their eyes, wrapping me firmly in their embrace, holding me too close, too tight. No one listens when I scream for them to stop.

Work the next day was excruciatingly long. Yael had sent me a text that morning saying that Noah was off to work and that I shouldn't worry, but I didn't hear anything else until my shift was almost over and she sent me another one to let me know that they would both be home that evening. I still didn't know what that meant, but I tried my darnedest to believe that it was a good sign.

On my way home, I stopped to get pho, hoping to use it as a peace offering, especially if Christine was there to make good on her promise of free cream puffs. When I asked for her, though, the manager told me with a frown that she didn't work there anymore. It figured. It was that kind of day. I really hoped she hadn't been fired for giving away baked goods.

I cut through campus and saw the goth kid eating his sandwich. He looked about a million times more depressed than usual, black lips turned down at the corner. I threw him a sympathetic smile. It seemed like everyone was in that boat today.

By the time I got home, I was pretty sure the whole city was in a funk. It wasn't even raining, but it was getting to be that time of year where the lack of sunshine hit home in a very real way, and grey and cold became the standard all around.

Yael was in the kitchen when I came inside. "I brought food," I said, holding up the plastic bag in illustration. "Is he home?"

She shook her head. "He's on his way, but he's...pretty upset."

"Yeah," I said. Setting the bag down on the table, I plopped myself into a chair and started unpacking plastic containers, mechanically dividing the contents into an assembly line. "I really freaked him out yesterday. I should have known better." Yael had made it too easy for me. I couldn't expect anyone else to take it as well has she had.

I didn't see her hand coming until it had already thwapped the back of my head good and hard. "Ow!"

"Asshole," she said.

"Don't you mean, 'freak'?"

"No, I mean asshole."

I must have looked as confused as I felt, because she rolled her eyes as she pulled out three bowls, and dropped into the chair opposite to help me with the unpacking. "You did freak him out, but that's not why he's upset."

"Then why?" I asked, rubbing the back of my head, almost certain she'd left a bruise.

"Because you knew Steve was a fairy and you didn't say anything? And because you didn't trust him enough to tell him what you told me."

"I didn't have time! He ran out on me."

"Not yesterday," she said, rolling her eyes again, exasperation in every feature. "Before. You didn't tell him when you told me."

"He was busy with Steve! I never saw him."

She just arched an eyebrow as she carefully poured the broth into the bowls.

"What? Was I supposed to track him down to tell him his roommate is a freaky, plant-whispering witch?"

"Yeah," she said, and then repeated it more gently. "Yeah, you really were."

I frowned, tearing a jalapeño into tiny chunks. "I just....I was scared."

"Of course you were, doofus," came a voice from behind me. I jumped a little, not having heard the door open. "But you still should have told me."

I tried to turn to look at him, but before I could manage it, I was enveloped from behind by Noah's arms and almost lifted off my chair.

"Hey!" Yael protested, chair scraping as she rushed to my side of the table. "If this is a roommate hug, I want in on it."

Before I could argue, I had a lap-full of Yael and was squished between them, Noah's grip mashing my face against Yael's shoulder.

"Guys?" I said eventually. "I love you both, but I can't breathe."

"Deal with it," they said in unison.

Chapter Twelve

Finn and I had cut our coffee down to once a week. It seemed like a better idea, both financially and emotionally, though neither of us acknowledged the latter. We were getting close to finals too, which meant that time for socializing of any kind was harder and harder to come by. Even when Sharon and I met for coffee on Sunday, I spent most of it working on my final essay for the Personal Writing class. There was no way I was going to write about what had actually been going on in my life since September, but I had managed to distill the most innocuous parts of my dreams into something I thought worked as a cohesive whole. The class was starting to seem like way more effort than I had thought it would be when I picked it up to fulfill that last English requirement.

To her credit, Sharon seemed content to sit with her coffee and her knitting, watching me work. She got us both refills whenever we ran low, and listened patiently as I grumbled about all the things I couldn't say.

Eventually, she had to go to an appointment, and I found I was genuinely disappointed as she got up to leave. We hadn't even been talking much, but she seemed to know what to say and when to say it, and having her there made me less stressed about...everything, really. About the essay and the roommates and how Creepface was still showing up in my dreams even if he wasn't in my reality anymore.

I was trying not to think of her as a 'special witchy friend,' but the longer I spent with her, the more I thought that she might be exactly what I needed: someone calm and stable, who was already so good at making me feel comfortable. It didn't hurt that she was really quite beautiful, forty or not. Her eyes were bright, they sparkled when she laughed, and the laugh seemed to twinkle through the room wherever we were.

When she got up to go, I started to pack my things as well. "You don't have to see me out," she said. "You should stay and finish your essay. You're almost done."

"Yeah, but...."

She cut me off by leaning down and kissing me. It was as much of a surprise as Finn's had been, but not as unwanted, and she pulled back before I had the chance to decide how to react to it. "Stay and finish," she repeated with a smile. "I'll see you tomorrow."

"Yeah," I said, a little dazed. "Yeah, see you."

She left, then, and I stayed. I really was almost done, and within the hour, I'd finished the essay and sent it off to my professor. I wasn't entirely happy with it, but I thought it was enough to get me a B, at least, and that was all I needed.

As I was packing up for the second time, he dropped into the seat across from me.

"That's twice now I've run into you all the way out here, gorgeous," he said.

Twice. He'd seen me twice in West Seattle and once on the water taxi, and I had to shake my head to clear it a little. Why had I ever thought he'd disappeared from my life?

"No, that won't do," he said, reaching across the table to take my hand, holding it firmly enough that I couldn't pull it away without causing a scene. "I can't have you falling into that old question again. It was useful to begin with, but we've moved past that." His voice dropped a little, and he spoke calmly and firmly. "You're not going crazy. You're all too sane, in fact. You're just having a little memory trouble."

It wasn't until he finished talking that I realized I was looking him in the eye, and I struggled to tear my gaze away. "What do you want with me?" Even as the memories started trickling back in, I couldn't seem to work it out. What did he need me for? What was my information giving him? It seemed like it should be obvious, but the pieces refused to fit together.

"Tell me about your friend," he said, still in that calm, firm voice.

My mouth opened almost against my will, and I started to tell him about Sharon. I got as far as, "She's just..." before I managed to clamp my mouth shut. I couldn't tell him about Sharon. I *wouldn't*.

"Tell me," he repeated, voice harder now, "about your friend, gorgeous."

My teeth ground together with the effort to keep my mouth shut. I closed my eyes, focusing hard, reaching out for any plants that might be nearby. Part of me was hoping I could do something with the coffee beans, but they were roasted too much for me to feel. I thought of how easy it was to manipulate plants at Sharon's house. I thought about Sharon's laugh and her smile and how she was always making sure everyone was comfortable. I thought hard about it, and the harder I thought the more determined I became not to tell him about her.

"Tell me," he said again, just a hint of anger in his voice now. I could practically feel the effort he was putting into the command. "Tell me about her."

I couldn't hold it in any longer. I had to tell him something. Not about Sharon, though. I couldn't tell him about Sharon.

"There's this girl," I blurted out, when I couldn't hold it in any longer. My eyes flew wide open. "This girl in...in the coventry. Katie. She's...she makes things levitate. She's getting really good."

He let go of my hand, then, almost throwing it from him in disgust. "I see," he said. "Well, that's a start at least. We'll have to work on the other one. It's...cute that you think you're protecting her."

When I finally shouldered my bag to leave, there was this sinking feeling in my gut. Guilt laying heavily in my stomach. I'd done something stupid. Something unforgivable. I just didn't know what it was.

I had known coventry would be different now that we'd decided to become the Number One Sibyls Detective Agency, but I hadn't quite been prepared to walk into Sharon's living room and see a giant cork board tacked with all the bits of paper we'd filled with notes the week before. Pictures had been added to some of them, smiling faces that no one had seen in weeks, months, however long since they'd disappeared. Color-coded highlighting seemed to be differentiating between those who were still missing and those who'd eventually come back. On a notecard off to the side was scrawled the word "Dead?" with a red string dangling underneath it. So far, we had no confirmation of any deaths, but speculation seemed to be running wild. There was a weight in my stomach as I looked at the card.

"Fred put it together this week," Sharon said, her hand resting momentarily on the small of my back as she pressed a cup of coffee into my hands. "Just how you like it," she added. "I think we'll be alcohol free for a while."

Finn gave me a look as she slipped off to get a plate of cookies, and I shrugged, not quite ready to share whatever it was that was happening between Sharon and me, certainly not with Finn. We'd just gotten over our last awkwardness, and I was in no rush to start more.

"So this is everyone?" I asked, looking over all the names, all the pictures, all connected with colored string to the area of Seattle in which they'd last been seen.

"Not quite," Davis said, stepping up to the board.

As I watched, he thumbed a pin into the map on Capitol Hill, just a few blocks from campus, a pink string dangling from it, connected to another pin. He lifted the other pin and used it to tack a name and picture to the board.

For a moment, I could only stare, willing the picture in front of me to shift into something else, but there she was, smiling and cat-eyed in black and white on cheap photo paper, Christine Omatsu scrawled underneath it in thick, black marker.

The guilt that had been slowly fading since the day before slammed back into my gut, and a deep sense of horror almost overwhelmed me. My mug slipped out of my hands, creamy brown liquid spreading out to stain Sharon's carpet. I spun away from the board, my eyes darting from Finn to Fred to Jerod to Katie.

"Oh, god," I said, feeling Finn's arm slide around me and vaguely conscious that it was the only thing keeping me upright in the face of that guilt. Katie's eyes met mine, confused and worried as I spoke. "I'm sorry. I'm....I'm so sorry."

I just didn't know what for.

Part Three

But it's really fear you want to talk about
and cannot find the words
so you jeer at yourself

you call yourself a coward
you wake at 2 a.m. thinking failure,
fool, unable to sleep, unable to sleep

buzzing away on your mattress with two pillows
and a quilt, they call them comforters,
which implies that comfort can be bought

and paid for, to help with the fear, the failure
your two walnut chests of drawers snicker, the bookshelves mourn
the art on the walls pities you, the man himself beside you

asleep smelling like mushrooms and moss is a comfort
but never enough, never, the ceiling fixture lightless
velvet drapes hiding the window

traffic noise like a vicious animal
on the loose somewhere out there—
you brag to friends you won't mind death only dying

what a liar you are—
all the other fears, of rejection, of physical pain,
of losing your mind, of losing your eyes,

they are all part of this!
Pawprints of this! Hair snarls in your comb
this glowing clock the single light in the room

"Insomnia" by Alicia Ostriker

Chapter Thirteen

My apology hung in the air.

The room around me was quiet, and if it weren't for the steady pressure of Finn's arm around me, I think I would have slid to the floor and melted into Sharon's pristine carpet. Everyone's eyes were fixed on me.

At some point, Sharon had ended up next to me, her hand resting lightly on my shoulder, and Finn stepped away. He stayed close though, and somehow shrinking away from his worried expression pushed me toward Sharon as her hand moved to grip my shoulder more firmly, and I leaned back into the touch, avoiding Finn's questioning gaze.

On my other side, Fred was frowning, mustache twitching in concern. "What are you sorry for?" he asked, glancing from me to Katie and back again.

"You haven't done anything," Katie added, her usually sanguine face drawn into a furrow between her eyebrows. "Have you?"

"I...don't...." I stammered, trying to gather my thoughts, to hold onto the fleeting explanation for why those words had flown out of my mouth, but it had already gone. My apology was just as incomprehensible to me as to everyone else in the room. "I don't know. I don't think so..."

I shook my head, vainly attempting to jar my thoughts into some kind of order. "I'm sorry," I said again. "I don't know why I did that."

"It's okay." Finn's hand hovered over my forearm like he wanted to touch but wasn't sure he was allowed. "Do you need...?" He trailed off, and I could see that he wanted to help and was coming up with nothing tangible to offer.

"Maybe some air," Sharon suggested, tugging me gently toward the door that led to her balcony.

"Or tea?" Jerod added, tugging the hem of his worn flannel shirt.

"Or both," Fred offered. "Why don't you let Finn take you home," he continued, and Sharon stopped her subtle guidance.

"You don't have to go," she said. "You can stay the night again."

"Again?" Davis asked, and Katie gave him a not-so-subtle shove.

"Not now," she muttered under her breath, only slightly more subtly.

There was something comforting in the thought of staying, even if I just slept in the guest room, but Finn was giving me that same look he had when Sharon had brought me coffee, and that pulled at something inside me. Things had been weird between us, sure, but he was still Finn, still my anchor in this stormy port. Sharon had been great to me, and I still wanted to explore whatever was starting to grow there, but Finn...Finn was the one with answers.

"No, that's okay," I said, pulling reluctantly away from Sharon. "Fred's right. I think I need to head home. I'm sorry for breaking up the coventry."

"Don't even worry about it," Katie said. "You're probably just stressed. It's getting close to finals, right?"

"Yeah, that's...that must be it," I muttered, glancing around the group. Everyone's faces were bathed in concern. Except Davis. He was just frowning, grumpy and suspicious, but that was fairly normal for him.

"Come on," Finn said, finally touching his fingers to my elbow to encourage me toward the door. "Let's get you out of here."

I nodded and mumbled an apology in the general direction of the group, though I watched Sharon the whole time.

"I'll call you in the morning," she said.

"Thanks."

And then we were out the door, and Finn let his hand drop, though he stayed close enough that I could feel the warmth of his arm next to mine through both our jackets. We were quiet all the way to the car, and my thoughts were in a muddle, bouncing off each other and ricocheting around my skull. I didn't know what had made me apologize or why seeing Christine's picture had sent that gut-wrenching guilt through me. It was still there, sitting heavily in my stomach, and I had no idea what to do with it. How do you deal with guilt that has no source? How do you make amends when you don't know what you need to amend?

I hardly noticed Finn opening the door and shuffling me into the car. Somehow, when I looked up, we were on the West Seattle Bridge, heading toward the interstate.

"I'm sorry," I said, voice croaking from my throat.

"You have got to stop saying that," he teased, though his expression was a little grim.

"No, I just mean…." I paused. I wanted to be sure I explained myself well. I didn't want this to be another untethered apology. "I mean for making you leave."

"You didn't make me do anything," he assured me. "I want to make sure you're okay."

"I'm not."

"Yeah, I figured. You'll feel better at home."

I wasn't sure I would, but saying that wasn't going to help anything, so I just nodded and settled back into the seat, leaning my head against the cool glass, watching rain drops chase each other down the window.

Before I knew it, he was stopped in front of my house, pulling up the emergency brake. "You want me to come in? I could…I don't know…make you some tea?"

My first instinct was to decline, brush aside the offer of help. I didn't want him to see me like this, messed up, confused, completely out of sorts. But I didn't want to go inside and sit by myself either. Yael was with T the O-Chem boy, and Noah was working. The house sat dark and lonely.

"Yeah," I said after a moment's deliberation. "Would you?"

"Of course." He cut the engine, and we both got out. Trudging up the walk, with Finn keeping pace beside me, I couldn't help thinking that it was so much more comfortable than the last time we'd done this, and I was wondering if I should say something about that when we got to the front step, and Finn said, "I promise not to kiss you."

I laughed as I fumbled my keys from my pocket, the sound a little shaky, definitely nervous. "Thanks? I mean…I'm sorry about…."

He cut me off. "Nope. No more apologizing from you tonight. We're just going to have tea and maybe talk and just let you…deal. Deal?"

"Deal," I said with a firm nod, my lips twisting into something like a smile.

He had offered to make tea, but I couldn't just sit and do nothing. I couldn't fix that guilty feeling, but I could at least fix some tea. Finn sat at the table, and I moved around the kitchen almost in a daze, filling the kettle, putting it onto the burner, finding two mugs, dropping tea bags into them.

"You're not going to make it in the mugs are you?" he asked.

"You sound like Yael." I kept on with my method, and he didn't stop me.

"Clearly Yael knows how to brew tea properly."

"Her mom's Greek. She has theories on these things."

"Well, my gran's Irish. She practically has a Ph.D. in tea-making."

The kettle whistled, and I moved to pour the water carefully into the mugs. "Well, if I ever meet your gran, I'll be sure to make tea properly. Until then, this is what you get."

I offered him the mug, moving to sit across from him with my own, but he stood.

"Can we go to the living room? Tea deserves a comfy chair."

"All we've got's a couch," I said, though that didn't sound like a bad idea. Enough of tonight had been uncomfortable already. I didn't need to compound that with bad seating.

"It'll do in a pinch," he answered, and we moved into the cozy cave of a living room. I settled myself into a corner of the couch, and he took the opposite end. Yael's blanket sat between us, and I toed off my boots to tuck my feet under it.

"Sorry," I said, then shook my head. "I mean...I'm not sorry. But the heater's kind of a piece of shit. We just pile on the blankets until it's livable."

"I can handle that," Finn said, pulling off his own shoes and slipping his feet under the blanket as well. I could see them moving, lumps sliding under the fabric. They stopped just a few inches shy of mine, and I was grateful for the space, though I couldn't help remembering his nudging in coventry and wondering if that was something I'd lost by turning him down that night. I wondered, too, when he'd become someone I was comfortable letting into my strictly defined personal bubble.

For a moment, we just sat, hands curled around our mugs, until I bobbed my tea bag a few times and then tossed it onto an abandoned plate lying on the crates we used for a coffee table.

"Do you want to talk?" he asked after a moment. "I mean...would that help with...." He made a vague gesture that somehow managed to encompass all of the weirdness that was going on, both that night and in the weeks since I'd left him on the stoop.

"Maybe?" I said, frowning into my steaming mug. "I just don't know what to talk about."

He nodded, pulling his own tea bag out and dropping it next to mine. I watched the brown puddles seep together to create one happily soggy pile.

"I feel like I've missed a lot since I went to Portland," he admitted, clearly offering it as a prompt. "Maybe you could start there? Fill me in a little?"

That didn't really make it easier, but at least it gave me a direction. "Um, yeah," I said, pausing to blow into my tea. "Well, when you were gone, and we were…."

"Being incredibly awkward?" he offered.

"Yeah, that," I agreed. "Anyway…I kind of needed someone to talk to."

"So you went to Sharon."

"Sort of? I mean…she offered, and you weren't around, and…she's really easy to talk to."

He nodded, but his brow was furrowed, and he definitely didn't look happy about it. "Yeah, she is."

For a moment, we were both silent, sipping our tea. Mine was still a little too hot, and I burned my tongue, but the pain felt like a little bit of penance for whatever was causing my guilt, so I sipped anyway.

"I'm glad for you," Finn said after a moment. "You need somebody, and Sharon is…."

"Old enough to be my mother."

"Not quite," he said, laughing and shaking his head. "She's good, though. She's been a big help to you, I can see."

I didn't know what to say to that. She had been a big help. Even without all the other complicated stuff, I knew that was true. She'd been there when I needed her. "Yeah," I said quietly. "Thanks."

"You don't have to thank me," he said. "It's good for you to have the support."

"You're taking this awful well." I hadn't expected that. Not after how awkward things had been for the last few weeks.

He shrugged. "Remember my Irish gran? I talked to her the other day. She had some things to say about how to be a good person. How to be a good friend."

"Yeah? She sounds pretty cool."

"She's the best."

I knew that we should be talking about the coventry and Katie and Christine and my weird, compulsive apology, but I just couldn't face all that right now, and the couch was cozy, and the tea was warm, and the proximity of Finn's toes to mine was just about perfect, so I said, "Tell me about her?"

I don't know how long we sat there, tea cooling in our mugs, as Finn told me stories about the woman who had taught him how to be a good person and a good sibyl and a good friend, but eventually, I was starting to nod off, and Finn was telling a story that had his whole face lighting up.

I sort of hoped I just imagined saying, "I missed your smile."

I'm not sure I wanted to be imagining hearing him come back with, "It missed you too."

"We should talk about the apology," he added, and I roused a little and attempted to pretend I hadn't by burrowing further into the blankets.

"Tomorrow," I muttered, and his answer was nowhere near as sleepy as mine.

"Okay. Tomorrow."

I woke up the next morning to the sound of quiet voices from the kitchen. Somehow I had ended up under a pile of blankets, still on the couch, my feet poking out from the cocooning warmth just enough to keep the heat from being too much. The voices slowly coalesced into something familiar, and I rolled off the couch, keeping one fluffy quilt wrapped around me as I shuffled toward them.

Finn was at the stove, flipping what looked suspiciously like pancakes, Yael was brewing coffee, but the scent of bacon drowned out pretty much all the rest of the pertinent sensory input.

They were both laughing softly, and Yael turned a smile toward me and then nodded at Finn. "See? I told you bacon would do it."

"Do what?" I asked, the words scratching out of my throat.

"Get you up," Finn clarified.

I peered over his shoulder at the sizzling pan on the back burner. "So you're telling me this bacon has ulterior motives."

"I'm afraid so," Yael admitted.

"I'll never look at pork products the same way again," I said, shouldering past Yael to fill a mug with coffee. When I dropped onto a chair to doctor the drink a little, I noticed Finn looking back at me over his shoulder. "What?" I asked, running a self-conscious hand through my hair.

"Nothing," he mumbled, turning away quickly with a bit of a flush to his cheek. "It's a good look on you."

"What is?" Because the hair definitely was not. I was not one of those people who could roll out of bed and straight into a photo shoot.

"Comfortable."

I'm sure I would have had something to say to that, but Yael was mouthing, "I like him," at me behind Finn's back, and then Finn was sliding a plate full of pancakes and bacon in front of me, and I got well and truly distracted by food.

"You know," Yael said after we'd both worked our way through half a stack of pancakes, "if you wanna fall asleep on our couch more often, I would totally be okay with that."

Finn laughed and I looked between the two of them, smiling myself. For a moment, I had the urge to play matchmaker, and then I remembered T and the barely-overcome-weirdness with Finn, and that I didn't even know if Finn would be into that, and I shook my head.

"What?" Finn asked, the smile that was hidden behind his mug evident in his voice.

"Nothing," I said. "Just...you're right. It's a good look. On you too, I mean."

Comfortable. I didn't get a chance to just be comfortable much anymore. I didn't think I'd ever really been comfortable around Finn, though I'd gotten close once or twice.

Finn was still smiling, and I looked away, meeting Yael's eyes, which was not much better. She was grinning, and I rolled my eyes.

"So," she said, leaning forward and drawing the syllable out. "How'd you sleep? You two looked really cozy this morning."

"Fine," I muttered, and then a laugh came bubbling up from my chest. "Wow, I...didn't dream," I added, only just realizing that.

"You've been dreaming?" Finn asked, that all-too-familiar expression on his face that let me know I'd just said something that I should be worried about.

"Yeah? I mean...it's not a big deal. We've been keeping dream journals for this class of mine? And ever since I've started having really vivid dreams." Not strictly true, of course. The dreams had started before the journaling, but I didn't want to worry Finn any more than I already had.

"It might be a big deal," Finn said. "Do you dream often?"

"Not really?" I glanced over at Yael. She was still leaning forward, fascinated and a little concerned. "Not until recently. I mean, probably I do. I know everybody does, but I don't usually remember them." His lips twitched a little, settling into a frown, so I asked, "Is that bad?"

"It's not bad, exactly. It might not be bad. Just...."

I tilted my head, eyeing him warily. "Just what?"

"Well...." He hesitated, dragging a piece of bacon through a puddle of maple syrup on his plate. "Remember how I said I didn't like the term 'seer' because it sounds like we see the future? Sibyls who don't usually dream...when they start dreaming, they're usually more like...visions. It's kind of like being an actual seer."

The room was quiet except for the low hum of the refrigerator. Both Finn and Yael looked at me expectantly. Eventually, I managed an eloquent, "Oh."

"It might be nothing," Finn offered quickly. "Sometimes they're just little hints of what's going on in your life."

"But you don't think so," Yael said to him. Her brows were knit in worry when she looked back to me.

He hesitated again, and I could practically see him sifting through words to find the right ones. "With everything that's been going on? I kind of doubt they're all innocuous. Can you...do you mind telling us about them?"

I took a deep breath and a slow sip of coffee. I noticed I was clenching my jaw and made an effort to relax it. "Yeah," I said eventually. "Yeah, I can tell you what I remember." I wasn't going to tell him everything—not the one about Sharon, at least—but this definitely went beyond the issue of my comfort, so I couldn't exactly say no. "Mostly they're about Sebastian," I began.

"Sebastian?" Finn asked. Yael got up to refill all our mugs.

"Creepface. The uber-glowing vampire dude."

Finn nodded, but he was clearly upset by the answer. "Um...when did you learn his name? Was it in one of your dreams?"

I frowned. Until that moment, I hadn't realized that I did know his name. I certainly hadn't been thinking of him as Sebastian. My hand slid under the quilt I still had around me, fingers curling around the shape of my phone in my pocket. "I don't know. I don't think so. I don't remember it, anyway." I knew I was sounding repetitive, but I was too thrown to really care. "It must have been, though, right?"

Yael dropped back into her seat, and it wasn't until then that I noticed my mug was steaming again. "You...haven't been talking to him have you?" she asked.

"No, of course not!" was my immediate response, and then I stopped, frowning. I knew it was true, but something about that didn't seem right. I looked from Finn to Yael, hoping one of them might have the answer to what was missing from this puzzle, but they both just looked at me, waiting for something more.

"I just...," I started again, then paused. It felt like all I had were questions, and I didn't know where they had all come from suddenly. "I think.... I think I might be forgetting things."

"Like what?" Finn asked gently, scooting his chair a little closer. His hand closed over mine around the mug I hadn't realized I'd reached for, and I didn't pull away from the touch.

"Like...I don't know. I keep getting these feelings? And I don't know what they're from."

On my other side, Yael had shifted so her knee bumped mine. "Can you give us an example?" she asked, then looked to Finn. "Not that I think I'll be much help here, but it can't hurt to have an extra brain working on it, right? Even if it's just a regular old human one?"

"No, of course," Finn assured her, giving her a quick smile. "It's a good idea. The more specifics, the better."

"Well," I said when they were both looking at me again. "Like last night." I tried not to squirm. I didn't like being the center of attention like this. "When I saw Christine's name on the board.... I felt incredibly guilty. Like it was my fault or something. And Katie...."

"Christine the pho girl?" Yael asked, and it occurred to me that she really had no idea what we were talking about. I'd filled her in on most of what went on at the coventry, but I hadn't seen her since last night.

"She's missing," Finn clarified before turning back to me. "Tell me about Katie."

"I don't know what it was. I just...knew I'd done something to her. Something bad."

"Something to do with the disappearances?" he asked, and I nodded, then shook my head.

"Yes? Maybe? I don't know. I have no idea where that came from. It just...hit me. Really hard."

He was still frowning, and Yael was still looking at me like she was afraid I might spontaneously combust or faint or something. I shifted in my chair, pulling into myself, away from both of them, and wrapping the quilt tighter around me.

"I think we should bring Steve in on this," Finn said after a moment.

"Fairy Steve?" I asked at the same time Yael said, "Noah's Steve?"

"Yes?" Finn said, glancing between us. "Fairy Steve, at least. I don't know about Noah...."

"Fairy Steve is Noah's Steve," I offered helpfully.

"Everybody has cooler friends than me," Yael grumbled.

I rolled my eyes again, more fondly this time, and asked Finn, "Why do we need Steve?"

"Fairies have empathy, right?" he said, and I nodded. Yael did too.

"Yeah, of course," she said. "Duh. Everybody knows that."

"Be nice," I chided.

"Right, sorry," Finn said, smiling a little, his nose wrinkling sheepishly. "Anyway, fairies have empathy, and that sometimes gives them a little insight into the subconscious. I think maybe we should have him hypnotize you."

"Right," I scoffed, still not used to having these kinds of conversations at breakfast. So much for comfortable. "I should definitely get hypnotized by a fairy."

"Now who's not being nice?" Yael nudged my knee with hers.

"Sorry."

"It's fine," Finn said, his smile ridiculously reassuring in spite of everything. "Anyway, it can sometimes help with repressed memories. I think it might be able to help you." He got up to start clearing the table, and Yael and I immediately moved to help. "You have a final this morning, right?" he asked me.

"Yeah, in like...," I glanced at the microwave clock. "Jesus. Half an hour?"

"Okay," he said. "Go to your final, I'll call Steve and have him come over at around 4:30. It's best to do this at twilight."

I was clenching my jaw again, hardly aware of it. Finn looked over at me and made another sheepish face, like he'd done something he hadn't meant to. "I mean...if you want. We don't have to, but if you are okay with it, I think it might be good. Totally up to you."

I took a deep breath and let it out slowly. As weird as it all seemed, I could see that this was a sensible course of action, inasmuch as anything was sensible in this situation. Having Finn give me the option made me strangely okay with it. "No, yeah. We should do it. It's a good plan."

He nodded and gave me a faint smile. "Should I call Sharon too? It might help to have someone...special there."

We had come such a long way from comfortable, but I nodded as well. "If that's cool? I can call her if you'd rather not."

"No, I've got it. You go take your final. Do what you need to do. Just trust me to take care of the other stuff. I'll even do the dishes. You don't want to be late."

"Oh my god, you guys," Yael said, throwing up her hands.

"What?" I asked, already moving to find my book bag and my boots.

"You're in the middle of a full-on supernatural mystery with vampires and fairies and dream sequences, and you're still having an awkward relationship moment."

I very diplomatically told her to shut up.

My final was a disaster.

I mean, I didn't get it graded immediately or anything, but I'm pretty sure on that front. It was for my sociology class, and I'm usually pretty good with that, but I couldn't focus on the test, and I think I must have left about a third of the questions unanswered. It was hard to care about that, though. I was too busy worrying about Katie and Christine and being hypnotized and—in an astounding display of screwed up priorities—having Finn and Sharon over at the same time.

I hadn't managed to grab lunch on my way out, so I stopped by a sandwich shop to grab something quick before my afternoon final. Econ at 1:30. I had almost forgotten that Finn was going to be there until he waved me over to a desk near his.

"Hey," I said, dropping my bag and sliding into the seat.

"Hey," he answered, smiling in a way that was both sympathetic and collegial. "How did it go?"

"Shitty." I smiled, though. It felt strained on my face.

"Hopefully this one will be better?"

"That's the idea." I glanced up as Dr. Sternquist came into the room. Her hair was more frizzy than usual, and her cardigan was...somehow less mustardy.

"Hey," I said, nudging Finn's elbow with mine. "Is it just me, or is she a little...."

"Dimmer?" he offered. "Yeah. I've noticed it, too."

"Do you think we should ask her about that?"

He started to wave off my concern and then stopped himself. "You're really worried about her?"

"Kind of? I like her." I shrugged. "Besides, she might have some answers nobody else does. Especially if Creepface is involved."

For a moment, he just looked at me, expression serious. "Okay. After the final. We'll ask for a meeting."

"Thanks." I nodded, feeling a little less stressed. I'd come a long way if talking to my vampire professor was relieving my stress instead of adding to it.

Before we had a chance to talk more, Sternquist was moving between the rows to hand out the exams, giving us all directions and wishing us luck. I wondered if luck from a vampire carried any weight. I certainly hoped so. I'd never be able to explain to my parents why I'd failed this quarter.

Finn finished his exam first, and I could tell he was killing time waiting for me to be done. He kept flipping back and forth through the pages, frowning at questions and erasing things only to scribble them back in a moment later. I didn't know how he could be so focused on it, but I supposed that came of being a little more used to this sort of supernatural peril than I was.

I managed to finish more than two-thirds of this test, and when I was satisfied that nothing more was going to be squeezed out of my brain that afternoon, I glanced over to Finn and nodded. We both gathered up our things and took the exams to the front, handing them over to Sternquist. Finn looked at me and arched a questioning eyebrow. It seemed it was up to me to set up the meeting.

"Dr. Sternquist?" I said quietly.

"Yes?" her expression was distracted as she glanced up from the pile of essays she was apparently grading while we all worked on the test.

"I was...we were wondering if maybe we could meet with you sometime. Soon?"

Her gaze sharpened a little, and she sniffed softly, looking us both over. "Of course," she answered, managing to sound welcoming and wary at once. "Tomorrow? I have office hours from two to four."

"We'll be there at two," Finn said, glancing to me for affirmation.

"Yeah, thanks," I said, offering her what I hoped was an encouraging smile. "See you then."

"Do you think we worried her?" I asked Finn as we stepped outside. It was windy enough that I zipped my hoodie up higher, hunching my shoulders against the cold. "I mean, she knows we're sibyls. Two sibyl students come up to her after the final, wanting to talk? She's got to know something's up."

He shrugged. "I guess? She probably already knew. Everyone in the community knows something's up. I can't imagine the vampires are oblivious."

"Yeah, you're probably right." I nodded, and I found that we were heading toward the coffee shop as if on instinct.

"Shall we?" he asked, inclining his head toward the entrance.

"Might as well."

Really, I thought it would be nice to put off going home for a little longer. Going home meant getting ready to be hypnotized, made to remember things I'd rather have forgotten. I couldn't decide if I hoped it worked or that it didn't. Your brain blocks things out for a reason, right?

"My treat today," Finn said as we stepped inside. "If that's okay?"

I didn't feel like arguing, and I knew he was trying to be a better friend or person or whatever. "Yeah, cool. I'll get a table."

I found a table as far into a corner as the shop offered, and by the time Finn brought our coffees over, I was tucked as far into that corner as I could manage to get.

"You want to get them to go?" Finn asked.

"Hmm?"

"You're barricaded in back here. I thought maybe you'd rather be at home."

"Nope. Here is better." Going home was one step closer to hypnosis.

He nodded, and we sipped our drinks for a few moments in silence.

"I called Sharon," he said eventually.

"Yeah?"

"Yep." He was quiet for another moment. "She's coming. Steve too."

"Cool."

Awkward silence.

It was maybe the awkwardest of silences.

There was a lot of sipping and eye contact avoidance.

Eventually, I couldn't take it anymore.

"Are you...cool with that? I mean, Sharon being there?"

"Sure, yeah."

More awkward silence.

I was in the middle of sip/avoidance when he said, "Actually, no."

"Oh."

"Sorry." He shook his head, frowning a little. I didn't know what to say or do or anything. "That was something Gran said too. About being honest. So honestly? I'm not okay with it, but I think it's probably good for you to have her there, so...I'll deal."

"Oh."

I was totally winning this conversation.

"Well," he said. "That got awkward fast."

"I think it's been awkward for a while now."

"Yeah." He dragged the word out into a slow drawl. "I shouldn't have said anything, huh?"

"No, it's….." I was going to say 'good,' but that didn't sound right. "I'm glad you did. It's useful to know?" I just didn't know what to do with the information now that I had it. "You...don't have to come."

"Do you not want me there?"

It was a deceptively simple question, and in the back of my mind, I could see Yael throwing up her hands again, so I took my time in answering rather than saying what etiquette dictated I should.

"I want you there," I said, surprised by how true that was. I didn't want to do this without Finn there. I wasn't sure I could delve into a new part of the supernatural community without him. "But if you'd rather not be there, I'd understand."

"I'd rather not be there," he said, and I had a quick, supportive comment all ready, but he continued with, "but I want to be." His face screwed up in frustration. "Does that make sense?"

"Yeah, it does." It sounded like a polite affirmation, but it was true. I knew what he meant, and I appreciated it, more than I was probably making clear. His support meant a lot, despite everything that was weird and awkward between us. It was good to have something stay the same.

"Thanks," he said, like he didn't quite believe me but was accepting it anyway. His aura got a little brighter, and that made me relax some. It really was a good look on him. I knew I wasn't supposed to be thinking that, not with whatever was happening with Sharon, but it was true, and I figured it was okay to be happy when your friends were happy. Or comfortable when they were comfortable. Something like that had to be okay.

It was a little less awkward after that, at least, and when we finished our coffee, I felt a little better about heading home, so we hopped the next bus going that way.

Yael was in the kitchen when we got there, stirring something delicious-smelling on the stove.

"I didn't know what to make for a hypnosis party," she said by way of greeting before turning to actually see us. "Oh, hey, fish-boy!"

"Hey," Finn responded, smiling a bit. It wasn't quite his usual smile. There was something stiff and awkward to it. I was pretty sure he was obsessing over the upcoming guest list as much as I was.

"It's not exactly a party," I pointed out, leaning over the pot to see what was inside—some sort of liquid, possibly soup.

"There's people, and there will be food and probably booze. Sounds like a party to me."

"Booze might not be a good idea," Finn said.

"Booze is for after," Yael returned. "So is soup, for that matter. Hypnosis really works up an appetite."

"Yeah, I'm sure I read that somewhere," I said, rolling my eyes and moving to put my bag aside and hang up my hoodie.

"How long before people get here?" Yael asked, and Finn checked the time on his phone.

"Anytime, now. I told them we wanted to get started at 4:30."

Right on schedule, there was a knock at the door, and then it opened. Finn looked surprised and a little concerned, and it took me a moment to connect that with what he might think of Sharon feeling that comfortable in my home already.

"It's Steve," I muttered, and then Steve appeared in the kitchen doorway.

"Hey!" He pulled me into a surprisingly comforting hug before turning to do the same to Finn and then Yael, whom he picked up off the floor, making her squeal a little.

"Jesus! When did fairies get to be so big?"

"I'm only half," Steve pointed out.

"I don't ever want to meet your dad," Yael affirmed.

"He's the fairy side," Steve said with a grin, waggling his eyebrows.

I stepped in before anyone could make any further speculations on Steve's parentage. "So, what do we need for this whole spiel?"

"Just a comfortable place for you to lay down," Steve said.

"You don't have to, like, burn some herbs or something?" I asked.

"It's a hypnosis, not an exorcism."

"Right."

"Though I guess if we need to do some exorcising later, it wouldn't hurt to have some sage," Steve added, and I couldn't tell if he was joking or not from the casual expression on his face as he looked around the room.

"Uh huh," I said and glanced over at Yael to see how she was taking things.

"Do you want the cozy quilt?" she asked me, concern on her face and in her voice.

"Maybe?" I couldn't tell if I was joking or not either, but Yael just nodded and headed down the hall, presumably to find the quilt.

"That's good," Finn said. "Anything that makes you feel comfortable should help. Right Steve?"

"That is the theory," Steve agreed. "Are we still waiting on someone?"

I glanced over at Steve as Yael came back into the living room, dragging her quilt with her. "Yeah, um...Sharon's still on her way, I think." Yael was laying out the quilt across the couch as I fished in my pocket for my phone to see if Sharon had texted. Before I could even get it woken up, though, there was a knock at the door.

"I hope that's her," Steve said. "We're running out of twilight."

It was, and she pulled me into a quick hug when I answered the door. "Hey," she said quietly, not quite letting go enough for me to pull back. I must have used up all my decision-making on my exams because I honestly couldn't tell if I wanted her to or not. "How are you doing with all this?"

"Hard to say," I said. "Okay, I guess? I'll feel better when it's over."

She hugged me again before finally letting go. "I'm sure you will."

"Are you okay?" I asked, all too aware of the voices wafting our way from the living room. "You seem a little tense." And she did. The lines around her eyes were a little deeper than I remembered, and her embrace wasn't quite as easy as it had been before.

"I'm fine," she was quick to assure me. "Just a little worried about you."

"Then I guess we'll both feel better soon."

She just smiled and tilted her head in the direction of the voices. "We shouldn't keep them waiting."

"Right."

I took her hand and gave it a quick squeeze before leading the way to the living room.

"So what's the deal with twilight?" Yael was asking. "And don't tell me it's because of the vampires."

"It's an in-between time," Finn said, nodding a greeting to Sharon. "Not quite day, not quite night. Barriers are thinner then."

"What kind of barriers?" I asked, moving to take a seat on the couch on top of the quilt and immediately wishing I hadn't since everybody else was still standing.

"Lots of them," Steve clarified. "Between magic and mundane, between light and dark."

"Between conscious and subconscious," I guessed.

"Exactly," Steve said with a smile before turning to Sharon and offering his hand. "You must be Sharon."

"Yes, hi," she said, giving his hand a quick shake and then moving to take the chair closest to the couch.

"Sorry," I said. "I thought you knew each other." After everything I'd been told about how close the supernatural community was, it hadn't even occurred to me that they might not.

"Nope," Steve said. "But I've heard a lot about you," he added to Sharon.

"Good things?" she asked, joking through the awkwardness I knew she must be feeling with Finn standing right there.

"So far," Steve answered, but his face was a little strained. I hadn't ever seen it looking like that before. I hoped it didn't mean the hypnosis was dangerous.

"So...are we gonna do this or what?" broke in Yael, looking around the room. She had to have been the most relaxed out of all of us, and I was grateful for it. Even in this weirdness, I could still count on Yael.

"Right, yeah," said Steve, clapping his enormous hands so hard that Sharon jumped a little. "Let's get going. You wanna lie down for me?" he asked me, and I nodded, stretching out on the couch.

"What should we be doing?" Finn asked. "I've never actually been part of a hypnosis before."

"Very little," Steve assured him. "You're mostly just here for moral support." As he spoke, Sharon reached out to touch my hand.

"We're right here with you," she said. "I'm not going anywhere."

I nodded. "What do I need to do?" I asked Steve.

"Close your eyes," he said, hunkering down on the makeshift coffee table. I kept them open long enough to see Finn settle in on the floor near my head and Yael take the last remaining chair before complying.

"Okay," Steve said, and his voice was just as deep and resonant as always. "I want you to imagine yourself at the top of a staircase."

"A staircase?" I heard the skepticism in Yael's voice. "Isn't that a little...cliché?"

"If it works, why change it?" Steve answered, and then he turned his attention back to me. "Go back to the staircase." As he spoke, something in the sound of his voice made me want to do just what he said. It was soothing and sweet, and I could see the staircase immediately. "I'm going to count down from ten," he continued. "At ten, I want you to picture yourself walking down the stairs slowly. Each number will bring you closer to the bottom of the stairs where there is an enormous feather bed waiting. When I get to one, you're going to fall into the bed and sleep. Okay?"

I nodded and then figured I should probably actually say something. "Yeah, got it," I said. My voice already sounded like it was coming from a long way off, from someone else entirely.

"That's good," Steve said. "I'm going to start now. Ten...." It was all too easy to match my breathing to the rhythm of his words. "Start down the stairs." He spoke slow and even, and his voice was like a warm blanket, sliding over me. "Nine. Take it nice and easy. One step at a time. Eight.... Seven.... One foot in front of the other. Six.... Five.... Breathe with the movement of your feet. In and out. Four.... Three.... Down the stairs. Two.... Almost there. And one.... Drop into the bed. Let yourself sink into the softness. Let it hold you. Relax completely. Keep your breathing nice and steady."

I could still hear his voice, but everything else seemed to slip away. I could feel the soft, rich warmth of the feather bed around me, and I was sliding out of consciousness, letting sleep overtake me. I thought, if hypnosis was nothing more than a good, long nap, it might not be so bad.

"Can you hear me?" Steve's voice came through the fog of sleep, cozy as one of his hugs.

"Yes," I said, in that voice that wasn't my voice.

"Okay," he said. "I want you to think about Christine."

"Christine," I repeated.

"Yes. Tell me about Christine."

I took a deep breath and let it out slowly, focusing on the image that came to my mind. "She has cat eyes."

"Good," Steve said. "What else?"

"I saw her at the shop," I added, remembering her holding up the top. "She came in to buy a shirt, and we talked. She promised me cream puffs."

"When was the last time you saw her?"

"At the shop," I said, certain of this. "I didn't ever get cream puffs."

"You're sure?" There was a tense sort of urgency in his voice that made me focus, made me concentrate on the memory of the waitress.

"Yes," I said eventually. "I didn't see her after that."

"Did you talk to anyone about her?"

I thought again of Christine's face and then another one came into my mind. "Just Sebastian."

There was silence for a long moment, and during that time, Sebastian's face grew in my mind, expanding until it seemed he was staring right into my brain. He wasn't happy. His eyes were flashing, and his pupils were a vertical slit, narrow and angry.

"What else did you tell Sebastian?" Steve asked. As he spoke, Sebastian's face receded, pulling away from me. Instinctively, I tried to pull him back, tried to focus on his face, but it was rolling away. I reached for him to pull him back, but he slipped through my fingers. "I don't know," I said. "I can't...I can't remember." I wanted to. I wanted more than anything to remember what I was doing with Sebastian, why I had his number, why I'd been talking to him about Christine. "I'm trying!" I added, voice strained.

"It's all right," Steve said. "Let it go." It took more effort than I'd have liked to stop grasping in the darkness for the shining beacon of Sebastian's face. Steve waited though, and by the time he spoke again, I was laying back in the bed, relaxed and sleepy again.

"Tell me something else about Sebastian," he said. "Tell me how you met."

"On the water taxi," I said, and then I shook my head, though I could clearly see him standing on the deck next to me. "No. No, it wasn't...it was...."

"At the bar," came a voice so far away I couldn't identify it.

"Shh," said Steve. "Don't think about the bar," he added to me. "Tell me about the taxi instead."

"I was leaving West Seattle," I said, focusing again on the reality of standing on the deck, the comforting presence of the aquatic plants, the sharp shock of his hand on my back, his voice in my ear, the warmth of his hand on my cheek. "I...it was cold. He was close to me."

"How did you feel?" Steve asked. "Focus on your emotions. It will connect your memories."

"I felt...." There were so many things I wanted to say. Repulsed. Scared. Angry. "Comfortable."

There was a muffled mumble of something that could only have been profanity.

"Okay," Steve said. I'd expected disgust in his voice or, at the very least, hesitation, but it was still warm and soothing. "Focus on that feeling. Focus on anything connected to that feeling."

I tried. I thought about any time I'd felt that comfortable, that at ease with what I was doing, what I was supposed to be doing. "Last night," I said, grasping for more details on when I'd felt comfort like that. "The couch...and...Finn...."

Before I could elaborate more, Steve said, "No. That's...not quite it. Not quite the same feeling. Go back to the taxi."

I tried, but it was difficult to pull myself out of the warmth and comfort of tea and Finn's gran. I thought of the taxi, though, concentrating hard. I thought about the seaweed and how it had surrounded the boat, just out of reach. I thought about the pressure of Sebastian's hand on my back. I leaned back into the touch, into the memory. "He wanted something," I said, focusing again on the warmth of his touch, the surprise of it. "He wanted me to do something."

"And you wanted to do it?" Steve asked, though it was less a question than a prompt.

"I did," I answered with certainty.

"Okay, think about that," he said. "Think about that desire. Think about fulfilling it."

I concentrated again, thinking about how much I'd wanted, in that moment, to do what he asked.

"Think about that desire and that comfort from before. Try to put them together."

I thought again, tried to connect the two feelings. Eventually, I said, "On the bus. I was on the bus, and I told him...I didn't tell him anything."

"Okay, good. That's good. Think about that same feeling. Think of another time you felt it."

I thought hard. I tried to come up with another time I'd felt that way. Only... "It was different on the bus," I said. "Different than before. There was...I didn't want to help him."

"Even better," Steve said. "Think about that. Think about fighting him."

I thought. I focused. I threw everything I could into finding another time I'd warred between the deep-seated desire to do what he said and the urgent need to keep something from him.

"In the coffee shop."

"Tell me about the coffee shop."

"I was there. I was...writing. I wrote, and then...." Something had happened. Something with Sebastian. I was trying to remember, but there was a part of me that didn't want to, a part that told me if I remembered, I would ruin everything.

"I told him about Katie," I said, and a panic rose in my chest. My heart picked up speed, and my breath came fast and uneven. "I didn't mean to. I couldn't help it. He...he wanted to know...."

"What did he want to know?" That urgency was still present, but somehow Steve's voice managed to be gentle and soothing all the same.

There was something more, something else Sebastian had wanted to know about, and it was just out of my reach. Sebastian's face filled my vision again, expanding bigger than before, a smug smirk on his lips.

"Keep your breathing even," Steve said. "He can't hurt you here. Nothing can hurt you here, but you need to remember. Focus."

The smirk twisted, mocking me, slipping into a snorting laugh, and it was too much for me. I tried to relax, tried to focus on my breathing, but all I wanted was to wipe that smirk off his face. I felt something brush my hand, and it hit me suddenly. "Sharon!" I exclaimed. "He wanted Sharon!"

"Okay, okay," Steve said, the struggle for calm evident in his voice. "I'm going to count back up to ten, and I want you to get out of the bed. Remember the bed?"

It was hard. Sebastian's face was still enormous, livid now, snarling.

"The feather bed," Steve was saying. "Soft and comfortable. Warm. You're just napping in it. Remember the bed."

I concentrated hard, working to see the bed. Steve's voice softened with every word until it was like the bed itself, and then I could see it. "I remember."

"Okay," he said again. "I'm going to count up to ten, and you're going to climb out of the bed and walk back up the stairs. Got it?"

"Got it." I didn't know how I was going to get out of the bed. It was so soft, so comfortable. Whatever was at the top of the stairs was difficult and complicated, and things were so much easier here.

"One," Steve said, a firmness to his voice that hadn't been there before. "Sit up. I know it's hard but start by sitting up." I strained to pull myself upright. "Two," he continued. "Get to your feet. Three.... That's good, keep going." I didn't know how I managed it, but I pulled myself from the bed, gripping the rail of the staircase, pulling myself along. "Four.... Just keep walking, keep lifting your feet." It was so much harder going up than down. "Five.... Six.... You're almost there. You can see the top." I could. I was getting closer. "Seven.... There's a door at the top of the stairs. A light is coming from underneath it." I saw the door, reached for it, the knob just out of reach. "Eight.... Hold out your hand. Nine.... Grip the doorknob." My fingers closed around it. "Ten. Open the door."

I blinked my eyes open, surprised to find myself still lying on the couch. It had gotten much darker since I closed my eyes, and no one had bothered to turn on the light. Sharon's hand was on top of mine, and everyone was looking at me in concern.

"Did it work?" I asked, memories of whatever had been at the bottom of that staircase already slipping away in a disturbingly familiar way.

"Yeah," Finn said, a deep frown pulling his whole face downward. "Yeah, it definitely worked."

"Do you remember any of it?" Yael asked. Sharon's hand tightened around mine.

"Sort of?" Everything was fuzzy. I remembered Sebastian. I remembered something about Sharon. "What did I say?"

Concerned looks bounced between Finn and Yael and Steve. Sharon just stared hard at our joined hands. The silence spoke volumes until Yael cut through it with a frustrated. "Fine! I'll say it."

"Say what?" I asked, not sure I wanted to hear it.

"Give it a little time," Sharon said. "We could all use a rest before talking about this. Why don't we eat whatever that is that smells so good first?"

There was no way I could get down any of Yael's delicious soup before knowing what I'd said that had everybody so on edge, so I blurted out, "No, tell me. It's better to know, right?"

Yael glanced to Steve who nodded at her. "You...well, you've been telling Creepface about the people who are disappearing."

"What?" I sat up, unconsciously pulling the quilt around myself. "No, I haven't!" Even as I said it, I knew it wasn't true. "Have I?"

"At least Christine," Finn said.

"And Katie," Sharon added, pulling my hand into her lap.

"But you did it to save Sharon," Finn was quick to put in, glancing over to her as if for confirmation.

"So...thanks?" Sharon said, a weak smile sliding across her face and off again.

"You're welcome," I muttered, feeling my own face drawn into a frown.

There was more silence as we all sat and let the information sink in slowly.

It was Yael who broke it, jumping up from her seat and firmly proclaiming, "Soup! We're having soup, and we're...figuring shit out. Soup will help. And booze. So much booze." This last was added as a mumble mostly to herself, I think, as she made her way to the kitchen.

Before anyone else could add their opinions the door opened, and in a moment, Noah appeared in the living room. His face broke into a smile upon seeing Steve, but before he could even cross the room to him, his expression fell again. "Um...I missed something, didn't I? What did I miss?"

"Fill him in over soup!" came Yael's voice from the kitchen.

Chapter Fourteen

I don't know that the soup necessarily helped things, but the booze certainly loosened everyone up. Sharon refrained, reminding us that she had to drive home. The rest of us dutifully dug into our steaming bowls and washed it down with beer and/or whiskey and/or whatever concoction Noah whipped up into a punch-like substance from the remainder of several different bottles. The others filled Noah in while we ate. I kept pretty quiet, not sure I had much to add.

"So," Noah said. "You're part of a supernatural kidnapping ring."

"Noah!" Yael and Steve said in unison.

"That's hardly fair," Sharon chimed in, touching my shoulder lightly.

"But it's true, isn't it?" I asked.

"I wouldn't say that," Finn answered cautiously.

"Is that a thing vampires can do?" Noah asked, looking to Steve. "Just...make people forget things?"

Steve looked to Finn who looked to Sharon who looked to me and then away.

"Not usually," Steve said after a long moment.

"It's theoretically possible," Finn said.

"Very theoretically," Sharon added.

"And not with a sibyl," Steve pointed out.

"Yeah," Finn said, chewing on his bottom lip and looking over at me. "That's the really worrying part."

"Why?" asked Yael.

"Because he shouldn't be able to glamour me," I said, the realization sinking in. "Right? Vampires aren't supposed to be able to glamour sibyls."

"Exactly," Steve said with a nod. "That's what I can't figure out."

"Maybe I'm just a shitty sibyl," I suggested.

"You're not," Finn said firmly. "You're coming along great, and it's not even about how good you are."

"Well," Sharon said carefully, leaning forward like she was nervous about what she was about to say. "It is possible."

"Is it?" I asked, leaning forward as well, eager to hear something that might make this all make sense.

"I guess?" Steve said, rubbing the back of his neck.

"Will somebody just fucking tell us what's possible and why?" Noah burst out. "You're ruining my buzz here."

"If the vampire is old enough," Sharon began, "they could possibly glamour a sibyl."

"But they'd have to be really old," Steve interjected. "We're talking well over 500 years, and there hasn't been a recorded case of a vampire that old in…well…centuries."

"Still," Sharon said. "It's possible."

"I thought that was just a myth," Finn said, and I couldn't help but laugh.

"Finally," I said, when everyone turned to stare at me. "Something Finn doesn't already know."

He gave me a sheepish smile and shrugged. "Even sibyls have legends."

"So what's the legend?" I asked, more genuinely curious than I could remember being since this all started.

"The story goes that there was a really, really old vampire," Finn said. "One of the first, or possibly the second generation. She was intent on living forever."

"Vampires don't live forever?" Yael broke in.

"Nope," said Steve. "Just a really long time."

"Sucks for them," Yael said. "All that blood and no immortality."

"Anyway," Finn continued. "She thought if she could steal the powers of other supernatural creatures, she could translate that power into eternal life. So she…." He broke off a moment and swallowed, like this was difficult to say. "She fed on them."

Steve, Finn, and Sharon all looked horrified. Yael, Noah, and I just looked at each other like we'd missed something important.

"It's just a legend," Sharon said after a moment.

"It's not a legend," Steve said. "It's true."

Everyone turned to look at him. "How do you know?" asked Sharon.

"Because my grandfather was there."

"Jesus," Noah said. "How long do fairies even live?"

"A long, long time, sweetheart," Steve said, slinging his arm over Noah's shoulders. "Anyway...he was there. He helped stop her."

"How?" I asked. I didn't know for sure that was Creepface's plan, but I figured it couldn't hurt to ask.

Steve shrugged. "I don't know. He never said."

"Can you ask him?" Yael said, getting up to start clearing the table.

"We live a long time, but we don't live forever," was his answer.

"Sorry," I said, and Noah leaned his forehead against Steve's temple.

Silence slid around the table again, and we all watched Yael as she moved around the kitchen, refilling drinks and loading up the dishwasher.

"Do you think that's what he's doing?" I asked eventually. "You think he's feeding on them?" As I spoke, I could see his face clearly, cat-eyes glaring at me.

"I hope not," Steve said. "Grandpa didn't talk about it a lot, but it was pretty bad last time around."

The alcohol was starting to settle in all around, and everyone looked maudlin. Sharon was the only one who still seemed to be in good shape.

"I think I should go," she said, glancing to Steve and then to me.

"Why don't you stay?" Finn asked before I had the chance. "Really. It's...you should stay."

"The others should know about this," she argued, shaking her head. "I need to call Fred and maybe Eleanor."

I glanced from Sharon to Finn. There was a tension there you didn't need to be part fairy to feel. Still, Sharon's reason seemed as good as any, and I didn't want her staying if she wasn't comfortable. "Thanks for coming," I said.

"Of course," she answered, smiling as she stood and bending to kiss the top of my head. "Talk to you tomorrow?"

I nodded, wondering if I should walk her to the door, wondering what Finn would think if I did.

"I'll see myself out," she said before I could make up my mind. "Goodnight, everyone."

Farewells were tossed out all around me, and then everyone fell silent again until we heard the door click shut behind her as she left.

"Okay," Noah said once she was gone. "I missed something in this hypnosis thing, didn't I?"

I had been thinking the same thing, but I didn't want to ask while Finn was still there.

"Yeah," Yael said, dragging the word out a little. "Nothing much, just...." She looked from Noah to me. "You um...you kind of said the last time you felt really super comfortable was...last night with Finn."

"Oh," I said, at the same time Noah said, "Oops."

"Yep."

I looked around the table as silence settled in around us. Maudlin still seemed to be the theme of the day, though Steve had that deep frown on his face again.

"What's wrong?" I asked, not seeing any reason why the weird pseudo-triangle between me and Finn and Sharon should have him frowning.

He shook his head. "I was just wondering why you had me come over."

"To do the hypnosis," I answered. "Finn said fairies are better at it."

"We are," he said. "But why didn't you just have Sharon do it?"

Silence again. I was starting to really understand that Simon and Garfunkel song.

"What do you mean?" Finn asked after a long moment.

"Well...she's part fairy too."

I wondered if I should start counting the minutes we spent in silence. Maybe it was significant.

"How...how do you know?" I asked at the same time as Finn said, "Are you sure?"

"Yeah," he said. "It's a fairy thing. Couldn't you see it in her aura?"

Both Finn and I shook our heads. "It's just...green," I said. "Yours is kinda...goldish."

"Well, she's definitely got fairy in her. I'd say half. A fourth at the least."

It occurred to me then that I didn't have any idea what Sharon's gift was. I'd never seen her manifest it, and I'd always just assumed she didn't have one. I wondered now if it was something like Steve's empathy, and that opened up a host of doors I'd rather keep closed, so I tried to focus on what was happening right then. "You didn't know?" I asked Finn.

"I had no idea," he said. "She never said. Maybe Fred knew?"

"Maybe," I agreed, but I was starting to wonder about that too. "Weird that she didn't mention it when you called, though."

"Yeah," Finn said slowly, chewing his lip again.

We were all avoiding each other's gaze. I desperately wanted to have something to say that would make this new mystery disappear.

"I think," Steve started, speaking slowly, his voice taking on that soothing tone I remembered from the couch. "I think we should maybe call it a night and pick this up tomorrow. Twilight's long gone, and like it or not, life still goes on. Finals and all."

I nodded, frowning, and Finn's knee came over to nudge my own. "We're seeing Sternquist tomorrow," he reminded me. "Maybe she'll have some answers."

Nods rippled around the table, and we all slowly got to our feet.

"You okay to drive?" I asked Finn.

"Yeah," he said. "I didn't drink all that much."

"Party pooper," Yael teased as she slipped past us toward her bedroom.

Finn shrugged smiling, and we both sort of watched awkwardly as Noah and Steve disappeared as well.

"So," he said.

"So," I echoed.

"For what it's worth...I hope it's nothing. This thing with Sharon. There's probably a totally simple explanation for it. Not every fairy is good at hypnosis."

"Really?" I asked, not sure I could buy it.

He paused for a moment like he was thinking it over. "Yeah, really. You should be happy. I mean...ideally we'd all be happy, right? But I'd like it if you were."

"How come?"

"You've had a rough quarter. You deserve something good."

I didn't point out that he'd had a rough quarter too, or that I was apparently causing some of the roughness myself. It didn't seem like the time. Instead, I said, "Thanks," and walked him to the door.

"Is it cool if I hug you?" he asked, and I nodded. His hugs weren't quite as good as Steve's, but they were very...Finn, and that was just what I needed then.

Chapter Fifteen

I DIDN'T HAVE a final for my Personal Essay class, so I was home free for the next day—other than the final essay I still needed to finish—which meant my morning was spent trying to sleep in so I didn't have to wonder about Sharon or Sebastian or what I had actually done or why or how. It didn't work particularly well, and by the time I actually let myself leave my room, Noah and Yael were both gone to work or finals or wherever. There was a noise from the kitchen, though, and when I got there, Steve was pouring himself a mug of coffee.

"Morning!" he boomed, smiling at me. It wasn't quite his usual grin, but it was miles better than the frown he'd had last night. "Coffee?"

"Mmm," I groaned in response, mostly for show. I'd been awake for the better part of an hour and was just ignoring that fact.

Steve was kind enough to let me sit quietly at the table while he poured me a mug and doctored it for me. He even let me be the first one to speak once he'd deposited it in front of me and settled into the chair opposite.

"Don't you get tired of serving people coffee?"

He shrugged, smiling over the rim of his own mug. "I like to think of it as a public service. Doing good for the community."

"No argument there," I said after I had a sip. "You've got the gift."

"So I've been told."

He let me sit another moment just sipping before he spoke again.

"What's going on in your head?"

"Can't you tell?" I didn't mean to sound snarky, but it did sort of come out that way.

"I can tell you're thinking awfully hard on something," he said, leaning back in his chair like he was giving me space for all that thinking.

I nodded, but I took another little while before I answered. "Do you think Sharon's been lying to me? To us, I mean?" Because if Finn didn't know she was part fairy, then this could be much bigger than me.

And back came the frown. Noah's "Might Be Whiskey" coffee mug looked small and insignificant cradled in Steve's hands. "I think," he said slowly, "that she could have any number of reasons for not having told you. But I also think it's more than a little suspicious that she didn't say anything when Finn called. I like you and all, but hypnosis is much more effective with someone you know and have a strong connection to."

"I don't know how strong a connection we have," I started, but he shook his head.

"It's pretty strong."

Then it was my turn to frown. Whatever Sharon and I were actually doing, we hadn't been doing it all that long. Not long enough to have anything I'd call a strong connection. "Is that...something you can tell? Like part of your empathy?"

"It's related," he admitted. "A little different, though. I see connections, kind of the way you see auras. I think it comes from fairies being connected to the land. I wouldn't say that you two are inextricably connected yet, but you're forging something significant."

As much as that sounded like the start of a really bad romance novel, something in Steve's tone made me wary about it.

"Oh," I said, falling back into my scintillating conversational tactics.

"I try not to judge," he said. "But I don't think it would be a bad idea to be cautious."

I didn't know what to say to that, but he checked his watch just then and pulled himself to his feet. "I gotta get to work," he said. "Are you gonna be okay on your own?"

"Yeah, thanks."

I watched him as he pulled his jacket from the back of a chair and tugged it on. Just having him taking up so much space in my kitchen was comforting, and I really needed comfort now, but I knew the world around me wasn't going to stop just to wait for me to get my head on straight.

"Call me if you need anything," he offered as he headed for the door.

"I will," I said. Then, "Steve?"

"Hm?" he turned in the doorway to look at me.

"You said it gets easier, right?"

"It does."

"When?"

It took him all of two strides to cross the kitchen to my seat and lift me up into a hug.

"Wish I knew, kid."

I met Finn outside Dr. Sternquist's office at 1:55, and he gave me a sheepish smile and then an awkward hug.

"How are you holding up?" he asked as I extricated myself from his embrace.

"Well," I said, not knowing how to start or where. "I'm here? And nothing catastrophic happened this morning."

"I guess we'll take it, huh?"

"I guess we have to."

We sat in the well-worn chairs in the Business Department's lobby, watching the clock tick its way toward two. Neither of us said anything, and any time we caught each other's eye, we smiled awkwardly and looked away again.

It was a long five minutes.

I wanted to say something, but everything that was in my head was going to make things less comfortable, not more. I needed to talk to someone about Sharon, but Finn seemed like the very wrong person to try that with. Really I needed Yael and Noah, which was a good long way from me thinking I wanted to keep them out of this part of my life, but it still wasn't something I was entirely ready to accept. They were for school and relationship issues. Finn was for magic and fairies. But those lines had already blurred so much that I didn't know which way to turn, no matter what I wanted to talk about.

Eventually, the earth turned enough to make it two, and we each looked over at the other and nodded.

"Let's do this," Finn said, and we both got up and headed down the hallway to Sternquist's office.

I knocked lightly on the door frame and peeked my head in. "Dr. Sternquist?"

Her office was exactly as I would have expected it to be if I'd given it any thought before. There were precarious piles of paper and files littered around the room on various surfaces, some of them punctuated with books and pens. Her degrees were framed on a wall behind her, but one of them was slightly askew. Several framed photographs showed her with a woman who looked a little older than her in various famous locations: The Great Wall, The Arc de Triomphe, Buckingham Palace, the Taj Mahal.

"Hm?" There was a pencil tucked behind her ear when she turned to see us. "Oh! Yes, hello. You said you'd be coming by, didn't you?"

"Yeah," I said, stepping into her office. "Thanks for seeing us."

"Of course," she said, and she did seem genuinely happy to be meeting with us, or at least not put out by it. "Have a seat." She gestured to a few chairs kept free of piles as she moved to close the door behind us. Finn and I glanced at each other and then each took a seat. He squirmed a little as he sat and then reached underneath himself, pulling out a pen and holding it up to me with a smile.

"Ah, thank you," Sternquist said, snatching the pen from his hand and dropping into the last free seat.

"You're welcome?" Finn said, watching her in barely veiled amusement as she settled herself.

"So," she said eventually. "I'm guessing you want to know about the disappearances."

"Yes," I said eagerly. It looked like we finally might be getting some useful information. Finn leaned forward in his chair, elbows braced on the arms. "Do you know who or what's behind them?"

"Nope," she answered, shaking her frizzy head.

"Oh." The disappointment was clear in Finn's voice, and he leaned back again. "Then why...?"

"Why else would two sibyls request a meeting with their vampire professor?" she said in the same tone she used when someone asked an incredibly obvious question in class.

"So you...don't know anything?" I asked.

"I didn't say that. I have my theories."

"Why haven't you been sharing them?" Finn asked. I flinched at the accusation in his tone.

She sat up a little straighter, tugging at her cardigan. "The supernatural community has been ostracizing vampires for centuries," she said. "I didn't want to butt in where I wasn't wanted."

"But I thought…," I started, glancing over at Finn who was shaking his head. Clearly the line between vampires and other supernaturals was a little more complicated than I had been led to believe, but now was hardly the time to dredge that up. "Never mind. Can you tell us your theory?"

She looked from Finn to me, considering, and then nodded sharply. "I think it's entirely possible there is a vampire behind it all."

"What makes you think that?" I asked, jumping in before Finn had the chance to offend her again.

"There's a legend passed around in the vampire community. It says that if you feed regularly from a supernatural creature, you can absorb their abilities."

"But," Finn said before I could stop him, "that's not true, is it? That's the sort of thing shifters tell their kids at night to keep them in their beds."

"Oh, it's all too true," Sternquist said.

"Then…how come we don't hear about it more often?" I asked. I could only assume that if it were widely known, it would have been the first place people looked when supernaturals started going missing.

"Because we have taken steps to assure it doesn't happen," Sternquist said firmly. "We like staying under the radar, as it were. There's no need to cause a commotion by letting one vampire get more powerful than all the others. It could end in chaos."

"What kind of steps?" Finn asked, leaning forward again. "I mean…if you can say," he added in response to my warning look.

"Hm." She sniffed and turned her gaze to me briefly. "Part of it is simply the natural resistance most supernatural creatures have to being glamoured. It makes the process much more complicated, harder to get away with. And really, we don't need the entirety of Faery after us. Most of it, though, is fear of the Council."

"The Council?" I asked.

"The Council of Vampires," Finn clarified, obviously intrigued. "I've heard of it, but no one I know has any information on it."

"Of course not," came Sternquist's sharp answer. "It is our own affair and affects no one outside the community. The Council was put in place to ensure that we remain a peaceful race. When someone steps out of line, the Council puts them back in their place."

"And if the Council can't convince them to toe that line?" Finn queried.

"Then the Council eliminates the problem."

I winced, glad I was a sibyl and not a vampire. I wondered if there were a

Council of Sibyls somewhere that no one had bothered to tell me about. I wondered if colluding unknowingly with a vampire was grounds for elimination.

"So why aren't they stepping in here?" Finn asked.

"I have a theory on that as well," Sternquist said.

I cleared my throat, pushing aside thoughts of elimination. "Can you share that with us?"

She glanced around the room a moment, as if concerned that someone might be listening in. "I think the culprit may be a member of the Council."

We'd had our share of silence the night before, but this silence carried an entirely different quality. It wasn't shock, exactly. To be shocked at the revelation, we'd have had to been thinking something else was the answer. It wasn't even horror. It seemed almost apt that a member of the Vampire Council might start breaking the rules. Absolute power and all.

It was more like the slowly creeping realization that we might be in over our heads. I guess I'd been feeling that way for a while now, but it had always seemed like as long as Finn knew what he was doing, everything would be fine. From the look on Finn's face, he had no idea how we were going to go up against a Vampire Council.

"Oh."

It was Finn who uttered the syllable this time, but I'm certain my expression echoed it.

"Indeed," Sternquist said.

"Do you...do you know who it might be?" he ventured.

Sternquist's eyes narrowed at the question, and she looked from Finn to me and back again. "I think you'd better ask your friend," she said to Finn.

"His friend?" I asked, and it wasn't until she turned her gaze back to me that I understood what she'd meant. "Me? What? Why would I know?"

"Don't play innocent with me, child," Sternquist said, and I did find myself feeling like a child in the face of her tone and expression. She seemed so much older than she had before. I realized that the other woman in the pictures was likely much, much younger than the professor.

"Dr. Sternquist," I protested, reaching over to touch Finn's arm to stop him speaking for me. "I honestly don't know what you mean. If you think I should know...." I trailed off, not knowing what to offer her or what to ask her for.

"You reek of it," she said, nose turning up in disgust.

"Of what?" I asked, desperate to have some answers even if I could already tell I wouldn't like them.

She turned to Finn again as though sick of the sight of me. "When you find out whose blood your friend has been ingesting, you'll have your answer."

"What?" It was Finn who stood first, jumping to his feet, face indignant, brows furrowed. "How dare you? No one has been...drinking vampire blood. That's...that's disgusting."

"Indeed," said Sternquist calmly. Her tone was icy. In all my musings about her cardigans, I had never imagined she had the capacity for ice in her voice.

I stood a moment after Finn, though I was trying to be the calm one here. Someone needed to be. "Dr. Sternquist...I promise you, I haven't been drinking anyone's blood. Certainly not a vampire."

"You can deny it if you wish," she said, slowly pulling herself to her feet and stepping closer to me. I wanted to back away, but my calves hit the chair and there was nowhere to go. She may have been small, but having her so close was intimidating, and she looked me over slowly, then inhaled deeply through her nose. "There's no mistaking that scent."

I looked to Finn for some support, but he was looking me over carefully as well, sizing me up as though he'd never seen me before. "What?" I said. "Finn...stop it. Stop looking at me like that. Stop it both of you."

Sternquist took half a step back, but Finn just shook his head. "She's right," he said softly. "You're...there's something wrong with your aura. Something...brighter."

"Don't say that!" I was on the verge of begging. I just wanted someone to look at me like I wasn't a freak of nature. "I'm not...there's nothing wrong with me." Even as I said it, though, I thought back to the night before, to what was waiting for me at the bottom of those stairs.

"Sebastian," I said quietly. "Oh fuck."

Finn offered to drive me home, but he spent the bulk of the ride calling everyone from the coven to ask them if they could meet at my place in half an hour. I sent a text to Noah and Yael, adding Steve to it after a moment's consideration: *Emergency vamptervention. Come home ASAP.*

Noah was working, I was pretty sure, but I hoped the other two would be able to make it.

By the time we got there, Steve was sitting on the front steps waiting for us. He took one look at me and pulled me into a tight hug. "You look awful."

"Thanks," I mumbled into his bicep.

"What happened?" he asked when he finally let me go, looking between me and Finn.

"Let's wait until everyone gets here," Finn suggested, and he gestured to the front door. I fumbled for my keys, hands shaking, until Steve finally took pity on me and pulled out his own set, unlocking the door and holding it open for us both.

"Coffee or booze?" he asked, heading straight for the kitchen while Finn steered me toward the couch.

"Yes, please," Finn and I said in unison.

I gave an exhausted laugh as I dropped onto the couch. After a momentary hesitation that seemed to say so much more than Finn probably meant it to, he sat next to me.

After a moment, his hand found mine and gave it a squeeze. "It's gonna be okay," he said. "We're gonna figure this out, and everything's gonna be okay." I nodded, more because I didn't want him to worry more than because I thought it was true.

By the time Steve came back with three steaming mugs of Irish coffee, Fred had arrived, Jerod tagging along behind him. Davis showed up a few minutes later, and we were just about to start explaining things when Yael practically ran into the room.

"Don't you dare start without me!" she said, and I smiled in relief, glad to have someone there I knew would be unequivocally on my side. Finn shifted over and I followed with a grateful smile, making room for her on my other side. The quilt appeared seemingly out of nowhere, and Yael wrapped it around the three of us. "Noah's working," she said to me. "Does that mean I'm the last one?"

"We're still waiting on Katie and Sharon," Fred said as Steve passed a mug to him as well.

"I...I don't think we are," Steve said quietly. Everyone looked at him. "I think Sharon might be...giving you some space after last night," he said to me, and then, after a moment, "and we may have to accept the possibility that Katie...can't be here."

"Oh god," I whispered. Both Yael and Finn wrapped their arms around me. I had to put down my drink; my hands were shaking too hard to hold it without spilling.

"What happened?" Davis asked. I glanced up in surprise. It wasn't accusing, nor was it cynically accepting. His expression was almost sympathetic when his eyes met mine, and I thought that maybe I had more allies than I'd realized.

Steve stepped in then, filling everybody in on the hypnosis. He skimmed very quickly over Sharon's fairy status, and I wondered if that was in deference to me or because he didn't think it was important. Either way, I shrank further into the couch, and there was a wave of unease across the room at the suggestion that she'd been hiding this.

"We met with Dr. Sternquist today," Finn said, glancing over to me. "You want to tell them what we found out?"

I really didn't. Everyone was already looking at me like they thought one wrong word might shatter me. I shook my head. "You do it."

Finn calmly filled them in on our meeting, looking to me occasionally for confirmation. When he was done, Fred tugged on his mustache, frowning deeply beneath it.

"Well," he said after a moment. "We have a serious issue on our hands."

"Isn't this a coven matter?" Jerod asked, looking pointedly at Yael and Steve.

"No," Fred said firmly. "We've moved beyond that. This clearly involves the whole supernatural community, and...everyone connected to it," he added, nodding to Yael.

"Thanks for the inclusion," she said dryly. "Happy to be part of the club." I elbowed her in the side, and she frowned at me. "What?"

"Look," Davis said, shifting in his seat. "Nobody wants to say it, but we've got a list of questions a mile long and one very obvious direction to go for answers."

"What do you mean?" Yael asked.

While everyone looked to Davis for an explanation, though, I said, "Sharon."

"Exactly," Davis said, nodding.

"Maybe not," Finn offered. "She could have had any number of reasons for not telling us...."

Fred cut him off. "I'm afraid Davis is right. Steve, you said she told you she'd fill me in on what happened?"

"She did," Steve agreed. "And Eleanor."

"Well, I don't know about Eleanor, but I haven't heard from her for days."

"Then what are we waiting for?" Jerod asked, jumping to his feet. "Let's go get some answers."

"Let's not rush into anything," Finn said hesitantly.

"Why not?" Jerod said, clearly ready to spring into action and finally get something resolved.

"I think she just said she'd fill you in as a reason to get out of here last night," Finn said.

"Why was she in such a hurry, then?" Davis asked, for once both on the same page as Jerod and calmer than him.

Finn looked at me, almost for permission to explain, but before I could do anything, Yael jumped in. "Because things were super awkward after the hypnosis. I think she was trying to give Finn a chance."

"A chance at what?" Fred asked.

"At me," I said, rolling my eyes. "And I don't think it was like that. But...things were pretty awkward."

"Then maybe I should go check on her," Fred said, and there was ripple of nods around the room. "Fill her in on what's going on."

"No," I said again. "I'll go. She deserves to hear it from me. We're...," I glanced over to Steve, "connected."

Steve frowned, but he nodded. "I think that might be for the best."

"Let me go with you, then," Finn said.

"I don't want her to feel like we're ganging up on her," I said.

"No," Fred insisted. "You of all people shouldn't be going anywhere alone. I'll go with you."

"Me too!" Yael offered. "Someone's gotta give good, old-fashioned, human emotional support."

Finn looked like he wanted to offer, but Fred cut him off before he could start. "Finn, you, Davis, and Jerod should go check on Katie. We don't know that she's missing, and if she's not, she may be in trouble. Either way, we owe it to her."

"I'll hold down the fort here," Steve said. "Call me if you need backup."

I really hoped he was joking this time.

About half an hour later, I was at Sharon's condo. It had taken some convincing to get Fred and Yael to wait in the car, but in the end, I got them to agree that if

Sharon were avoiding me, I was the best person to bring her back in. That, and it seemed like Fred really didn't want to get in the middle of any potential relationship drama.

I couldn't tell from the outside if Sharon was home or not, but when I got to the front door and knocked, it swung open.

"Sharon?" I called, stepping inside. The front hall looked normal, and so did the living room, but when I got to the hallway, it was clear someone had been tearing the place up. I wondered for a moment if Sebastian had gotten to her, and a wave of panic rolled over me. Had I told him about her after the coffee shop? Had we just missed it in the hypnosis?

"Sharon!" I called again, louder, rushing down the hall toward her bedroom.

When I got there, I saw her. She didn't seem to be in any distress, but she was hastily shoving clothes into an open suitcase. She looked up when I entered the room and just laughed.

"Oh, sweetheart," she said, clearly amused. "You just don't know when to walk away, do you?"

"Sharon...we need to talk," I said carefully, taking a few steps toward her.

"No, we don't," she said. "It's sweet that you came all this way, but you really should have stayed home."

"I was worried about you," I said, taking another step.

She laughed softly, shaking her head. "It's almost a shame you're so earnest," she said.

From behind me came a voice that made my heart stutter. "Good to see you, gorgeous."

Part Four

Lord, we know what we are, but not what we may be.
—Ophelia, Hamlet
—William Shakespeare

Chapter Sixteen

Any response I might have had to Sebastian got stuck in my throat, wedged there by my surprise at seeing him and my inability to quickly process what that meant. In my hesitance, he lunged at me, hands outstretched as if to grab me. I didn't remember much of anything from the encounters we'd had recently, but I did know enough to work out that he'd done something to keep me pliable, to prevent me from fighting back. It annoyed me that he'd been able to, that he'd chosen me for some reason, and that he'd taken away my autonomy.

Something in that anger must have been sufficient to stop him from doing it now. I didn't have time to think about how to protect myself, but in my fury and determination, I called out to the faint traces of plant life I could feel in Sharon's room. A flowering plant in her windowsill responded, shooting out a stalk toward Sebastian. It cut between him and me, and he jumped back, hissing.

"You know, gorgeous," he said, his voice tainted by his own outrage, "I'd hoped to put off this particular tryst for another day, at least. Don't get me wrong," he added, and somewhere outside the room, I heard the door swinging open and footsteps in the hall. "I'd hoped you would come, but this would be just so much easier if you hadn't brought your friends."

I didn't know what he meant until Fred appeared in the doorway behind me.

"I think it's about time I stopped making things easy for you," I said. Not the most eloquent comeback, but I was still watching for anywhere else I might need to be throwing plants.

"I knew you'd be trouble," Sharon cut in, scoffing. Looking at her now I wondered what I'd seen in her. Her face was twisted into a deeply unpleasant sneer, and she rolled her eyes like a sullen teenager. "I tried to warn him…"

"Enough," Sebastian interrupted. "I have had so much more than enough of your whining. You've long outlived your usefulness."

I'd always thought he was creepy, but the expression he turned on Sharon at that moment sent a shudder through me. He'd been angry with me during the hypnosis, but his feline eyes at that moment seemed to glow a fiery orange, and I honestly thought they would burn into Sharon. Instead he turned his gaze to her suitcase, and it began to wriggle in her grip, wresting itself away and flopping onto the bed. We all stared in amazement as the zipper burst open and an enormous, leather-bound book flew out of it, toward Sebastian's waiting arms. Sharon tried to intercept it, leapt for the book, and actually managed to take hold of a few of the pages, but they tore off in her grasp as Sebastian's fingers closed around the book. With a feral growl, he raised the book up and swung it at her, catching her square across the cheek and sending her tumbling to the floor near Fred's feet.

"This was all I ever really needed from you, helpful as your little friend has been."

He cast one more scathing look in my direction before making a leap for Sharon's window, crashing through and soaring off into the sky, disappearing into the overhanging clouds.

For a long, long moment, Sharon, Fred, and I all stood gaping at the shattered glass that recently been a window. I think we would have stood there forever if Yael had not come bursting in, tire iron gripped in her hands.

"I know you told me to wait in the car, but....What. The. Fuck?" As she stopped and gaped as well, the rest of us turned our attention to her. Or at least Fred and I did. Sharon attempted to take the opportunity to sneak out

"Oh, you have so much explaining to do before you get out of this," Fred called after her. And then he was gone. Literally. He just...disappeared, and a moment later, I heard Sharon grumbling in the living room.

"Get your hands off me."

Yael and I rushed toward the voice in time to see Sharon trying to twist free of Fred's firm grip on both her arms. I briefly thought that I really should have taken a survey of what the coven's full list of abilities was so I could stop being taken so off guard by it.

"A little help here?" Fred pleaded, looking in my direction. I didn't know what to do at first, but Yael nudged me and nodded toward the plant I'd been using to practice on during our coventries. I closed my eyes and concentrated. It wasn't as natural as when I'd let my anger call the shots earlier, but it was still easier than it had been in a while to call out to the tendrils, encourage them to grow and wrap around Sharon firmly. Not too tight, though. I couldn't bring myself to hurt her. I was still hoping there was a good explanation for all this, though that seemed less likely with every passing moment.

"Want me to call in the cavalry?" Yael asked, finally dropping the tire iron to pull her phone from her pocket.

"Yes, I think so," Fred affirmed, wrestling the bound Sharon onto the couch and yanking the torn pages from her grip.

"Let me go!" Sharon insisted.

"Can you shove a flower in her mouth?" Yael asked me. "I mean…I'm assuming she's the bad guy here, right?"

"Yeah…I guess she is," I said, frowning at Sharon's struggling form and then almost unconsciously sending a few more tendrils to hold her in place.

"You do not want to do this," Sharon insisted.

"I think whatever leverage you might have had in this situation flew out the window with that book of yours," Fred responded, frowning deeply as he looked over the pages in his hands.

That seemed to work as far as silencing Sharon went, and for a moment we all just looked at each other, clearly unsure where to go from here.

"New plan," Yael said. "You two call the cavalry, I'll make tea."

By the time everyone had gathered, Yael had made an enormous pot of tea from whatever she found in Sharon's kitchen. There was much explaining to do, both to the coventry and to Steve, as to why, exactly, we had a sulking Sharon tied up on the couch.

"Wait, wait," Steve said, eyeing Sharon warily. "She's been working with a vampire?" He sounded utterly disgusted by the idea.

"It seems that way." Fred looked from Steve to Sharon and then back to Steve. "At the very least, she's been copying the Grimoire. She doesn't seem too keen on sharing more than that." Yael and I exchanged a look, but before I could ask what the Grimoire was, Fred continued. "How good are you at interrogation?"

Steve grimaced. "I can handle it. I'll need back-up, though. Truth potion or something would help a lot."

"Interrogation?" Yael asked. "That sounds a lot worse than it probably should."

"It's ugly," Steve admitted.

"How ugly?" I asked.

"Let's just say I'm glad Noah's still at work."

"Problem," Davis said. He hadn't taken his eyes off Sharon since he walked into the room. "She's our best spell-worker, and I'm guessing that book your bloodsucker took with him has her potion recipes in it."

Sharon said nothing, but she looked smug.

"I'll call Eleanor," Fred offered. The smugness slid right off Sharon's face. "I'm willing to bet everything she learned came from the Grimoire anyway."

"The Grimoire?" I asked. Now that it had been mentioned twice, I figured it was okay to ask. It was clearly important somehow, more important than I was grasping.

"It's a book of spells," Fred answered. "Very old, very important. Eleanor has care of it. It's been in her family for centuries now."

"It's more than that," Steve added. "It's a history of the sibyls and the werewolves. It's a sacred trust, and if Eleanor knew Sharon had been copying from it, she'd be livid. That information is too powerful to be out in the world, especially in that vampire's hands." When he mentioned Sebastian, Steve turned a glare on Sharon. I'd never seen that kind of anger in him before. I wouldn't have thought him capable of it.

"Then let's leave her punishment up to the pack," Finn suggested.

I'd almost forgotten he was there. Since he'd arrived, he'd kept to the sidelines, saying nothing, though I felt him looking at me more than once.

"I don't think Eleanor will leave us much choice in that matter," Fred agreed.

Sharon went pale.

"Werewolves don't take kindly to being crossed on matters of such importance," Steve added, looking grimly pleased.

Fred left the room to call Eleanor, and the rest of us sipped our tea quietly, always watching Sharon from the corners of our eyes. After a long while, Yael nudged me. "You okay?" she whispered.

"No," I admitted.

"We'll figure this out," Finn offered quietly, touching my shoulder just for a moment. "Steve will manage the interrogation, and we'll get the answers we need to fix it all."

I nodded, but I wasn't sure on that at all. There seemed to be far too much to fix, and how could any of us know if it wasn't already too late for Eli and Christine and Katie and everyone else who'd gone missing? I didn't think Sharon had all the answers we'd need for that.

By the time Eleanor got there, we'd taken to watching Sharon in shifts, one on duty in the living room while the rest of us gathered around the dining table. Several of Sharon's neighbors had stopped by to ask about the glass-breaking earlier, but Fred managed to send them on their way with a vague explanation of a shelving incident. There was some bickering over whether we should be planning our next move, but no one quite seemed to know how to do that without getting some information from Sharon, and she was in no mood to talk, it seemed. I had a million questions that I couldn't bring myself to ask, but Yael was more than making up for that. She wanted to know what had happened before she arrived with the iron, and I explained it in as much detail as I could.

"His eyes were...." I trailed off, not quite up to mentioning the detail. It seemed unlikely to be true, even after it had shown up during the hypnosis and again in Sharon's bedroom.

"Distinctly feline," Fred finished for me. "I noticed that as well. It worries me some."

"Do you think it's maybe related to feeding on the shifters?" Jerod asked.

"That's my best guess," Fred answered with a nod.

"Does that mean he can shift now?" I asked. The possibility made my stomach drop, especially when I thought of Christine and her promise of cream puffs and her own, distinctly feline eyes.

"Let's hope not," Finn said. "Last thing we need is a shapeshifting vampire."

We all jumped when the doorbell rang. Fred went to answer it, and a few moments later he was escorting Eleanor and two men I didn't recognize into the dining room. I thought back to when I'd first met Eleanor. She'd seemed a little on edge but was mostly pleasant and cheerful, clearly trying to lighten the mood in the midst of the crisis we'd been in.

Tonight she was nothing like that. She stormed into the room, and her usually twinkling eyes darkened to the color of a storm cloud as they scanned the room.

"Where is she?" she asked, the tension in her body holding her perfectly rigid as she reverently laid the satchel she was carrying on the table.

"In the living room," Fred began. Before he could get any further, Eleanor was moving toward the door, both men stepping after her. I could swear I heard her growling as Fred took hold of her arm to stop her. "You can have her when we're finished," he promised, "but we need some information first."

Her tempestuous eyes moved to Steve. "You're interrogating her?"

He nodded.

"Don't be gentle," she said, a snarl in her voice. "I'll make the potion." She picked up the satchel again and disappeared into the kitchen before anyone had a chance to respond.

"What's with her?" Yael asked, eyes wide and fixed on the kitchen door.

"Werewolves can get…kind of intense when it comes to pack business," Jerod said with a glance at the strangers.

"And Eleanor perhaps more than most of us," said one of the men.

Fred interjected with an introduction. "This is Soren, everybody. He's Eleanor's husband and the head of Seattle's pack."

Yael mouthed a silent, "Werewolves?" at me, and I shook my head. I could fill her in later.

"To be fair, Eleanor's really the head," Soren answered with a shrug. It was clear he was trying to keep things from getting too intense here, but he held himself stiffly, spine perfectly straight, even as he shook some of his shaggy, sand-colored hair from his face. He wasn't nearly as built as Steve, but he was muscular enough that I fully believed he led a pack of werewolves.

"I thought Eleanor was a sibyl," I commented, though after what I'd just seen of her, I was perfectly willing to believe there was a wolf in her.

"She is," Finn said. "Very rare crossbreed. Even my gran doesn't remember the last one."

"I'll get you that book," Steve said to me, voice dry and smile twisted.

"Yeah, I think I'll need it after this." I wasn't actually sure there would even be an 'after this,' but if there was, I was going to spend the rest of Christmas break researching all the stuff nobody seemed to tell me until after I needed to know it.

We fell into another awkward silence. Steve and Yael spent much of it texting. I was pretty sure they were talking to Noah, and I was pretty sure it was about me, even though both of them were careful never to look at me when their phones were out. It was at least another half hour before Eleanor came out of the kitchen, face set in a firm line, shot glass in hand.

"Is that it?" Jerod asked, nodding to the amber liquid in the glass. It looked fairly innocuous. Like whiskey or rum or something like that.

"You were expecting blue and glowing?" she asked. I wanted to believe I saw a little of her former warm nature in the comment, but her face was still hard and determined.

"At least." Jerod tried a smile, but there was very little humor in the room.

We all stared at the glass a moment longer, and then Steve held out a hand for it. It looked even smaller held in his grip, and he nodded once Eleanor had handed it over. "I guess we should do this."

Almost as one we stood and filed into the living room. Davis was watching over her, and they seemed to both be deliberately ignoring the other when we entered. It was a surreal moment. We moved in rhythm with each other, one by one dropping into seats in a circle with Sharon at the center. She'd been moved from the couch to a wooden chair—possibly because someone thought she shouldn't be so comfortable when she'd caused so much trouble. Steve took the seat directly in front of her. Her eyes dropped to the glass in his hand and then back to his face. Somewhere in her defiance, I thought I saw something like fear. Her aura brightened, flickered, and settled down again.

"Hold her head still," Steve requested. His voice was soft, and there was something in it that sounded suspiciously like regret. I wondered again what was involved in this interrogation and if Steve had ever done one before or had only seen them done.

Fred moved to hold Sharon's head firmly between his hands. She struggled wildly. Davis and I had to step in to keep her still—even Soren lent a hand when she flailed at us—while Steve's enormous hand pried open her jaw and he poured in the liquid. He held her mouth shut then and pinched her nose so she couldn't breathe until she'd swallowed. She coughed and struggled, her face turning red. I thought she'd make herself pass out before she gave in, but just when she couldn't possibly have held her breath any longer, she swallowed violently, and everyone stepped back. She gulped in air and sent a glare around the circle until her eyes fell on me.

"You won't let them do it, will you?" she pleaded, gaze softening, coaxing me to agree with her.

I couldn't answer. I was held somewhere between disgust and sympathy. I think sympathy might have won out, but I felt Finn's hand on my shoulder as everyone moved back into their places, and he squeezed gently. I looked away.

"How long will it take?" Steve asked, glancing over at Eleanor.

"She should be feeling it already. You can begin."

Steve nodded. It seemed like I could feel the air being displaced by the movement. A ripple of tension slid around the room and settled in everybody there. I had a strange urge to fall over into Yael, just to see if we'd all do a domino topple in our circle. I'm pretty sure we were all holding our breath.

Only Steve was left near Sharon. He placed both hands on her shoulders. She avoided his gaze, but he whispered something in a language I didn't understand, and she looked up, their eyes locking.

For a moment, neither of them moved. They were frozen in place and so were we. None of us could have looked away if we'd wanted to, I'm sure of it. Eventually, Steve leaned in closer, his face a hard mask, determination written in every feature. Sharon flinched but didn't look away. Her face twisted into a grimace, and Steve leaned closer still, his forehead nearly touching hers. She looked terrified, and I almost cried out, pleaded with Steve to stop, to let her go.

When the silence was finally broken, it was Sharon, not me, who shouted. It was a mixture of pain and fear, and I sucked in a sharp breath at the sound of it.

"I'm in," Steve said, voice strained.

I didn't exactly know what was happening, but I could get the gist of it. He was invading her mind. I wondered how this compared to what he'd done with me and the hypnosis, but that hadn't been at all painful to me, and it was clear Sharon was hurting. Every now and then, she'd let out a whimper, though her eyes never once left Steve's.

I wouldn't have known where to begin an interrogation like this, but Fred, his voice even and emotionless, said, "Tell us about the vampire. About Sebastian."

"That's not his real name," Sharon said. Her voice was flat, almost disinterested, though pain was still etched in every feature of her face. It was like she wasn't controlling it, like someone had turned it on with a switch and it was just playing a recording of itself.

"I didn't imagine it was," Fred told her. "Tell us what he wants."

"To live," she said. "Just like all of us."

"To live?" Eleanor said, and Steve's expression hardened further.

"Forever. To live forever," Sharon affirmed.

"How is he trying to accomplish this?" Fred asked.

She flinched again, but her voice was calm. "The Grimoire."

Eleanor growled softly, but she held herself back. "What does he need for the ritual?" she asked after taking a moment to compose herself.

"Blood," Sharon said, and it seemed like that was all she intended to say, but Steve gritted out, "Not so easy," between his teeth, and I could see his fingers digging tighter into her shoulders.

She cried out again and added. "Blood and solstice and sacrifice."

"What else?" Eleanor asked, stepping toward them a little. Fred stopped her with a hand on her arm.

"I doubt he was more specific than that with her."

It seemed for a moment like Eleanor would fight him. She tensed under his hand, then nodded.

"What were you getting out of this?"

I didn't immediately know who had asked the question, but once it was spoken, everyone but Steve and Sharon looked to me, and I realized that's what I'd been wondering this whole time. Why had she done it? Why had she been working with him? I couldn't believe she wasn't getting something big.

"Life," she said calmly. "Eternal life."

"That's a hell of an incentive," Jerod muttered.

"If he'd intended to pay up," Davis added.

Sharon's head jerked a little at that, but Steve's gaze held her firm.

"What kind of sacrifice?" I'd been surprised to find myself asking a question, but I was far more surprised to hear Yael asking this one.

Sharon's voice answered as evenly as before. "A sibyl just come into their power."

I broke the circle then, only vaguely aware of the rippling murmurs in the room as I turned and walked out. Yael and Finn followed a few moments later, and I heard Fred's voice saying, "Keep going. We're not done here," before I stepped out the back door onto Sharon's patio.

"Fuck," Yael said when they'd followed me out there. "Couldn't you have your freakout inside where it's warm? I mean, nobody's arguing that you don't deserve a freakout after that, but warmer is generally better."

"Sorry," I mumbled, and she insinuated herself under my arm for an awkward side-hug.

"You gonna be okay?" Finn asked.

"Hard to say," I answered, "but somehow I think I don't get a choice on that."

"You get a choice," Yael said. "It just doesn't change what you have to do."

She was right, of course. I could be as not okay as I wanted, but I had to do...*something*. I didn't know what yet, but it was clear I was a part of this. I had to help in stopping it. "Then I guess I'm okay."

It wasn't entirely a lie.

Chapter Seventeen

We stayed outside until I was pretty sure I could go back in without shaking so hard that I was in danger of breaking something. From the sound of it, they were finishing up things in the living room, and before long Fred came out to where we were gathered in the entryway.

"You should come back in," he said to me. "If you're up for it. We've got some things to discuss."

I nodded and Yael and Finn sort of flanked me until I took a step in front of them. They fell back after that, and I noticed as I got into the room that Sharon was gone and that they'd left my usual spot on the couch open for me. I dropped into it gratefully.

"The wolves took her," Steve said before I could ask, and it was only then I noticed Soren and the other man weren't there anymore either. "They'll take care of her." The hardness in his voice stopped me from asking what exactly that meant. At the moment, at least, I didn't want to know.

Eleanor sat next to me, satchel in her lap, and though I could see she was still tense and angry, she turned to me with a sympathetic smile. "How are you holding up?"

"Well, it's not every day you learn you were supposed to be some kind of vampire sacrifice."

"You weren't supposed to be any such thing," Eleanor said, nudging me with her shoulder. "Supposed has nothing to do with any of this."

"Yeah," Yael agreed, taking up Katie's usual spot by my feet. "Creepface doesn't control fate. Sounds more like he's trying to interfere with it."

"Either way, we're going to stop him," Steve added. He was sitting in Sharon's big, cushy easy chair, and he looked...wrecked. There were dark circles under his eyes, and he seemed exhausted, slumping in the seat, head drooping.

"How?"

It was Finn who asked, but the question was on my mind as well.

"Easy," Yael said, turning to look at me. "We just keep you from Creepface as long as possible, right?" As she finished, she looked around the group. Fred had a pained expression on his face.

"Maybe," he hedged. "But…"

"But?" I asked.

"He has contingencies," he continued. "There is…a very young sibyl who is just discovering her gift in Kirkland."

"So if he doesn't get me…." I trailed off.

"How quickly can we get to Kirkland?" Yael asked.

"We're working on that angle," Steve said quietly. "But we have to assume she's not the only option for him."

"Why is he after me at all, then?" I asked. "Wouldn't a younger, newer sibyl make for a better choice?"

Fred offered an answer. "We thought so as well. It seems Sebastian is somewhat fixated on you."

"But why?" I asked, my face sore from frowning.

"We're not sure why he did to begin with…," Steve started, then hesitated.

"What is it? What don't you want to tell me?"

"It turns out that stealing from the Grimoire isn't the only thing Sharon's been doing," Jerod said, tugging at the hem of his shirt.

"Okay," I said. I knew that was likely to be the case. She'd looked pretty cozy with Sebastian before he double-crossed her. I looked to Fred for an explanation.

"She's been…feeding you Sebastian's blood," he said. Something in his voice said he was trying to sound calmer about this than he felt. Finn inhaled sharply. I felt sick.

I thought back to all the times I'd taken a drink from her, trusted her to refill my glass. I wondered if that was why Sebastian could glamour me. Had she started as far back as Thanksgiving? Had it been building up longer than that?

Yael's voice broke my thoughts. "And that's…bad?" she asked, looking from Fred to me and back again. "I mean, worse than just, 'Ew, ick, blood'?"

"That's horrific," Finn clarified. He took a step away from me and rubbed the back of his neck. I thought back to our meeting with Sternquist.

"Sebastian's on the Council," I said. "That's what Sternquist said, right? She said whoever's blood I was drinking was the traitor on the Vampire Council."

"I don't know," Fred admitted. "The Council is a closely guarded secret. Only the vampires know who's on it, and not even all of them do."

"If he is on the Council, he's already older than he should be," Steve warned. "They only take the oldest vampires."

"I thought you said 500 was older than any vampires alive," Yael prompted.

"The Council is different," Eleanor answered. "Those on the Council tend to...want power. And people who want power that badly don't like to give it up."

"How do I not know *any* of this?" I asked, and for the first time I was truly angry that I hadn't been told all of this before. It wasn't fair to ask me to handle these situations without all the facts. I felt as though the people I'd trusted most had been keeping things from me. More than just Sharon.

"Very few people do," Fred pointed out. "Even in the sibyl community, knowledge of the Council is vague at best. The werewolves on the other hand...."

Eleanor interrupted, straightening next to me. "The werewolves keep the secrets we must, but we share when it's necessary."

I'd always thought of her as a sweet young woman, plump and pleasant and helpful. A little over-empathetic. Now I could see her as an actual leader, of a coven or a pack or perhaps both. She had a strength that was well hidden behind her smile.

"It's necessary," Steve said quietly.

"And I'm here to share it," Eleanor pointed out.

"Fucking politics," Finn muttered, and a few people gave him a tense smile or a nervous laugh.

"Okay, okay," I said, holding up a hand. "So...why feed me his blood? Is that what's made him able to glamour me?"

"We have to assume so," Fred answered. "And we believe that's why he wants you for the ritual instead of anyone else. He thinks you having his blood will make it easier for him to keep you in check."

"Okay," I said slowly, working out the possibilities here. "So again...how do we stop him?"

Eleanor shifted. "It seems Sharon's been copying from the Grimoire whenever I let her borrow it. Many of the spells are meant to be shared and passed around. Others are...quite powerful. It's part of why we guard it. Something he found in there made him think he can perform a ritual to make him truly immortal. That means our answer has to be in there somewhere."

Yael cleared her throat. "How can you be sure?" Everyone looked at her. "Look, I wanna be Miss Optimistic too," she argued, hands up in surrender. "Just...y'all don't even know what kind of ritual he has planned. How can we even know there's a way to stop it, let alone be sure that it's in the book?"

Finn started to argue, but Fred cut him off. "She's right. The answer may not be there, but it's where we have to start."

"Doesn't hurt to be realistic," Yael muttered.

"Leave it to the mundie," Jerod said with a smirk. "Way to pull your weight."

"Thank you," Yael said primly, flipping her hair over her shoulder.

Everyone was quiet then, and it took me a moment to realize they all kept glancing at me. I wasn't sure why at first, but it hit me eventually. They were looking to me to make a decision. It made sense, I supposed. My involvement with Sebastian—and to a lesser extent, Sharon—had gotten us into this mess, so I should be in charge of fixing it.

"Okay," I said finally. "Research time."

There was only one Grimoire, and Eleanor was understandably protective of it, but Sharon had some old spellbooks around the house, and Jerod and Finn took to the internet for their research. We were all hunkered down in our own projects for the long haul, it seemed. I didn't even realize how late it had gotten until the doorbell rang and Steve answered it to let Noah come rushing in, tackling me for a hug and sending the tome I was perusing flying across the room.

"Jesus," I muttered into his shoulder.

"You scared me! And you!" This last was directed at Steve who was the next target for embrace. It was a strange thing to see Steve almost melting into Noah, like he was soaking up some kind of energy from him. (That was going on my list of things to ask about fairies once this vampire thing had been sorted out.)

"Oh, sure. Nobody worries about me," Yael complained, and in a moment she was pulled into the hug as well. Then me. Then Finn. Then, inexplicably, Fred and Eleanor. Even Jerod got one. Davis just stood back and shook his head.

"Weirdos."

"Everybody gets a hug!" Noah exclaimed, extricating himself from the group to chase Davis down. Once he had Davis pinned to the wall, he said, "I'm Noah, by the way. Nice to meet you all."

We recovered slowly, and Steve shifted over in the easy chair to make room for Noah so he could fill him in on anything they hadn't already discussed over text. They looked relaxed and comfortable, and while there was still a sense of urgency in the room, Noah's appearance had broken some of the tension. It was easier to focus now, less fraught. Fred got up to make some coffee, and we all sort of settled back into the research routine. Coffee was made again and again as needed, and before I knew it, the sun was rising over the city.

I was up stretching my legs, and I stopped by the living room window to watch it tinting the skyline a soft pink and orange, glinting warmly off Elliott Bay. It was hard to believe that we were fighting against a would-be immortal vampire while the city slept, hard to think that there was danger in a place that seemed so peaceful, so beautiful.

"Hey." I turned my head to see Finn standing beside me, offering me another mug of coffee. "How are you holding up?"

I shrugged. "I'm still here? Honestly...I don't even know what I'm looking for or what I'll be able to do with it once we find it."

"That's why we're here, though," he said. "So you don't have to do it alone."

"It works like that, huh?" I asked, dry and sarcastic.

"It does," he answered, perfectly serious. "That's why things like Sebastian haven't ever taken over the world."

"What's why?"

"They always want to do it alone. The good guys win because...." He laughed softly, shaking his head. "Well, because we've got friends. Cheesy, but true."

"Cheesy, but true," I echoed and turned completely then to look at the group, studiously searching for anything that might help. I sipped my coffee and nodded.

Eventually, real life intruded, even into the emergency vampire research session. Fred and Davis had to go to work; Jerod had a final to get to. People trickled out one by one to their daily business, stumbling blearily into the dim, morning sunshine. Before long, all that was left were me, Finn—who had called in sick to work—Eleanor, Steve, and Yael.

Steve insisted that we sleep in shifts. "Nobody's going to find anything if we're all drooling in the books," he pointed out.

I took my Steve-mandated nap around two in the afternoon. By the time I stumbled back to the living room two hours later, Jerod, Finn, Yael and Eleanor were all crowded around Eleanor's Grimoire.

"What did you find?" I asked, subtly pushing my way between their shoulders to take a look.

"I think this is the ritual he's attempting," Eleanor said, flipping back a page. I scanned the book quickly. There were vivid diagrams of the procedure of the ritual, and scattered around them were several instructions in a language I didn't understand. There were a few passages that seemed to be translations though, some of the original text, some of another translation. By the time I worked out which bits were actually in English, I still hadn't managed to make any sense of what was in front of me.

"Sparknotes it for me."

"Basically, Creepface needs a balance of a whole fuckton of things," Yael answered. "Something old, something new, etc."

"What kind of things?" I asked, peering more intently at the book than before.

"Old and new, like she said," Eleanor answered. "You're the new."

"What's the old?" Instinctively, I looked to Finn for the answer, but he shook his head.

"It's not specific. But I'm guessing he'd go as old as he could. I don't even know what that would be."

"The *Leann?n Si*." Eleanor spoke the name softly, reverently. I almost missed the sound of it.

"Is that even real?" Finn asked. "My gran used to tell me stories of the *Leannán Sí*, but it's just a legend, isn't it?"

"The *Leannán Sí* is very real," Eleanor said. "Very real and very, very old."

"Okay, are you really going to make me actually ask?" Yael broke in, face scrunched in annoyance.

"The *Leannán SíLeannán Sí* is like...the Irish version of a muse," Finn answered, running his hand through his hair sheepishly.

"She's a vampire," Eleanor said.

"So which is she?" I asked, impatient for some answers.

"The Irish tell stories of the *Leannán Sí* inspiring poets, giving Ireland its eloquence," Eleanor elaborated. "But some of the stories talk about her taking where she gave. The poets gave their life for their craft. The *Leannán Sí* is the oldest vampire. She speaks only truth, and she inspires those who wish to speak truth." She really talked like that, like something out of a book. Or, no. More like she was repeating something she'd memorized. "For many generations she allied herself with the Sisters of the Sight, the sibyls. She gave us her truth, and we learned our work from her, honored her with truth-telling. In the end, she abandoned us, fearing our growing connection to the world of Men." She shook her head, then, breaking whatever trance she'd been in. "The *Leannán Sí* is the oldest living creature on Earth."

"What are the odds she lives in Seattle?" Jerod piped in.

"Actually..." It seemed to be Eleanor's turn to look sheepish. "The *Leannán Sí* always resides near the Wolfsight."

"Now you're just making things up," Yael protested.

Eleanor rolled her eyes, and her answer came back with some of the growl she'd lost in the last day. "It's what they call me. I have the Wolf and the Sight."

"So because you're double-dipping the magic, this thing is within Creepface's gruesome grasp?" Yael scoffed. She looked immediately contrite. "Sorry, sorry. I'm running on pure caffeine right now. Got a little snappy."

"This *thing* is a living creature and deserving of your respect," Eleanor sniped back. For a moment, I thought there'd be a fight. "But yes," she continued. "She's here because of me, which makes keeping her out of this my responsibility."

"Hey, just a thought," said Jerod. "Um...where exactly is it she's staying?"

"She lives in Soren's cabin," Eleanor answered. "It's near Enumclaw."

"So...when those werewolf dudes came by before, they took Sharon where?"

The knowledge settled across the room like a lead blanket.

"Well, fuck," Finn said. We all silently agreed.

Chapter Eighteen

WE MOVED QUICKLY, but I think all of us were afraid it wasn't going to be quickly enough. Eleanor tried calling Soren, but she couldn't get through.

"It's remote," she explained. "We usually can't get a signal there."

When she tried the landline, she got a busy signal, which pushed us all into a higher gear. Finn offered to drive, and he, Eleanor, Jerod, and I piled into his car. Yael protested only a moment before agreeing that she was probably the least use to us in this and offering to stay behind in case anyone came back to the house.

The drive seemed much longer than it actually was. We hit Enumclaw a little after five, but the cabin was way out in the boonies, and it was another half-hour before we made it to the gravel drive that led up to the house.

"Something's wrong," Eleanor said as we approached. Her eyes glinted brightly, and she shook her head, rolling down the window and leaning her head out to sniff the air. "There should be a sentry posted."

I bit back my instinctive, sarcastic remark about sentries and medieval fortresses. Finn had just barely started slowing the car in front of the cabin, and Eleanor already had her seatbelt off, the door open, and was all but leaping from the car. I took a little longer to untangle myself from the stiffness of roadtripping, and Jerod and I stumbled out just as Finn was throwing the car into park.

We were almost at the door, which was dangling from its hinges, when I heard first a feral growl, and then a full-on, actual wolf-sounding howl, echoing out into the woods around us.

When I crossed the threshold, I had the fleeting thought that I should be impressed by this cabin. On a normal day, it was probably exactly what a cabin should be. If what you wanted from a cabin was a warm and inviting feeling, vaulted ceilings, and cozy furniture.

On a normal day.

On this day, the cozy furniture was in pieces and scattered around the main room. A few windows were shattered, and there were shreds of quilts and throw pillows everywhere I looked.

"Jesus," Finn said as he loped in through the door behind us.

It took me a moment to trace the still-resounding howl to its source. Behind one-half of what might once have been a loveseat, I saw Eleanor's foot. I rushed toward her, not sure what I could do to help or even what she was so distressed about, but feeling the need to try *something*.

She was huddled over a prone body, cradling the torso in her arms and caught between tears, growls, and utterly inhuman noises of grief. Once the body in her arms came into focus, I could see that it was Soren. A moment later, I let myself look more closely around the room and saw several other bodies in similar states. Jerod was crouched over one, feeling for a pulse.

"They're alive," he said. "Must be some sort of spell?"

"That bitch," Eleanor spat out, and then she shifted, laying Soren's head in her lap and whispering something I couldn't quite catch. She made a gesture with her hand, fingers coming to rest on his lips, and Soren's chest expanded as he sucked in a deep breath, sitting up abruptly. He shoved Eleanor away and leapt to his feet, a deep rumble emanating from his chest as his eyes danced around the room.

His gaze lit on each of us in turn, and without glancing down, he reached a hand down to Eleanor. She took it and pulled herself up. "When did it happen?" she asked, moving quickly to each of the other unconscious forms and performing the same, strange ritual.

"About four," Soren answered, helping the others up as Eleanor revived them.

Finn, Jerod, and I stood and watched, separate from this scene and helpless to offer assistance.

"Sharon?" Finn asked.

Soren nodded, helping the last of the wolves to her feet. "It was a complex spell," he said, flinching away from Eleanor's touch as she dabbed at a cut on his temple with a scrap of fabric from the wreckage. "She must have found it in the Grimoire."

"I'll kill her," Eleanor said, calm but for the persistent growl in her voice.

"We have to find her first," Soren pointed out, and she nodded. They must have come to some sort of an agreement in that conversation that I didn't pick up, because Soren looked at her briefly, then nodded to the other wolves. They all began stripping out of their clothes and heading for the door.

"Whoa, what...?" I started, and Finn touched my arm.

"Don't worry," he said, and Jerod nodded, adding, "They're not gonna start a big, wolfy orgy or anything."

"Wrong time of the month," Soren agreed, and he winked at me without losing the intensity of his eyes. With another nod to the other wolves, he dropped his jeans and leapt out the front door. I turned to watch in amazement as the wolf raced off into the woods, four others following in short order.

Eleanor stopped the last before he could follow. "Check the sentries. They were missing."

He nodded and leapt after them, a blur of dark fur slipping through the trees.

"Fuck," Jerod muttered as he watched them go.

"Exactly," Eleanor answered grimly. "It seems she's picked up a few tricks from the Grimoire that weren't just for Sebastian."

I wasn't sure I wanted to know just what sort of tricks she'd had access to, and it didn't seem terribly important to be that specific at the moment. The far more important question was, "What now?"

"Now we...go back to research," Eleanor said, her voice trailing off as though even she realized what an immensely un-useful answer that was, growl fading from her tone as she went on.

"There has to be something more we can do," Finn protested.

"I'll make some calls," Eleanor offered. "But until we have more information, we've nothing to go on. The pack will cover clean up at the cabin. We need to focus on finding out where Sharon and Sebastian might be hiding. They won't stay there forever. They still need the final element for the ritual, and they're running out of time."

I knew I was the final element, and it wasn't a thought that inspired confidence. "How are they running out of time?" I asked. "Is he on a tight schedule?"

"He has to perform the ritual at the solstice," Finn said. "In the middle of the longest night of the year."

"Shit," I said. "That's...tomorrow. What are the chances we can figure this out in twenty-four hours?" I asked, trying to sound more optimistic than I actually was.

"We're gonna need help," Jerod suggested.

Eleanor nodded as we trudged dejectedly back to Finn's car. "I'll make some calls."

By the time we got back to Sharon's place, there were cars parked all down the street. Yael met us at the door.

"Oh, thank gods," she said when she saw me. "I am running out of hostessing skills." Then she paused, her eyes widening briefly. "Oh my god. Are there actual gods? Am I going to be smitten? Smote? Smited? Never mind." She took my elbow and pulled me inside, leaving the others to follow. "I don't even want to know, I just want someone to tell me where I can find more coffee."

Jerod took one look at the living room packed with what I was now comfortable enough with auras to say were sibyls, shifters, and werewolves, and said, "I'll run out and get some more."

Finn tossed Jerod his keys. "Maybe try and find another coffee maker while you're at it." Jerod mumbled something in the affirmative, and rushed out the door.

I could immediately see why Yael was feeling overwhelmed. There were easily twenty people crammed into Sharon's tiny living room with more in the dining room and, from the sound of it, more still down the hall in the bedrooms.

"How many calls did you make?" I asked Eleanor.

She shrugged. "Phone tree."

"Werewolves have a phone tree," I said, no longer surprised, just vaguely amused by the idea. "Do we have enough books for everybody to be looking through?"

"Most of them brought their own," Yael said. "The rest seem to be using the internet like regular people."

"We are regular people," Eleanor reminded her, though the growl she'd had earlier was no longer evident. She seemed tired more than anything.

"Sorry," Yael mumbled. "Just trying to lighten the mood."

"So where's Soren?" Davis asked, weaving his way through the crowded room to join our conversation.

"Soren is utilizing other methods of searching," Eleanor said.

"Sniffing out a trail?" I held back a snicker at Finn's question, especially since it seemed to be perfectly in earnest.

Eleanor nodded. "He's trying to, at least. Magic trails are much harder to follow."

"I'd imagine so," Yael said before turning to pick up a stack of books and pass them out to us. "I figured you'd want some primary sources when you got here."

I nodded. "What exactly are we looking for now?"

"Something to counter Sebastian's ritual," Eleanor answered, taking up a spot on the floor with her Grimoire. Actually, that's not quite right. She didn't take up a spot on the floor so much as the wolves in that area slid aside until there was room for her. I thought at first it might be something to do with her being the Wolfsight, but then I saw that all around the room the groups of wolves seemed to have organized themselves in this fashion. Everyone looked as though they had shifted as a unit to make a place for everyone there.

"How will we know when we've found it?" Finn asked, taking a book from Yael and wiggling himself between two sibyls who were frowning at their tablets.

"The ritual is translated to something like 'eternal night'," Eleanor said, accepting a glass of water pressed into her hand by the wolf to her left. "So you can look for mentions of something similar, or you can look for something that roughly translates...."

"Take back the night?" Yael suggested.

Eleanor smirked a little. "Or something to that effect, yes."

"You know," I said, squeezing into the space Finn made for me next to him, "finals are over. I'm not supposed to be doing research anymore."

"Like I said," Eleanor answered, "supposed has nothing to do with any of this."

It should have gone faster with so many additional eyes from the pack and various covens from around the city working on it, but the evening seemed to drag on forever. Jerod eventually came back with coffee and two extra coffee makers, but even so, we could barely keep up with the demand. Steve, Fred, Davis, and Noah found their ways back to us in the next few hours as well, and we found them all places to do their own versions of research. Someone from

Eleanor's pack made another coffee run around eleven, returning just as we used the last of what Jerod had picked up. At some point, pizza was ordered. Also Thai. Also Indian. Werewolves can really eat. Eleanor finished half a combo pizza all on her own, plus salad and breadsticks.

I couldn't eat. My stomach was twisting and bubbling uncomfortably, and the coffee was making me jittery. Steve very sternly insisted that I at least have some rice, and Noah, Yael, and Finn joined him in ganging up on me until I agreed.

I did feel better after, but I nonetheless found myself absently twirling something between my fingers for about ten minutes before I realized it was a tendril from Sharon's ivy plant. I glanced around the room, expecting looks of surprise or shock or horror, but no one was paying any attention to me. Noah looked up at the same time, but he just smiled, shook his head, and shifted to lean more comfortably against Steve's leg.

It was closing in on midnight—some of the werewolves were starting to take turns napping in a cozy-looking pile near the fireplace—before someone stumbled down the hall from the bedrooms with a tentatively victorious expression. "I think I found something," he said. I think he was a sibyl from Eleanor's coven.

"Let's see it, Daniel," Eleanor said, holding out a hand for the book. It looked older than a lot of the ones Sharon had available, and I wondered where he'd gotten it, if there were some secret stash of sibyl lore somewhere. A supernatural library. It got added to the list of questions I was going to ask if we ever got this resolved.

Eleanor looked over the book for several minutes, frowning, occasionally nodding, her brow furrowed. Eventually, she nodded more vigorously. "I think we might have something here."

There was an immediate influx of sibyls closing in around Eleanor, though the werewolves seemed content to stay back, giving her space. I wasn't quick enough to find a space where I could see the book in Eleanor's lap, so I had to content myself with asking, "What do we need?"

"That's where it gets tricky," Eleanor said, handing the book over two girls' heads to Steve, who took it and looked it over closely.

"Tricky how?" Finn asked.

"Balance is key," she said. "That's the foundation of magic. Sebastian is trying for balance with his ritual, but it's a precarious one. He needs old and new, but he's forgetting about darkness and light. He wants a night that will last forever: his own night. At least, that's what it seems to me."

"And night isn't a balance," I said, starting to get an idea of what she meant.

"Precisely. The solstice, just one at least, is the opposite of balance. It's all darkness; it's as dark as you can get."

Everyone was quiet a moment, digesting this. I started twirling tendrils again.

"How do we tip his precarious balance, then?" Noah finally asked.

"With a stronger balance," Steve answered, putting the book down. "But it will be difficult to find in time."

"What's the balance we need?" I asked.

"The one he's forgetting," was Eleanor's answer. "We need to balance both solstice and equinox."

"I don't get it," Yael said. "How the hell are we supposed to do that?"

"This ritual requires elements from each," Steve said. "We need someone born on each equinox and the summer solstice. It isn't so much a counterspell as it is...a hijacking."

"Can you break that down for the uninitiated?" Noah asked.

"The power he'll create with the spell is too much to be destroyed, but we can divert it," Eleanor said. "We can give that life to someone else if we can wrest control of it from Sebastian."

"No," Finn said. The firmness of his reply caught me off guard.

"What do you mean, 'no'?" I asked. "We have to stop him. We can't let him get any more powerful than he already is."

"No," he said again. "Didn't you hear what she said? We're not stopping the ritual. We have to let him complete it."

"Yeah, but then we're going to steal it from him," I insisted.

"*After* he completes it," Finn said. I still didn't understand his reluctance, but apparently Noah did. He shook his head firmly.

And then it seemed to dawn on Yael. "Oh, hell no. Not going to happen."

"Seriously, guys," I said. "What is the problem?"

"If he completes the ritual," Finn answered, looking at me with an expression I couldn't quite place, "he has to complete the sacrifices."

Even then, I didn't quite get it. I guess the realization of your own mortality takes a little time to sink in. When it finally did, it was like the whole room narrowed to include only myself and the few people in it I actually knew. I sucked in a quick breath. "Oh," I managed. I wanted to reach out for something that might protect me from this knowledge, this thing that couldn't be unknown, but there was nothing to reach out for. At least, I thought there wasn't until I noticed the ivy tendrils curling around my feet, beginning to build a barrier between me and everything around me. I had to concentrate to stop them, and they slowly receded back toward their pot.

Gradually, the room widened out again. Everyone was looking to me, though the werewolves and the sibyls I didn't know at least tried not to make it obvious. Fred was frowning and tugging at his mustache. Davis rubbed the back of his neck. As I looked at them all, everyone I knew and everyone I didn't, it seemed so obvious what needed to be done that I was almost annoyed with everyone who was trying to stop it.

I thought back to one of my first conversations with Finn. This was the moment I had to decide. Up until now, I'd been just floating along with all the things that were happening to me. Now I had to actually choose if I was going to do something or do nothing.

"I'll do it," I said, already holding a hand up to stop the protests I knew would be coming. "I have...an obligation to use my gifts," I added, looking straight at Finn. He looked for a moment like he wanted to argue, but then he set his face into a firm line and nodded, reaching for my hand. I took it.

"Over my dead body," Yael said, arms crossed over her chest.

"Only if you make me," I answered, trying for a joke. She glared at me, and Noah looked back and forth between us several times.

"Yael," Noah said quietly. "If...we can't find another way..., you know it has to happen."

"I know," Yael said, gulping in air like she was gulping back a sob. "But I don't have to like it."

"It may not happen," Steve pointed out, picking up the book again. "We still need the rest of the ritual."

Yael's hand also found mine, and Noah and I met eyes and nodded. Something, at least, had been decided.

"What exactly do we need for this balance again?" I asked, determined to see this through if it was the only way.

"It's the same idea as Sebastian's ritual," Eleanor said, looking at me with something like a growing respect. It didn't make thinking about the ritual any easier, but it helped me feel like I was definitely doing the right thing. "We need something or someone born on each of the equinoxes and the summer solstice."

There was silence for a moment. I guess everyone else was contemplating what a horribly difficult task this seemed to be. I was just trying to hold in a surprised laugh. I failed.

"What?" Finn asked.

"You're kidding, right?" Yael said.

"I'm not," Eleanor answered, looking between the two of us with a frown. "What's...what's funny?"

Noah broke in to answer. "We have your balance," he said. "Right here."

"What do you mean?" Steve asked, sitting up a little straighter, his arm sneaking around Noah's waist as if to keep him closer.

"It's part of why we decided to live together," I clarified. "Fate, you know. We're each born on a solstice or equinox."

"You're kidding," Finn said, and I felt his grip on my hand tighten.

"I'm the solstice," I said. "Yael is vernal, and Noah's autumnal."

"No joke," Yael added.

"That's...too easy, though, right?" I asked, looking first to Steve then to Eleanor for an answer. "Of all the people Sebastian could pick for his ritual, he picks someone who can fuck it all up for him?"

Eleanor shrugged. "Fate, like you said."

"Sometimes supposed does matter," Steve added.

"This is...kind of too much, though," I protested.

Nobody answered right away. I thought they were probably all silently agreeing with me. "We don't go in much for prophecies these days," Eleanor ventured, "but that used to be part of the sibyl heritage. And they worked out like this more often than not. Whenever someone had a viable plan for shifting the balance firmly toward evil, the ingredients for us to shift it back to good have been available. It isn't a guarantee—nothing is—but it is an opportunity. There's always an opportunity."

It still seemed like a little much, but I wanted so badly for it to be true, that I tried to push that wariness aside. Except for one thing.

"What about your vampire lady?" I asked Eleanor. "You can't just...let her die, can you?" I thought if she was staying with Eleanor, or near her or whatever, she must be more like Sternquist than Sebastian on the vampire continuum.

Eleanor's brow furrowed, and she looked down at her hands. "The *Leannán Sí* makes her own decisions. I don't always understand them."

"What do you mean?" Noah asked.

"She means if the vampire lady had wanted to stop Sharon, she could have, right?" Yael said, touching the nearest part of Eleanor—her ankle—lightly.

"Right," Eleanor answered, glancing up and giving Yael a brief smile.

We were all quiet for a moment. I don't know what everyone else was thinking, but I was wondering what that meant about my own willingness to go through with this. Did that make me something like the *Leannán Sí*? Was it arrogant of me to even consider that?

"This balance," Finn asked eventually, "does it require sacrifice too?"

"It does," Steve said, and there was no way to disguise the protective way he pulled Noah against his chest.

"It does," Eleanor echoed. "But the sacrifice of the good is a different sort. Sebastian will take an unwilling sacrifice. In fact, for his purposes, it's better. For us...we need people who are willing to give up their own life for something greater."

"I volunteer as tribute," Yael said dryly. "No, but seriously," she added, looking around the room. "I volunteer."

"Me too," Noah said, though he didn't pull away from Steve's embrace at all. In fact, from the way the 'too' forced itself out, I was pretty sure Steve was just holding him even tighter. "Easy, big guy," Noah muttered under his breath.

"You guys," I said. "You...you can't do this."

"Why the hell not?" Yael asked. "You are."

"Yeah, but...." I knew I didn't have a good response to this just as surely as I knew I couldn't let my friends do this. "But I was born into this world. You guys just had the bad luck of knowing me first."

"Don't be an asshole," Noah said. Steve had loosened his grip a little, and Noah's voice came out forceful and a little annoyed. "We were all born into the same world. It's ours as much as yours. Just because we can't grow carrots on demand doesn't mean we don't have just as much right as you to protect it."

I wasn't sure I agreed with that, but I knew Noah well enough to know he wasn't going to back down, and I didn't have a good enough argument to make him. Anyway, I was pretty sure Steve was going to be making every argument he could think of as soon as they were alone. "Well, then," I said. "How are we gonna make this bloodbath happen?"

"Let's not get too ahead of ourselves," Finn said, something tentative and hopeful in his voice. "We could still find another option."

"We could," I said, nodding to him and then looking away quickly. "But we need to have a plan in case we don't find anything."

"We need Sebastian to think he's succeeding," Fred offered. I let out a breath. I hadn't realized how much I'd been wanting someone else to take charge until that moment. I let myself sink back a little, hardly aware of Finn's arm as it slid around me and I let my head rest on his shoulder. Or rather, not letting myself be aware of it, of how comfortable it was, how much I was going to miss it, wherever I was headed next. "We have to find a way to give him what he wants while making him think he's taking it from us."

"I have to go out alone," I said. "Or with someone he can easily overpower."

"No," Steve said. "He's not stupid. He'll know if we're handing you over. What we need is someone who will put up a good fight and ultimately lose."

"But not die," I added quickly. "Just lose." I didn't think I could handle anybody else biting it because of me. My two best friends were a big enough loss for the world we were supposedly saving.

"Okay, but we also need to figure out where Creepface is doing this thing, right?" Yael added. "Could we...GPS track it or something?"

Steve shook his head. "Sebastian will know to get rid of a phone or anything with a wifi signal, and we don't have the time to find something more stealthy."

"Yeah," I agreed, settling more firmly against Finn to think about this. I had no experience with how this thing was supposed to go, but it seemed like most of the people around me didn't either, despite having much more experience with the supernatural in general. I lit on an idea after a moment, but I needed to confirm it was doable. "Eleanor, you said magic trails were harder for a wolf to track. Is there a way we could make them easier?"

She considered this for a moment. "He's definitely put up some sort of barrier against standard locating spells. Otherwise we could easily have found Sharon. But we might be able to give you an object with a particular magical signature. Something we have a sensitivity to but Sebastian doesn't."

"Electricity," Finn said, sitting up a little straighter and pulling me with him. "If we could find a portable, electrical device for you to carry that doesn't have a GPS or wifi signal...."

"Does something like that even exist?" Yael scoffed.

"Yeah, Fred totally has something," Jerod came back with immediately.

"I do?" Fred asked.

"Yeah," Jerod said. "Your little...calendar thing."

"What this?" Fred answered, reaching into his pocket and pulling out something that looked like a half-sized, foldable e-book reader with an attached stylus.

"What. The hell. Is that?" Noah asked, leaning forward for a better look.

"It's a pocket organizer," Fred explained.

"Why don't you just use your phone?" Yael wondered.

"Because Fred's phone is from the Dark Ages," Jerod said. "It's a miracle he can even text on it."

"I thought it would come in handy for organizing on the go." Fred's face was a mixture of triumphant and embarrassed.

"He's right," Eleanor said. "And that might actually work. We can magically alter the signature a bit to make it easier for Finn to pinpoint."

"You can do that?" Yael asked, looking to Finn for confirmation.

He shrugged. "I think so. I've never tried it, but it's theoretically within my skill set."

"We can at least give it a try," I said, glancing over to the device in Fred's hand.

He was looking at it like it was his childhood dog and we were asking him to tie it in a sack and drown it. Then he looked to me, and his expression shifted. He nodded and handed it over. "If it will help at all."

"Thanks," I said. I knew that this sacrifice of Fred's was nowhere near on the level of mine or Yael's or Noah's, but it still felt significant. It felt like a recognition of my own somehow. Chances were good he was not getting this dinosaur back.

"Now we just need an excuse for you to be out without a full entourage," Steve said.

It was going to be a long night before we managed to get ourselves completely in order.

Chapter Nineteen

Before the night was over, Steve made us all sleep again, insisting that we would need all our strength if this plan was going to work. We left most of the werewolves and sibyls up and researching in the hopes that they would find something else that we could use, but the rest of us found a spot in one of the bedrooms and crashed.

I let Noah and Steve have the guest room to themselves, hoping they would make the most of their time there. Yael, Fred, Jerod, and Eleanor camped out in Sharon's room. One of the werewolves had nailed a bit of plywood across the hole Sebastian had left in the window. Davis opted to stay up with the others, since he wasn't on the roster for the big finale. That left Finn and I with a pile of blankets and pillows in Sharon's office.

I wanted to go home. I really, *really* wanted to go home. I wanted to spend my last night on earth in my own bed or, failing that, curled up in Yael's quilt on our couch.

I also wanted to spend it with Finn. Something about knowing nothing was ever going to come from this made it easier to admit to myself that Finn was what I wanted. Maybe not forever, but for tonight. He'd changed in the last few weeks, either from his gran's advice or simply from us knowing each other better. I'd certainly changed, and that also made it easier to admit that curled up under several blankets on a stack of throw pillows with my head on Finn's chest was precisely how I wanted to spend the next few hours.

Finn wasn't sleeping. I could tell that much. Neither was I, obviously, and I didn't think I was likely to. Who wants to sleep away their last night? Our legs tangled easily together, and everything about it felt comfortable, right, easy. I wished I'd realized this before. I wished we'd had more time to settle into each other. It didn't matter now, though, and I knew that what I was really doing was using Finn for my own comfort, that it wasn't fair to him to give him something so small right before I left for good, but I was selfish enough to believe I deserved it. Part of me thought I should feel like a hero for this, but I didn't feel terribly heroic. I just felt scared. Scared and determined. I knew it had to be done, and I knew I had to be the one to do it. That's all there was, really. How could I feel heroic for that?

"You're thinking awfully hard," Finn said, his voice small in the empty office space.

"Sorry," I murmured.

"It's okay," he said. "I'm pretty sure you're allowed to be thinking. You've got a lot to think about."

"Yeah."

After a moment, he came back with, "I'm not sure it's good for you to be thinking about it, though."

"Maybe not," I said. "But it doesn't really matter what's good for me anymore, does it? Not like I'm going to do lasting damage to myself." I didn't mean to sound bitter—I'd chosen this, after all—but it definitely came out that way. It started to hit me, then, that this really was the end. That if I wanted Finn to survive—and Steve and Fred and, god, my parents—I was going to have to...not.

"Don't say that," Finn said, and his arms tightened around me. It felt good to be held at that moment. I was beginning to feel like something that was being tossed away in favor of more important things, but Finn held me like something that he wanted to keep. Even knowing he couldn't didn't stop me from being glad of that.

"I'm sorry," I muttered, burying my face in his shirt.

"You don't have to be sorry either," he said.

We were both quiet for a long while, and his breathing evened out enough that I thought he might finally have fallen asleep when he said, "I...have to tell you something. I know it doesn't really matter anymore, but I have to say it anyway."

I wanted to tell him not to, that saying it was only going to make things worse, but there was a part of me that wanted to hear it, wanted to know that it was true, so I let him.

"I...really like you. Maybe I even love you. Anyway, I...I don't want you to do it. I get that it's your choice, and I respect that but...I don't want you to. I'd ask you not to if I thought it would make a difference."

It might have, but I didn't tell him that. I didn't want him to know he might have that power over me. "I...really like you too," I said. "I don't know about love, but I know that much. I...don't want to do this either, but I have to. I have to *because* I really like you. Because people like you deserve to live in a world that's not...broken. Not as fucked up as Sebastian would make it."

"People like me are people like you," he said, shifting in a way that forced me to lift my head and look at him. "You deserve that too."

"I don't think that's what matters here," I said. "What I deserve doesn't play into it. Just what I have to do."

"Yeah," he said, his voice dropping into resignation, his hand coming up to touch my cheek. "That just makes me like you more."

I was expecting the kiss this time, but it still took my breath away.

Early morning was early, as they say, and I didn't sleep at all. Not because Finn and I were up to any shenanigans; I just couldn't. I laid awake all night, listening to Finn's heart beat, matching my breathing to his when I could. He drifted off somewhere around three in the morning, and I spent the next couple hours trying very hard not to worry about the plan.

We'd settled on Fred escorting me back to my place as though I needed to pick something up there. Eleanor suggested that earlier would be better. We didn't want to risk Sebastian doing something like storming Sharon's condo to stage an enormous battle to get to me. Not that I would have made him do that even if we didn't possibly have a way to stop this. Knowing that if it wasn't me it was some poor kid in Kirkland, I wasn't about to walk away from this. At around four in the morning I started wondering if maybe Sebastian let that information leak to Sharon on purpose, knowing I'd find out about it, that it would be enough to make me give myself up if all else failed. I wondered if it were even true, though not for long. It didn't matter if it were true or not. It wasn't a risk I could take.

By five, I knew I couldn't stand just lying there any longer. I carefully extricated myself from Finn's arms. They tried on their own to pull me back, and I really wanted to let them, but I knew there was no use pretending I could put this off. I did pause a moment to get either really sappy or really creepy and watch

Finn sleep. I wondered if Fred and I could manage to sneak out without waking him up. It wouldn't be right, but it would be easier.

Eventually, I pulled myself away entirely and crept out of the room into the hallway. I could hear muted conversations from the living room and smell the ubiquitous coffee-brewing scent from the kitchen along with something that was suspiciously bacon-like. When I arrived at the dining room, Eleanor was carrying an enormous platter of pancakes from the kitchen to set next to the pile of bacon already waiting. When I gave her a curious look, she just shrugged.

"I cook when I'm nervous," she said and then disappeared into the kitchen again.

I surveyed the bounty on the table, which included bacon *and* sausage, some kind of coffee cake, fruit, scrambled eggs, and toast. Just as I was about to head into the kitchen in search of the coffee I was so desperately in need of, Eleanor returned with two steaming mugs. One of them was pressed into my reaching hands, and the other was offered over my shoulder. I turned to see Yael grumbling her way into the kitchen. She took the mug with a nod and a grunt, and I turned an impressed glance on Eleanor. "How do you do that?"

She shrugged again. "It's a wolf thing."

I made a mental note to look that up after this thing was over before remembering that there was no after. The thought made me shiver a little and swallow, gripping the mug a little tighter as I took a seat at the table.

"No luck in saving our asses?" Yael asked once her brain had been lubricated by caffeine.

Eleanor shook her head. "Nothing that's feasible in the time we have."

"Solstice is all day, though, right?" Yael continued.

"It is," I interjected. "But we need time to track down Sebastian, and to get everyone in place for their...parts." Their sacrifices. My sacrifice. It was too much to think about so I just dropped into a kitchen chair and focused on my own coffee.

One by one, all of us who had managed to sleep or at least pretend to sleep stumbled our way into the kitchen and sat down. From the looks of things, none of us felt like eating, but that didn't stop Eleanor from loading up plates for each of us and giving us her sternest glare—pretty darn stern, all things considered—until we tucked in.

No one said a word. Finn took the seat next to mine, his knee pressed against my leg. Across from us, Steve was eating one-handed, the other hand resting on the back of Noah's neck like he was afraid to break contact even for bacon. On my other side, Yael munched absently on a piece of bacon before tossing half of it onto her plate.

"All right," she said decisively, pushing her chair back. "We don't have to rush into this, but I cannot possibly shovel down another bite. No offense, Mother of Wolves," she added, nodding to Eleanor.

"None taken," Eleanor said, getting up herself and starting to clear the table. I got up to help, but Finn tugged at my hand.

"It's fine," I said, attempting to pull away. "I don't mind helping."

"No, it's just..." He dropped my hand and glanced at Fred.

"We should get going," Fred finished for him as a weight heavier than my breakfast settled into the pit of my stomach.

"Right," I managed, fingers grasping for Finn's hand again. It took longer than I would have liked for him to take mine again. I took a deep breath, swallowed, cleared my throat, and took another deep breath. "Okay, yeah. Yeah, let's go."

"Have you worked your mojo on the thingy-bopper?" Yael asked, and it was something of a testament to how welcoming the group had been to her that it was Fred who answered, "Yes," and me who said, "Huh?"

When I realized the significance of that, the weight in my stomach turned acidic. I had brought her into this. I was the reason she wasn't going to last to see another pancake. What right did I have to...?

There was a faint pressure on my palm as Finn squeezed my hand in his and I looked down. His face had all the resolve I didn't, but seeing it made me nod my own head and squeeze back briefly. "Right, yeah," I said when I'd found my voice again. "The calendar...thingy."

"The thingy-bopper," Yael affirmed with a nod.

"So we're good to go," I said, and Finn got up without letting go of my hand. I was glad. I didn't want to have to reach for it again.

"Whenever you are," Fred answered, getting up himself as Eleanor bustled around him, stacking plates, most of which were still full of food.

I nodded again. I had no idea how you were supposed to take leave of your friends and walk to your death. Even worse was knowing I was leading them to their own. I looked to Noah and Steve, both of whom were watching me carefully. I looked to Yael. Her brow furrowed like a Dickensian heroine's. I looked to Finn. His face was set into a firm line that was determinedly neither smile nor frown.

"Can we just...."

"God help me, if you say, 'get it over with...'," Noah started, but he was cut off when Steve abruptly frog-marched him around the table and enveloped both of us in a hug.

When I finally pulled back, a little winded, Yael looked at me and swallowed hard. "Yeah," she mumbled. "What he said." And then she was hugging me as well, quick and tight. When she let go, she turned to leave the room, and it was only then I noticed that everyone else had already left, leaving only me and Finn, who had kept hold of my hand throughout all the hugging. Once Yael was gone, he turned to me and opened his mouth to speak.

"Don't," I said quickly, hoping to cut him off. "Don't...just don't. If you say anything, I might start crying, and that's... We can't do that. Can't tip Sebastian off that anything's out of the ordinary."

"I liked it better when you were still calling him Creepface," he said, obviously attempting to steer clear of tears.

"Yeah, me too," I said. And then, because I could feel a lump forming in my throat, I hugged him, squeezing until he made a sort of squeaking noise.

When I tried to let go, he said, "No, it's fine," a little out of breath.

"Sorry," I mumbled into his shoulder.

"Don't. Don't be sorry. Don't be anything but here."

I didn't know what to say to that. I didn't know what to do either. I couldn't be here. Not for very much longer. I let him hold onto me, though, at least until I heard Fred softly clearing his throat on the other side of the door. Finn squeezed me, then, and I mimicked his earlier squeak.

"Jerk," he said affectionately, and that was almost too much for me, so I tugged myself out of his arms and tried to smile as I turned to go.

Fred touched my shoulder as I passed. "Okay?"

I just nodded, and he reached into his pocket to pull out the device I'd only seen the night before. I held out my hand for it, and Fred pressed it to my palm. The plastic was warm from his body heat, and it seemed so sad and unimportant in my grip. I could only hope Sebastian would think so too.

As I slid it into my back pocket, I felt another touch to my shoulder and turned to see Eleanor. "You know," she said quietly, "if I didn't know better, I'd think you were a wolf."

"Why's that?" I asked, stalling more than anything else.

"You're giving your life for the pack. There's nothing we honor more."

I was struck speechless again, and Eleanor gave me a brief hug. I couldn't remember the last time I'd been hugged so much. Probably last Christmas when my grandma kept forgetting she'd already gotten to me.

Steve and Noah and Yael each got in another one as well. It was clear they were trying to hold themselves together, and I wanted to do the same, so I kept my mouth shut.

Davis and Jerod were there as well.

"You're really...," Jerod started, giving me an awkward bro-hug. "Well, yeah. You know?"

I laughed, a choked sort of a sound. "Yeah, I think I do."

"You done good, kid," Davis added, ruffling my hair.

And then it was clearly time to go. Fred was at the door, carefully pushing it open, and I was moving to follow, hardly aware of my own actions, my feet simply shuffling forward after him. When I finally reached the door, I heard a soft, "Ah, fuck it," behind me, and then Finn's hand was on my shoulder, spinning me around, and he was bending to kiss me, firmly, definitively.

"You know?" he asked, breathless, when he pulled back.

"Yeah," I answered. "I definitely know."

It was a tense drive across the bridge. Fred glanced at me every now and then, and I tried to make vaguely encouraging faces at him, but I'm pretty sure I failed spectacularly. After a moment, I pulled out my phone. There was still one last goodbye to say, and I had no idea how to say it.

I was also a little bit of a coward. It was Friday, in the middle of the morning, which meant it was around noon back home. Both of my parents were at work. I glanced over to Fred and held up my phone. "I'm just gonna...."

He nodded, and I stared at the screen for a long moment before dialing their home phone number. I couldn't handle actually talking to them just now. I waited through the rings and the voicemail message they'd recorded with me before I went off to college. Three years, and they still hadn't changed it.

"Hey," I said once the beep let me know it was time to talk. "It's me. I...just wanted to call and say hi. And happy solstice? I'll...." I swallowed and cleared my throat and decided I could do nothing better than lie through my teeth. I couldn't possibly explain to them everything that had happened, what I was planning to do, and why. Not before the machine cut me off. "I'll see you in a few days." My voice cracked. "And I love you. I really love you guys. Always."

I thumbed the screen to end the call and sniffed, turning my face to look out the side window. Fred said nothing, but he touched my shoulder for half a second before moving his hand back to the gear shift.

It was still dark when we pulled up to the house, and early enough that most of the neighbors were not out and about. That was good. We wanted Sebastian to be over-confident, not to question his advantage.

I shot a quick glance to Fred when he'd parked, and he nodded. Taking a deep breath, I opened the door and got out. The idea was to spend just enough time out in the open for Sebastian to make his move, but to keep close enough to Fred that it seemed like I was being protected.

Fred was still getting out of the car when I heard a whoosh of air to my right. And then there was blackness.

Chapter Twenty

When I came to, I wasn't entirely sure I had. Everything in front of me still looked dark, but I could hear faint noises, echoing slightly, and it felt damp and close, claustrophobic, if I had leaned that way. The back of my head was pounding dreadfully, throbbing with every tiny movement I managed.

"You've awoken," said a voice behind me, and when I turned I was not at all surprised to see a soft glow emanating from my new companion. Whoever it was, they were clearly a vampire, but where Sebastian's voice had the power to make me shudder in both disgust and fear, this voice flowed like warm butter, settling into me and making the room itself seem rich and smooth. In what little light there was, I could see that we were in something like a cave, though the walls seemed to be man-made, and there was definitely cobblestones for a floor.

I knew who it had to be. "Are you the...?" Suddenly I couldn't remember what Eleanor had called her.

"The *Leannán Sí*," the creature answered. "We are."

I say 'creature' because whoever was in front of me was...clearly not human, though they possessed all of the traits a human should have and could likely have passed for human on any street. I still knew that they were something else. Something very much other. In addition, they were...well, Eleanor had described them as a woman, or at least as female. But they...weren't that either. Nor were they male. They were simply...them.

"You wish to know about us," they said, and there was amusement in that voice. I didn't understand how anyone could be amused in a place like this, and I wanted to be annoyed by it, but the voice was so soothing that I couldn't manage it.

"I wish to know a lot of things," I said warily. It was the strongest emotion I could seem to muster.

"And you will know many things," they answered. "In good time."

I knew suddenly, with blinding clarity, what Eleanor had meant when she said the *Leannán Sí* made her own decisions. This creature in front of me, peaceful and comforting as they seemed, had power. More power than anything I'd encountered so far. More power than Sebastian, certainly, which made me wonder how Sebastian had managed to capture them. Were they here willingly? Were they helping Sebastian?

"Foolish thoughts, child," they said. "The abomination deserves aid from no one, certainly not from us."

It was more than a little creepy that they could apparently read my thoughts, but I was somewhat comforted by the use of 'abomination' to describe Sebastian. That seemed to fit him to a T. "Okay, so...." I was tempted to just think my side of the conversation at them, but that felt a little rude, so I stuck to audible remarks. "How did you end up here?"

"The same way that you did," they answered with a slow nod. It was that nod, more than anything else about them, that made me understand just how very, very old this creature was. They moved with strength and elegance, but every motion seemed to radiate exhaustion.

"He hit you over the head?"

That seemed to amuse them a little. A faint smile teased at the corner of their mouth. "No, child. We used...deception," their face contorted as though they found this thought repugnant, "just as you did. We have both chosen to be here."

I thought of the girl in Kirkland, and I wondered who the *Leannán Sí* was protecting by going along with Sebastian's ritual.

"Does it matter?" they asked, and I felt my face twist into a scowl I'd meant to hide. It wasn't fair that they could do that. "The abomination believes this to be our weakness, that we would sacrifice ourselves for the sake of just one other."

"But we're gonna use that weakness against him," I said, remembering my conversation with Finn about why the bad guys kept losing.

"If you have the strength for it," they cautioned. "It is no easy thing to take a life, much less so when that life is your own."

"Yeah, I've thought of that." I'd thought of a lot of things. Eleanor said that my sacrifice had to be willing. I was kind of hoping that meant I just had to be okay with it. If this came down to me having to kill myself with my own hand, things could get tricky.

"When the time comes, you will find what strength you need," they said, certainty in that soothing voice.

"What makes you so sure?"

"We have the Sight, as you do, child."

Two things occurred to me at that moment. The first was that I still had so many questions about this world I'd landed in and how I was supposed to deal with it, and this was probably my last chance to get any answers. The second was that I should make use of whatever time Sebastian was giving us to get a look around at wherever he was keeping us. I stood then and tried to take care of both issues at once. The *Leannán Sí*'s light didn't illuminate the way Sebastian's did, but I could feel my way around the room with them in my sight, and my eyes were beginning to adjust a little. There must have been a source of light somewhere nearby.

"I thought you were a vampire." As I spoke, I felt my way around the space. It was small, maybe 10x10, and the walls were mostly brick. There was a door, but it had been boarded and barred over, and though I could see no other openings, I could feel a slight breeze, so there had to be some passageway somewhere else.

"We are that," they said, head tilted as they watched me move. "But that is a simple explanation. Too simple."

"'Oldest vampire' is too simple?" I asked, completing my circle and carefully settling myself onto the floor in front of them. It was too dark to really be able to look for that opening, and I doubted it was big enough to make use of. Besides, escape was not actually on the menu for tonight.

"Far too simple," they agreed. "Adding 'oldest sibyl' does not make it any more accurate."

"So you're like the Wolfsight," I said, thinking back to Eleanor's brief explanation of her own status.

"In some ways," they answered. "But no. Not like the Wolfsight. The *Leannán Sí* cannot be bred for. We require...a more complicated birth."

"Right. Because what we need in this world is more complication."

They were quiet a moment, then, but their eyes stayed on my face as though they were scrutinizing everything in my expression. "You disdain the rituals."

"Sort of?" I was too close to my imminent demise to bother lying about something like that. "I guess I just...don't understand the need for them. Why is everything so convoluted?"

"You are not alone in your confusion. The rituals are in place for just such a reason."

"To confuse people?"

"To keep power from the hands of those who think it should be simple to wield."

Well, that put me in my place. I guess I was too simple to get that on my own.

The *Leannán Sí* shook their head. "You are here and willing to die to protect that power. Whether you know it or not, that shows a great deal of respect for the ritual itself and for the power it creates."

I went quiet at that, wondering about the ritual, what exactly would happen and when. The notion of time made me reach frantically for my pocket, hoping to any and all higher powers that Sebastian had left Fred's weird little calendar thing. My breath came out in a rush when I felt it still in the back pocket of my jeans. I fished it out. I didn't know how long I'd been out, so I flipped the device open to check on the time. It was just past noon. That meant I had twelve hours to sit and fret about whether the others would find me in time, what would happen when Sebastian came back, and whether this was all for nothing in the end.

"Sleep is best," the *Leannán Sí* said. I was almost getting used to them knowing what I was thinking. I supposed it didn't really matter after all. Nothing much mattered now.

"I'm pretty sure I'm not gonna be able to sleep."

They smiled again, and there was a warmth to it that was more than just the soothing nature of their voice. "We can help with that."

"I'm also pretty sure I have a concussion. Aren't you supposed to stay awake after one of those?"

"We can help with that as well, if it's a concern to you," they said. "You will need your strength for what is to come."

"Don't tell me you're the oldest fairy too," I said, the memory of Steve's comfort coming on me so sharp and sudden it was almost painful. I squeezed my eyes shut and let my head drop for a moment.

"The Fae are a wise race," they said, definitely amused now, though after a moment, I felt a cool hand on my shoulder. "We will not force it on you, but the rest would do you good. Far more good than sitting awake and dwelling on the future ever could."

When I lifted my head again, their eyes met mine, silvery blue and bright in the darkness. I didn't know much about them, but I could see why Eleanor revered them so much. So much empathy and so much power in one creature. It was almost impossible to believe. "What would you do?"

"It's a simple spell," they answered. "You would sleep gradually and naturally, and you would awake refreshed."

After a moment, I nodded, the memory of Steve—and Finn and Yael and Noah—still tender. "Will you...talk with me until I fall asleep?"

"We will," they answered, shifting to settle back against a crumbling wall, their legs crossed. "Rest your head in our lap. We will gentle you to sleep."

I moved, still hesitant, still a little wary, but I eventually stretched out at their side, my head resting in their lap. "Where are we, anyway?" I asked, already feeling myself relax as they ran delicate, elegant fingers through my hair.

"Beneath the city."

"We're in Underground Seattle? Isn't he afraid a tour's gonna find us?"

"We are far beyond where tourists visit, child."

I was already beginning to drowse, but my fingers found the calendar again, clutching it, hoping that whatever they'd done to the signal was strong enough to work its way up out of the ruins here. I wanted to keep talking, but I was starting to lose coherence. "Hey, how come Eleanor thinks you're a girl?"

The laugh I got in answer made me smile drowsily. "The Sisters of the Sight saw us as they wished. Eleanor knows better, but tradition holds great sway with her."

"Weird," I mumbled.

"Indeed."

When I woke again, I was immediately aware of a coldness in the room. Where the *Leannán Sí* had given off a sense of warmth and comfort, this presence brought with it a sense of chill and...I think the only way to describe it is void. As though something had been sucked out of the room to accommodate its existence, only it didn't quite fill up the space left behind.

I sat up slowly, movements careful and measured.

My heart was racing, and my head throbbed with every beat, but I knew exactly who that presence belonged to, and I was damned if I was going to let Sebastian see me frightened. My jaw ached from clenching it, and as my eyes adjusted to the cave again, they immediately searched out the *Leannán Sí*. They were standing in the center of the room, spine rigid, staring straight ahead.

"Good morning, gorgeous," Sebastian said, his lips twisting into a satisfied smile. "Getting a late start, are we? I wouldn't have thought you'd be able to sleep."

I pulled myself quickly to my feet, ignoring the pain in my head as I mimicked the *Leannán Sí*'s stance. I said nothing. The abomination did not deserve an answer.

As the thought crossed my mind, I thought I saw the *Leannán Sí*'s eyes flick toward me for the briefest moment, but when I glanced over at them, they were standing perfectly still, eyes forward.

"Oh, come on now," Sebastian said, his voice nasal and mocking. "This is going to be a long, boring slog if you keep giving me the silent treatment."

There was so much I wanted to say to him, yell at him, throw at him, but I glanced again at the *Leannán Sí*, and their resolve strengthened mine. My fingers clenched and released, the tips of my right hand brushing over the solid plastic in my pocket, reminding me that I wasn't as alone as I seemed. I didn't know for certain that the coven had been able to track the signal, but I had to believe they had.

Sebastian heaved a sigh. "Well, fine. I guess I'll just have to content myself with the company of your girlfriend. Come along!" he added, his head jerking back toward the door he'd opened before I woke. Sharon was scowling as she came in. He made a gesture with his hand, and a coil of rope rose, hovering in front of me. "I'll let you take care of your little friend," he said to Sharon, and she came over to me, yanking my hands in front of me to tie them with the rope.

"You don't have to do this," I said under my breath. Despite everything, I still wanted to believe that there was something in Sharon that could be saved. There had to be something of the person I'd sort of fallen for in there. It couldn't all have been a show. Her eyes leapt up to meet mine for a moment, and she looked...like she was going to say something. Or perhaps like she had some measure of regret.

"I'm afraid you're wrong there, gorgeous," Sebastian answered for her. I glanced over to see him tying the *Leannán Sí*'s hands the same way Sharon had mine. "I'm all she has left. No other supernatural would have anything to do with her now. She's...tainted."

Tainted.

Hearing the word made me think of my own tainted blood. How long had Sharon been feeding it to me? If, by some miracle, I survived this, how would that affect me? Who would know? Who would treat me differently? I wished, rather than hoped, that I would at least be remembered positively, that Finn wouldn't shudder to think of the time we'd spent together now that he knew what was in me.

A tug at my wrists drew me out of my thoughts, and I looked up to see Sharon leading me out of the room into a damp corridor. The floor was uneven, and it was dark and stuffy. No one spoke for a long while as Sebastian led us through the maze under the city. Occasionally, light would filter through grating in the ceiling, but I could tell it was streetlight, not sunlight. I wished I'd been able to check the time again before Sebastian got there, but it seemed like it couldn't have been later than about ten. I tried for a moment to cast my thoughts out to find any plant life—moss or mold or fungus or...something—but I couldn't keep my mind on that and on not tripping over loose stones at the same time, and I soon had to give it up.

In spite of his earlier complaints about a lack of conversation, Sebastian kept quiet as he led us. His unnatural light seemed to illuminate the pathway we were taking. Rubbish and wreckage had been shoved aside haphazardly to clear the way, and I could almost feel how far we were coming from any entrances into the underground city with each step we took. Eventually, the silence became too much for me.

"So, how come we're down here in the underworld? Don't you have, like, a secret vampire lair somewhere?"

"Missing your flowers, gorgeous?" Sebastian asked, smirking. "Or did you really not even do that much research into what we're about to do?"

I hadn't, of course. I knew the basics of the ritual, but I didn't know what that had to do with our location. "Well, you know me," I said. "Homework's not really my thing."

As we kept walking I noticed that the walls became less and less like the underground city and more and more like actual caves. I didn't know where Sebastian was leading us, but I could tell we were getting further and further away from anywhere we might be found and interrupted.

"Really," he said, scoffing. "What do they teach children in their schools these days? Oh, that's right. You sibyls don't have schools anymore, do you? Nothing to teach your youngsters about the glorious tradition they come from." As he spoke he gave a rather harsh tug at the *Leannán Sí*'s rope. I saw them stumble, and it was my instinct to move to help them, but Sharon stopped me, and Sebastian only laughed. "Sadly, there will never again be a school for your kind. It's too late to pass on that tradition."

"Not entirely too late," I argued, curious now, and wondering just how much I could get him to monologue. Maybe he'd reveal some unintended weakness in his plan like a Bond villain and I'd be able to stop this whole thing before anyone else had to die. "You could still pass it on to me."

He laughed again, and even Sharon snorted. "Wouldn't that be rich. Learning about your heritage from a despicable vampire. Only too fitting, wouldn't you say, old man?"

It took me a moment to realize he was talking to the *Leannán Sí*. I glanced over at them, but they were walking as stiff as ever, though they seemed to be even more exhausted than before.

"Why not?" Sebastian continued. "Where we're headed, gorgeous, is a long-abandoned sacred site. You see, all these little rituals need to happen at a sacred site. The Sisters were always so insistent on that. There's something to it, of course, power pools in these sites. Each ritual performed there adds to the pool, and each successive ritual draws on that power. Of course, this site hasn't been used in centuries, but the power is still gathered there. I doubt even the oldest covens in the city know of its existence, but I sought it out. I discovered it. Your friends wouldn't know where to begin to look, even if they were stupid enough to try and stop me."

I wondered about that. Without being able to focus on possible plant life, there was very little I could do to even delay Sebastian, let alone stop him, but some of the others maybe could. Fred, for instance, or Steve or Eleanor. Or...

I looked over at the *Leannán Sí*. They could do it. I was certain of that. They could stop this happening, stop me having to die, and Yael and Noah. So why didn't they? I wanted to ask, but there was something about them that made the question impossible. Eleanor had said that they made their own choices and that they were hard to understand sometimes. I could see why. This was one decision I could not fathom making. I could feel anger building in me at the thought, but something made it impossible to grow enough to be a catalyst for something more. Perhaps it was the look in the *Leannán Sí*'s eyes when they looked over at me, that unbearable fatigue.

In that moment, everything seemed entirely hopeless. I couldn't stop this. The *Leannán Sí* wouldn't stop it. Sebastian was dragging us directly into it, and Sharon was either content to help or so cowed by Sebastian that she felt she had no choice. This was it, really. I was not coming out of this.

Still, something made me ask, "Is this where you're keeping them all?"

His head lifted and tilted. "Keeping whom?"

"All the people you've taken."

He grinned, his teeth glinting in his own light. "What makes you think they're not all dead?"

"I think if getting their powers were as easy as feeding once or twice, more of you people would have done it before."

"Smart and beautiful," he teased, chuckling. "All right, yes. They're still alive. Some of them, anyway."

I didn't want to think about who might or might not be. "So are they? Here?"

"That's an interesting thought," he said, seeming to mull it over a bit. "I suppose it would have been nice to have an audience for this, but no. I kept them much closer to home."

I was beyond annoyed that the only electronic device I had on me then was not capable of sending a signal. I wanted to text Finn and tell him to find out where Sebastian lived, to see if they could find the missing supernaturals. Before I could curse the situation any further, though, we stopped so suddenly that I bumped into Sharon's back. I was trying to peer around her to see why we'd stopped when Sebastian said. "Secure them. Then come help me set up the altar."

Sharon avoided my eyes as she pulled me over to one side of a circular cavern. She tied my wrists to a column there, and I had to try something, so I whispered, "It's not too late."

She shook her head, smiling wryly. "Oh, honey. If only you knew how late it is."

A moment later, she was securing the *Leannán Sí* to the column next to mine before heading for the center of the cavern. In Sebastian's light I could see that we were standing in a natural cave that had clearly been embellished. The columns we were tied to were of some sort of wood, polished and smooth. I tried to sense any remainder of life in them, but they'd been long, long dead.

As Sharon and Sebastian moved around lighting candles, drawing circles and symbols on the floor, and bedecking a circular table in the middle of the space with a black covering, I closed my eyes. I might have a moment here to concentrate and find some kind of plant life. It wasn't easy. I focused all my concentration on the task, cutting out any sound of Sharon and Sebastian, any knowledge of their presence. Still, I could just barely sense something outside the space. It wasn't anything very strong, nothing that even had the capability of growing large enough to do me any good. I couldn't tell what it was at first, but eventually I realized it was moss, clinging to the cave walls in spite of the lack of sunlight here. I wondered if it had something to do with the power in this cavern.

Just as I was about to give up looking for anything more when I felt rather than heard a warm voice say, "There is life and there is the potential for life. Do not discount either."

I had no idea what to make of that, but it encouraged me to try again. I concentrated harder. I could feel my face scrunching up tightly, my jaw locked. I almost gave up a second time when I felt the presence behind that voice pushing me on, stretching my consciousness further. Somewhere in the pile of moss was something I hadn't ever sensed before. Not life, but the potential for life. A seed. I didn't know what I could do with a seed, but now that I knew it was there, it was as though it, well, planted itself in my mind. Even as I drew my focus away from the moss, away from the faint feelings of life too far away to do any good, I could still feel both the seed and the warmth of that voice. I clung to them as I turned my eyes and my mind back to the preparations taking place at what Sebastian had called the altar.

They had drawn a circle around the altar, a lit candle at four points on the circle and one larger one on the altar itself. The inside of the circle was strewn with herbs and something that looked dark and ashy. Around the inner perimeter of the circle was some sort of writing, but nothing that I recognized. Even the alphabet looked completely foreign.

"Hurry," Sebastian was saying to Sharon. "It's nearly time, and I want to do this right."

She nodded firmly and pulled two last items from the satchel she was carrying, laying them on the altar to either side of the candle. I was just too far away to make out what they were, but something in her facial expression as she laid them out made me think they were nothing pretty.

"Bring them in," Sebastian said, and Sharon came toward me then, determination on her face along with something that I optimistically labeled regret.

It wasn't until she untied me from the column and started pulling me toward the circle that the full realization of what was going to happen hit me. I wanted to be stoic. I wanted to face my death heroically, knowing it was a true sacrifice, knowing something good was going to come from it. Instead, I found myself crying, almost hyperventilating, as much as I tried to keep calm. All that stopped, though, when Sharon pulled me across the chalk line of the circle.

It was hard to breathe at all inside the circle. I could feel the power Sebastian had been talking about. Remnants of every ritual that had ever been performed here were stuck in this place. I turned my head left and right, hearing faint, murmuring voices but unable to find any source for them. Sharon led me to the altar and pushed me to my knees. I wanted to struggle, but the sense of power was too much for me to overcome, and then Sharon whispered words in a language I didn't recognize. It sounded a lot like what Steve had used for the interrogation, and I tried not to think too hard about it as I felt my limbs relax outside of my control. I couldn't have moved if I'd tried. I couldn't even try. My mind relaxed as well, information and reaction slipping out of it. Before long all that remained were the seed and the warmth of the *Leannán Sí*'s voice.

I was still aware of what was happening around me, though. I watched as Sharon untied the *Leannán Sí* and brought them into the circle as well. I jumped slightly when they crossed the line. The air seemed to expand and then contract, like thunder without the sound. The *Leannán Sí* was led to the opposite side of the altar from me, and I met their eyes. They nodded, and I felt it as an affirmation, though I didn't know of what. I was dimly aware that I should be looking for something, for someone, but I couldn't bring my mind enough under my control to remember what it was.

As I knelt, Sebastian moved to stand behind me, resting his hands on my shoulders. I wanted to pull away, but my body wouldn't react as I wanted it to. Sharon took her own place behind the *Leannán Sí* and began to speak. Her words rolled over me, and I couldn't parse any of them, but I had a sense of what she was saying. A blessing, of sorts, if you could call it that. Over the circle and the altar and the tools. I could feel the power around me roiling as she spoke, building itself up to a frenzy.

When the blessing finished, both Sharon and Sebastian leaned over to pick up the tools from the altar, and for the first time I got a good glimpse of them. Even in my relaxed state, it made my blood run cold. Sebastian held a crude knife, black like obsidian, flashing in his reflected light. The handle was wrapped in some sort of hide, and runes were carved into the blade.

Sharon's tool was far more grisly: a curved, blackened sickle. This black was not from the material the blade was made of, though. It was black with crusted blood. If there were any symbols carved into it, they had long since been covered up.

Sebastian and Sharon both straightened then, and I felt the cold stone of the blade resting against my throat. My eyes rested briefly on the curve of the blade at the *Leannán Sí*'s throat before raising to meet their eyes. The strength in them bolstered my own, and whatever hold Sharon's spell had had over me loosened a bit. I remembered why I was here, why I wouldn't struggle even though I could now. I breathed out a silent plea that the rest of the coven had found us and were in place to hijack this ritual, that my blood would do more than add to the power of this site.

Sharon began to speak again, her voice taking on a deep resonance. I wanted to close my eyes, knowing what was coming for me, but the *Leannán Sí* never once looked away from me, and I couldn't abandon them at this moment. Sharon's words turned to a chant, and the chant grew in volume into a violent crescendo. I swallowed and just barely saw the flash of the blade before Sebastian's hand moved lightning-quick, dragging it across my throat.

I had expected pain, but the blade was sharp, and the hand wielding it was sure and strong. He cut deep, and I felt the warm flow of blood down my front before I began to choke, wondering for a moment what that gargling sound was before I realized it was me. I slumped, still enough under Sharon's spell not to flail as I saw my blood flowing toward the altar. There was a shallow trench carved into the floor around it, and I could see my blood begin to fill it, sliding around to either side of the altar. I knew the *Leannán Sí*'s blood must be doing the same, and I knew the moment our blood mingled.

There was a crashing boom, and over the continued chanting of Sharon's voice, I heard another voice, stronger, in yet another language. I had just enough awareness left to realize it was Eleanor's, and then the last of my strength bled out of me and I slumped to the floor.

Chapter Twenty-One

There was warmth and a seed.

There was darkness crying out to be dispersed.

There was a cool hand on my shoulder.

In a rush of energy and light and darkness and power, I saw beyond myself.

I was above the room where my body lay, still bleeding out its life. Sebastian screamed in rage and turned to where Eleanor stood behind him, only just inside the circle. Sharon's face twisted in confusion and then acceptance, and I heard her sob in relief, knew that it was relief. Her voice shifted, and she and Eleanor chanted in unison. The light from the candles grew, towering over the circle. With a gesture of their hands, both Sharon and Eleanor guided that light, not toward Sebastian but toward the lifeless body at Sharon's feet.

This was right. I could feel it. The *Leannán Sí* must be preserved.

"But I am only a vessel," came a voice, warm and soothing, beside me.

I turned my head to see the *Leannán Sí* floating as I was above the chaotic scene before us. Sebastian was lunging at Eleanor, but she pulled one hand from guiding the light to push toward Sebastian. A violent wind sent him sprawling backward, and as he went, a bone-chilling screech rent the air. His body twisted and convulsed, stretching and compressing, lengthening and shrinking, until he was lying in a heap on the floor, a gross amalgam of every creature he had tried to become. Grotesque and useless, limbs twisted at awkward angles, wings flapping pointlessly.

"I am only a vessel," the voice beside me repeated. "The *Leannán Sí* can be preserved without me."

"How?" I asked, frowning at the woman next to me. She was definitely a woman now—young and sweet, not the powerful creature I'd met earlier—and as that sunk in, I realized what she was saying. "You're...you hold the *Leannán Sí*, but you are not them."

"No one person can be. But we can be vessels."

"We?"

"You have the ability."

"Why me?" I protested. "I am...nothing special. I'm still not sure I'm not maybe-kind-of-crazy."

"You're right," she said, but the warmth and comfort was still in her voice. "You are nothing special, but you are here and you are needed. You must decide what to do with that."

I looked down at the struggle still happening below us. I could see Sharon and Eleanor trying to force the light into the *Leannán Sí*'s body, feel their panic rising as it was rejected again and again. I knew what she meant then. I was nothing special. Perhaps when she'd begun this, she was also nothing special. But we were there and we were needed.

I swallowed, pushing aside my own panic, and nodded.

Immediately the light rose up in a high arc, leaping over the altar. I watched in awe as it flooded my body.

I was no longer floating above the scene, but I wasn't lying in a pool of blood either. I could see so much more than the cavern I was lying in. I felt the power rushing through me, felt the damage it would do to the room we were in. I knew I couldn't stop it, but I also knew I didn't want that power, that life. Not all of it.

There were threads of light I could see connecting this room to other places around the city. Time in the cavern slowed as I followed the threads. One of them led me to a tiny boat bobbing in Elliott Bay. Inside the boat, I could see Steve clinging to Noah's limp form, rocking it in his arms. I reached across the thread for Noah, sending what light I could into his body. I heard him gasp as I raced along another thread. This one brought me into a field somewhere east of the city. An enormous bonfire was raging and a few feet from it, Finn sat, tears sliding down his face, Yael's hand clasped in his. I poured as much of the light as Yael's body would take into her, and Finn's eyes flashed with the reflection of it.

I wanted to stay and watch, but I felt myself pulled back to the cavern. "The potential for life," whispered a voice in the back of my mind, and I called out to the seed. Moss grew like never before, spiking and flattening as needed to roll the seed to the circle. I tried to start small, to ease the seed to life, but the light in me was not yet finished. It flooded into the seed, and burst it into a tree, racing upwards, through the open air of the cavern and into the stone above, rushing to the moonlight. It was all I could do to mold the growth of its base wrapping it around the altar and pulling the body of the *Leannán Sí* into its core.

I was certain I heard a soft, warm, "Thank you."

The moment the tree breached the open air, the cavern was rocked with an explosion. I felt myself part of my own body again, but more than myself. Inhabiting the space in a way I never had before. I was thrown back, but I had enough strength to turn my body from the explosion and place myself as a shield in front of the wolf with the sparkling eyes that leapt from the circle as I did.

There was hardly time to think after that. The cavern began to collapse, and the wolf and I sprinted through tunnels shaking with the force of the blast. We ran until I lost track of how long we'd run or where we were going, but part of the light that now inhabited my form guided me along until we came to an opening that led us out into the street, moonlight streaming down on us. I worried briefly about the attention we would garner. My clothes were covered in dust and blood, and I had a wolf walking beside me, but no one seemed concerned.

We made our way through Pioneer Square and wandered until we came to a bus stop where we could catch a bus out to West Seattle. I wanted Eleanor to change back. I had so many questions to ask her, but even as I thought of them, I found we knew the answers. We even knew why she wasn't changing back just yet.

The bus driver almost didn't let us on, but I heard myself speaking to her without thought, my voice warm and soothing, and she relented. As I sat with my hand on the back of Eleanor's neck, I closed my eyes, trying to find those threads of light again, trying to follow them as we had before.

It wasn't that I found no threads or that I couldn't manage to follow them again. It was more that when I closed my eyes, we saw millions upon millions of threads reaching out from me to everyone around us. Some were faint, tiny gossamer strands of light from me to the bus driver or to the drunk man sitting across from us. Some were incredibly strong. Eleanor's thread was thick and bright, sparkling like her eyes.

I chose the next brightest thread and carefully extracted it from the others, sending my mind along it until it settled on Yael and Finn, wrapped in blankets, seated on the remains of what may have once been a quite-comfortable couch by a fireplace, whiskey in hand. They were speaking to someone I recognized only vaguely at first. The more-than-me that was in my body, though, quickly clarified. Wolf. Leader. Soren, mate to the Wolfsight. We couldn't hear them, but I lingered a while, simply watching, satisfying ourselves that they were both safe for now. Next we chose another thread, also thick and solid, and I followed it carefully again. It took us back to the boat. Steve still clung to Noah, but there was joy in his embrace. The engine was running, and the boat was headed to shore. We watched again, almost, but not quite, detached from the situation, registering only the health and safety of the two of them. After a moment or two, Steve lifted his head, his eyes meeting mine. "Do you mind?" he asked, a bright smile on his cheerful face, and we accepted his desire for privacy.

There was one more thread to follow then, less one distinct thread than a tangle of polychromatic lights. We drew it from the web of light and flowed along it until it reached its home and split into a cascade of individual threads, each terminating in a drowsy form. I saw Katie and Christine before the others. They were unharmed but drugged, only half-awake. I also found Eli, his full beard making him difficult to miss. Only he looked up as we watched, giving a faint smile and murmuring, "Thank you." We nodded, though I knew somehow that he could not see it, and left, sliding back along the thread until we sat again in my body on the uncomfortable bus seat.

Eleanor rested her chin on my knee, and I glanced down at her. I knew what she wanted to know, though she didn't speak at all. "They are all fine," I said, then ruffled her fur a little. "Even Soren." She gave a soft woof of appreciation, and we settled into silence for the rest of the trip.

It was a bit of a walk from the bus stop to Sharon's condo, and we garnered a few more looks in West Seattle than we had in Pioneer Square, but we made it back without incident. When we got inside, Eleanor immediately shifted back. It looked painful, but I found myself fascinated by the process. She stood in the hallway, completely unselfconscious in her nudity, surrounded by her wolves and sibyls, and we did not look away. It was natural and right that she should allow this vulnerability to us. Eventually, she was handed a blanket which she absently wrapped around her shoulders.

Looking at us critically, she asked, "Do you know what you are?"

"We are the *Leannán Sí*," I answered, surprised by the sound of my own voice.

She nodded, and there were murmurs around the room. They looked on us with awe and respect, and we settled into the knowledge of it. "There are certain stories in the Grimoire that suggest the *Leannán Sí* has not always been as she was when I knew her, but nothing to say how she came to be or where she began. I would never have thought to be honored enough to witness her birth."

I wasn't comfortable with the way she talked about us, but when we spoke, the answer was, "You have indeed been honored, child. It will not be forgotten." I shook my head, struggling to focus on just one thing, on just myself. Finally, I managed, "I...I don't know what to do with this."

Fred wove his way through the crowd to touch my shoulder lightly. "I'm not sure any of us do. How do you feel?"

"Like...like there's too much of us. Of me."

Eleanor nodded. "You've taken on the *Leannán Sí*. It's bound to feel a little cramped for a while. How else are you feeling?"

I thought for a moment, struggling to separate the me from the more-than-me. "Tired," I said eventually. "Exhausted, really." We laughed, knowing now what true exhaustion was and knowing this was only a shadow of it.

"Do you want to nap? We can clear out the spare room," Fred offered.

"No, I...have so many questions." We knew some of the answers already, but it would take time for me to accept that. "Can I go home? Eleanor, would you drive me?"

When Noah and Yael and Finn got back, that's where I wanted to be. That's where I wanted them to see us.

"Yes, of course," she said. "Kind of my job now, after all."

"I survived the vampire apocalypse and all I got was a chauffeur?" I teased.

"Something like that."

She borrowed some clothes from one of her wolves, and we were soon on our way. It was a quiet ride. I closed my eyes, but we did not sleep. Closing our eyes on the physical world only opened up the supernatural world to us. I was too tired to follow any more threads, but I let the new information wash over us as we drove. When we reached my home, I asked Eleanor to come in with me. She readily agreed and made herself at home in the kitchen, finding a bottle of whiskey and two glasses.

"Can you tell us...me...what happened with Sharon?"

I had seen it. We had known something of it, but it was unclear to us still.

"She...redeemed herself," Eleanor said softly, frowning. I could see that she was warring between gratitude and anger.

"We cannot judge others based on how they have hurt us," we said. "Pain is a part of life. When confronted with the end of life, that is when we show who we truly are."

She nodded. "In the end of her life, Sharon chose goodness. I will...say nothing more of her."

I frowned then. "I don't know what to do when you talk to me like that. I'm still...me. I'm still just learning all this shit."

"Are you really, though?" Eleanor asked, tilting her head a little before taking a sip of her drink.

I took a drink as well, shaking my head. "No," we answered, but my voice was a little shaky. "Part of me is, though. I know...I know that you know us already, but I want to be me as well. I want people to treat us like me."

"You want people to treat the *Leannán Sí* like a new sibyl?"

"Yes?" I laughed and we did as well. "Is it so much to ask?"

She considered this a moment, and I didn't look at her thoughts. "It is more than I think you know, but I'll try. And I'll tell the others to try as well."

"Yeah, no offense, but I'm not living out in Enumclaw."

"But the...," she began to protest and we raised a hand to cut her off.

"We are the *Leannán Sí*, but we are something else as well, and that will take time to discover. We cannot do so in seclusion. Besides...," I felt something shift inside me, making room for me alongside more-than-me, "I'm not ready to give up all this." I gestured to the room around us and to the glass in our hand. "We'll still be your *Leannán Sí*. But I have to just be me sometimes too."

She took a deep breath, and we could feel her thoughts swirling around, struggling to take shape. When they did, we smiled and she nodded. "All right. I'll break it to the pack." She stood then. "In the meantime, I'll leave you to rest. I'm sure you'll want to greet your...friends in peace."

I walked her to the door and stopped her just as she was walking out. "Thank you. We know this won't be easy for you, for any of you, but it is necessary." She nodded, and I hugged her. It took her a moment to respond, and we laughed. "Many things will change," we said.

"So I see," she remarked, smiling herself as she turned to go.

I eventually managed to sleep. At least, I assume I did because when we woke, Finn was sitting on the coffee table, holding my hand a little too tight. "Careful," I mumbled, "I might need that hand someday."

"Sorry, sorry," he said, dropping my hand. We smiled, feeling his confusion and reveling in the forgotten newness of it. I reached for his hand and took it in mine.

"It's all right. I was only teasing."

"Good. Good, that's...good," he said, and we laughed and sat up. Immediately, he pulled us into an embrace, and there was a forgotten pleasure in that too—one that now carried the remembrance of many more such embraces in the arms of many more lovers—in the warmth of his body against us. And then we shifted again, and I pulled back only to look at Finn's face a moment before kissing him. The thread between us became stronger, brighter, and we were satisfied to let it, though he was a sibyl and so, so young.

"Okay, this is really weird," I said.

"What is?" he asked, trying for another kiss until I pulled back a little.

"I'm...did Eleanor tell you what happened to me?"

"That you're the...*Leannán Sí*? Yeah. She did." He pulled back more then, frowning at me.

"Well, it's like...when we kiss? It's like I've never done that before. No wait," I added. "It's more like *we've* never done that before."

"To be fair, we've never done it comfortably when no one was going to die," he pointed out, and we laughed and embraced him again.

"Sorry," I said. "I have a feeling we'll be doing it more now. At least, I hope we will."

"I have no complaints," he said, and we felt the motion of his body as he chuckled. For a long moment, we settled into his touch, and then he said, "Um, one thing, though...."

"Yes?" we said, and his confusion caught us by surprise. A new feeling.

"I just. Well, you're not...." He sat back entirely then, gesturing at our body.

I looked down at ourselves, and it took me way too long to work out what he was trying to say. I was myself, as I always had been, but as the *Leannán Sí*, we were more than simply myself, in all ways. "We...," I began, trying to find a way to explain it. "We contain too much to be confined by gender."

"Huh," he said, looking me over again.

"Is it...a problem?" I asked.

"Um...let me think about that," he answered, but the way he kissed me then said he didn't think it would be.

I was almost annoyed when Yael and Noah came tumbling in to catch us both in a tackle-hug.

Epilogue

WE TOOK OUR accustomed seat in the lecture hall, about halfway back. Dr. Sternquist glanced briefly up from her papers to nod at us as we took our place. We nodded in return. Sternquist would make a strong ally, would help in alleviating the animosity between the vampires and the rest of the supernaturals. She would help us make a change.

A newspaper was dropped onto the desk in front of us, and we looked up to see Finn smiling down at us. "Have I mentioned yet that I'm really glad we both failed Econ?"

"Only about a dozen times," we assured him. "What's with the old school news feed?" We asked, picking up the paper.

"You made the front page."

We looked down at the headline: Mystery Peach Tree in Bell Street Park Still Confounds Scientists.

"Are they still going with the student prank angle?" we asked.

"Looks like," he said, and we laughed, leaning back in our seat to peruse the article. "What?" he asked.

"Nothing," we said with a grin. "But perhaps we'll change our major to botany. Someone's got to solve these sorts of mysteries."

"Good luck with that," he said, leaning over to kiss our cheek just as Sternquist took her place at the podium.

We glanced at each other, smiled, and pulled out our sunglasses.

ACKNOWLEDGMENTS

There are too many people I need to acknowledge. It starts with my mom reading to me every night and moves through Karly Wygmans—my best friend at age 7, who spent countless hours with me at her kitchen table writing storybooks—to Mrs. Fickle—my middle school English teacher who introduced me to the wonder of sentence diagramming—to Professor Greg Wolfe—who was instrumental in helping me realize that creative non-fiction was not for me. All these and more.

Most especially, though, I want to thank my fellow *Four Windows: Seattle* authors. Without their patience, critical eyes (and ears), and encouragement, this book would never have been finished. Thank you all.

And thank all of y'all. I hope you enjoyed reading it as much as I enjoyed writing it (though perhaps with fewer moments of frustration).

ALSO FROM RAZORGIRL PRESS

NeuTraffic by Andrew Gaines

John Graham, Thought Commuter License 178, has a simple mission: deliver a message. In a near-future, post-revolution Seattle, he and the other underground messengers are the only tenuous threads that keep the fledgling New Cascadian Order from falling back into chaos. Careful, paranoid planning and incredible luck can only take the young Nation-State so far — and now even the Thought Commuter network's secret intelligence can't save them from a devastating air raid.

His route home destroyed, John is forced on an odyssey through the bizarre new environment of his changed city. Seattle is boiling under the threat of renewed chaos, and the new society's structures are threatening to dissolve...but that's the least of John's problems. Because as John journeys through the mental landscape of his past, he's beginning to suspect that society isn't the only thing unravelling. His own sanity might be coming spectacularly undone.

Brass & Glass Book One: The Cask of Cranglimmering by Dawn Vogel

When Svetlana Tereshchenko, captain of the airship The Silent Monsoon, catches wind that a cask of mythical Cranglimmering whiskey has been stolen, she and her renegade crew of outcasts fly off in search of it. With the promise of a reward worthy of the cask's legendary lineage from both the Heliopolis Port Authority and the head of the Kavisoli crime family, Svetlana and her crew embark on a breathless chase that takes The Silent Monsoon from one end of the Republic to the other.

What Svetlana assumes will be an easy search and recover mission quickly becomes more complicated as each step she takes uncovers secrets and lies about the cask and its contents. Now, with an ethereal Ghost Ship haunting their path, friends reveal themselves as enemies and alliances develop with the most unlikely associates. The lives of her crew hang in the balance as Svetlana makes the crucial choice of whom she can trust and whom she should fear.

Shifting Borders by Jessie Kwak

When a resurrection goes awry in a cold Seattle cemetery, mother-of-three Patricia Ramos-Waites finds herself possessed by the ghost of her sister's dead lover. God forbid her only problem be sharing her body with Dead Marco. Yesterday Patricia's only worries were her teenage son's new deadbeat friends, and putting her kids through college; today she's become the target of a Central American drug-smuggling gang who desperately want to get their hands on the ghost she's hosting.

On top of all this, Patricia is beginning to suspect that either Marco is an exceptionally powerful spirit, or she has ghost-handling abilities that haven't been seen in centuries. Will Patricia be able to stay out of the crosshairs long enough to fix this botched resurrection?

Trace by Ian M. Smith

Joanne Shaughnessy needs a job, and bad, which explains why in the course of 24 hours she has joined a shady medical study on the chi of amputees with a questionable physician at its helm, and agreed to buy antiques for an eccentric Chinese woman who seems to think Joanne has a supernatural affinity for it. She might just be taking advantage of two easy marks' open pocketbooks, but when she stumbles into a cache of mysterious letters, she starts to wonder if Ming is right, and if she can actually hear the voices of the dead.

To complicate matters more, she's being followed by a band of monocle wearing tech-heads desperate to harness her mysterious powers into unbelievable technological advancement.

Made in the USA
Columbia, SC
10 May 2019